A Pride & Prejudice Reimagining

Follies & Forgiveness

Kitty Bennet's Adventure
Book Six

NEY MITCH

Dedication & Author's Note

Readers, we're on Book VI, and you've reached the middle of the series. The journey is still unfolding. I never thought I would get the chance to pursue this story to such great lengths, and here is an *important note* for you before you delve into this part of the series. After all, what sort of writer would I be if I did not prepare you?

Before one begins, it is best to inform the reader that there will be some connections back to Miss Austen's other timeless and incomplete work, *The Watsons*. If the reader has not read *The Watsons*, never fear! The tale will be introduced in the plot of this novel, and work alongside the existing characters. Also, there is another of Miss Austen's novels that will make a brief appearance in this chapter. Yet I shall not mention which one, for a reader has a right to surprises. Lastly, every now and again, there will be a chapter that deviates from the heroine's perspective, to follow the actions of other characters. This is solely done so that the reader can be given vital information.

For you few, you happy few, who wish to continue following Kitty and every road that she chooses to bravely walk down, I thank you. *Primarily*, there is a special thanks to the first reviewer who requested this sequel as part of the series! Believe me, you will never be forgotten by me at all. You encouraged me to keep going, and that was the best thing anyone could give me.

A special love for my friends, family, and all who helped me get this work published

A special thanks to Helyn Roberts-Vickers and A. Madison for sticking with me. And lastly a wonderful thanks to Laurie Novo for helping me pursue my love for writing.

Chapter One

TWICE THE BLESSING, TWICE THE HAPPINESS

What would Lady Catherine say indeed!

The number 'one' has often been regarded as quite the lonely number. Two is always regarded as more profitable, for many common reasons. And in this circumstance, two would double our mother's joys, and two would also double Lady Catherine de Bourgh's agony.

For my sisters, Jane, and Elizabeth, by all accounts, had fulfilled another romantic plateau and achievement of marital joy: they had not only married two close friends on the same day, but they were also with child at the same time.

And now, here we all were, in Matlock, where Doctor Carney distributed the news. My own merriment was awakened, but my reactions would not be either lesser or greater than the rest in my company.

Mr. Bingley practically leapt out of his shoes, from mirth.

Mr. Darcy did not speak, but his face was overpowered, his sternness gave way, and there was a gentle exhilaration in his eye.

Mr. Atkins was very amused.

Arthur Philips clapped his hands in a way that reminded me of Sir William Lucas.

Enara, Georgiana, and Mary all gasped in excitement.

And Colonel Fitzwilliam turned to me.

"Two friends on the road to an even greater happiness," he noted. "What say you to this?"

I gave him a naughty smile.

"I think I am the most perverse creature in the world."

"And why so?"

"On this happy day, my mind wondered over to a joke. Now, I cannot fathom why in the world that was where it fell."

"And where did your mind fall?"

I looked squarely at him.

"With every rise of good news that we have here, must look like a tragedy to Lady Catherine."

I only uttered this to him, and it was enough to make Colonel Fitzwilliam guffaw. His eyes lit up, filled with mirth and, without thinking, I began to chuckle, touching his arm in the process. It was a small reaction—as organic and unconscious as anything. A gesture that is undergone, purely on instinct, is something of which we all are guilty. For as we chuckled to ourselves, I turned to see Lady Fitzwilliam looking upon us, with that familiar discerning eye that she possessed. Once more, it was neither a critical look nor a condescending one. On the contrary, it was simply the tendency of a woman who attended to, discerned, and observed more than she voiced.

Instinctively, I lowered my hand from her son's arm, and I stopped laughing. However, I did not stop smiling. For, I have learned very late in my life, that the second that you put on a shameful face, when you have done nothing that is actually wrong, you will be wearing that shameful face forever. For we humans spend our lives often saying, 'I'm sorry'. Sometimes the words need to be said. Other times, it's said as a bit of a default, a reactive statement that we utter because we are trained to walk around always feeling wrong.

Well, I tired of feeling wrong just for merely existing. It did not do, neither to my heart or head to spend my life feeling shame. Therefore, I maintained my composure and gave into the jollity of the moment.

"My sisters are having children," I professed, going to Mary and Georgiana. Taking their hands, I began to dance, forcing them to give way and we skipped in a circle. "We're going to be aunts, Mary, and Georgie! We're going to be aunts!"

"Yes, we will!" Georgiana laughed. "Now that will be the day."

Everyone watched us for a moment, even Doctor Carney. However, feeling compelled to dispose of the truth, despite the spirit of the moment, Doctor Carney cleared his throat.

"This is a joyous event, and it is always lovely to see a family receive such news. Yet, a doctor must do his duty and distribute both the good news and the potential ill."

"Potential ill?" Arthur commented. "What ill could come of this happy event?"

"A reality that every wife has to face, sadly. Both women appear to be healthy and full of vigor. Although, that does not always prevent the grim reality that, the first two months of a woman's time is fraught with possibilities."

"You refer to miscarriage," Lady Fitzwilliam deduced.

"I do, indeed." Doctor Carney turned to Mr. Darcy and Mr. Bingley. "Sirs, while such an event cannot always be predicted, I still would recommend that you encourage your wives to not do anything strenuous at all these next two months. It will help their future child along, I daresay."

The gentlemen agreed with this quite easily.

"Oh, my goodness," Bingley said, clapping his hands, "I feel so terribly nervous now."

"A natural reaction," Mr. Darcy assured him. "I myself...well, Doctor Carney, I believe that we may see our wives now? We desire to be with them."

"Yes, yes, yes," Bingley repeated merrily. Darcy raised his eyebrow and gave his friend an amused look.

"Of course, sirs. I believe the women may be happy to see you as well."

"Imagine if they didn't?" Bingley voiced, chuckling nervously, "and scolded us for being presumptive?"

"We married perfect women," Darcy responded, "you are imagining an event, Bingley, and I will not let you. No, friend, save any irrational behavior for when they go into labor. That is when a woman has the right to curse our very existence. I have often heard that women do so, when in the throes of such pain. And perhaps, they would be right to. They create, while we are the ones who stand there and be happy that we are spared such a fate."

They all laughed as Darcy turned to Doctor Carney.

"I would request that you visit Matlock every other day while we are here and tend to Mrs. Darcy and Mrs. Bingley."

"Yes, yes, yes," Bingley repeated. And now we all were looking at him, amused. Seeing this, Bingley decided to defend himself. "My wife is with child. I have every right to sound quite nonsensical all that I wish."

"No excuses are needed, man," Lord Fitzwilliam said. "We share your enthusiasm."

Both Darcy and Bingley went upstairs. Bingley always had an active step, but now, Darcy matched him. Soon, it became a competition, and both men were racing up the steps and dashing to their wives resting room.

We all were amazed.

"Did you see that?" I asked. "Did you actually see that?"

"Yes," Mary said, equally marveled. "Yes, I did."

~

"And what of us?" I asked Doctor Carney. "Can we see our sisters?"

"Yes," Mary added, "wouldn't they be expecting us to give our congratulations?"

"There will be no need," Carney advised us. "In times like this, the husbands are the best sort of company, for they are only two in number. The ladies are still in a slightly delicate state, and being so very much overpowered by the circumstances, it will be well for them to rest, with only Mr. Darcy and Mr. Bingley as company for about an hour. Then, when they are prepared to receive more company, they can come down at their choosing, and you can wish them all the congratulations in the world."

Turning to Mr. Atkins, Enara, and Arthur Philips, I arched my eyebrow, mischievously.

"Imagine if Elizabeth heard herself regarded as being too delicate to receive family? I wonder what she would say."

"She would prove herself fit by walking a mile after her rest," Mr. Atkins replied. "Unless I am mistaken, and do not know Mrs. Darcy at all."

"Oh, contrare, you do."

Doctor Carney turned to Lady Fitzwilliam, wondering if she had any servants in the household with any experience of tending to women who were early into their pregnancy state. Lady Fitzwilliam assured him that her servants, Vera, and Gabrielle, were adept to the service.

"Be rest assured, Carney," Lady Fitzwilliam said, "Gabrielle and Vera have a few sisters who they supplied as being midwives whenever their siblings gave birth. They are experts on the matter."

"I wonder if there is a Gabrielle and Vera in every house with extensive grounds," Georgiana whispered to me. "I never think of such things until now."

"I suspect that there is," I replied. "At Longbourn, our cook, Henrietta, and Mrs. Hill, assisted in delivering three children each."

"No! Truly?"

"Yes. As Henrietta once told us, she delivered her cousin's child by morning, and then was returned to Longbourn to make our supper by the evening."

"Really?"

"Yes. She did. This was when I was very young, so I never knew she did that. Hero in the morning and cook by the evening. Ah, the wonders of the common creature!" I looked at Georgiana, laughed and tickled her arm. "We're going to be aunts."

"Yes, we are."

Then her face dropped to alarm and anxiety.

"I have no idea how to be an aunt."

Ah, how contagious discomfort can be! At the fall of her expression, which transformed from excitement to fright, so did my will and way. I felt the suddenness of the change of having a niece or nephew quickly, and my brow furrowed, in the same style as hers did.

"No, nor do I."

"Do not think another moment on the matter," Enara coaxed us, "or do not do so in a way that it would cause you pain. No one knows how to be anything until they do it. You will learn to be kind, and you'll even learn to exude a maternal air about you."

"Besides," Arthur Philips suggested, "you have been my mother's companion very often when you came to visit."

"That's true," I realized, "we did."

"Yes, you did." His expression became wonderfully wicked. "And how would you feel if I decided to punish you for not thinking of her?"

"Oh, you wouldn't, Arthur! You had better do no such thing. Aunt Philips has been a great mentor for me."

"As well as Aunt Gardiner," Mary added.

"Yes. I only forgot them in this moment, but I will remember them in the next. There, Arthur, you had better not put me on the spot so horribly, will you?" I appealed to Enara, despite that I knew this was all spoken in jest. "Enara, convince your new beau that he is being too unkind."

"He needs no convincing from me in words," Enara acknowledged. "I sometimes have a habit of pressuring him with a look. Come, let us look sternly at him and see what happens next."

Mimicking her, we both looked serious at Arthur.

"Very well," Arthur replied, with a faux expression of contrition, "I give into the ladies, and will not bring you to the court of judgment, Kitty."

I touched Enara's arm.

"You do your service very well by being a wife."

"It is my way. Thank you for noticing."

After an hour of us all sitting around, discussing the future of the children, we were all granted entry to the bedroom where Jane and Lizzy were.

Lady Fitzwilliam proved herself to be the ultimate matriarch because she immediately found the comfort of ordering everyone around as if we all had known her for our entire lives.

"I will only let two people visit the ladies at one time," she instructed. "This way, they will not be overtaxed. They are at the special time in their lives where too much activity, or even conversation, can be detrimental to the child." Lord Fitzwilliam chuckled. "Are you laughing at me?"

"Never, dearest. Oh, very well, maybe a little. They are not altogether invalids, you know."

"When you deliver a child, then I defer to you on the matter. But since I was the one who succeeded at bringing three sons into the world, I must believe to being the authority on the subject. Besides, are you forgetting that, when I was first with child, you never let me walk more than three steps without ordering a servant to fetch something for me."

Lord Fitzwilliam slapped his lap, feeling found out.

"I was worried that you would bring that up."

"Yes, I did bring that up, Lord Fitzwilliam. And I would do it again, gladly."

Lord Fitzwilliam turned to the rest of us, taking out his newspaper.

"Single and newly married men, this is what you have to look forward to: your wife will keep minute details of everything, and then bring it up every few years, to remind you of what you used to be like."

"You like it, Father," Colonel Fitzwilliam said, "don't even deny it. You love it when Mother brings up the past."

"Yes, I do have a fondness for looking back. But teasing is important to any marriage, mark my words. Truly, take out a pen and set this down. Teasing helps a marriage vastly."

We all laughed.

"And here I tease you by taking control over the situation," Lady Fitzwilliam voiced. "You may own this house, my dear, but I have the joys of running it."

"I'll sit in this chair and make myself smaller, while you make yourself larger."

Lady Fitzwilliam smiled at us.

"He actually likes it when I rule our domain. It gives him the joys of sitting by the fire and having little to distress or vex him. Oh dear, now we talk in circles."

"I prefer circles. Going in a straight line is so unproductive."

Colonel Fitzwilliam rubbed his forehead.

"Mother and Father, at any other time, your witticisms would be welcome. We younger folk love when you older sort begin to speak so much and say very little to the purpose. You make up for when we have nothing to say. But once you allow us all to take our turns and wish the young ladies our congratulations, then you can go back to your public teasing."

"Very well, we will save our delicious nonsense for after I give instruction," Lady Fitzwilliam acknowledged. "Georgiana and Miss Bennet are the two sisters, so they shall be the first to see their sisters. Then Mr. and Mrs. Atkins, since Mrs. Atkins is another sister. Afterwards, Mr. and Mrs. Philips, you may follow. Then, Richard, you may go with me."

"Sound listing," Colonel Fitzwilliam announced.

Georgiana and I immediately rushed to the stairs.

"But you ought to stay for only five minutes before I send up the next set," Lady Fitzwilliam declared.

"Only five minutes?" I asked.

"Yes. Believe me, you will have many other days to talk with them about it more. Nine months full of it, I assure you. Now get along with you both."

Georgiana and I walked up the steps. While we did so, we overheard Colonel Fitzwilliam say, "Now Mother and Father, I believe you may return to your witty nonsense. For we truly do enjoy listening to it."

When we were on the upper landing, we finally felt like we could speak.

"So, Lady Fitzwilliam..." I began.

"Yes, that is my aunt," Georgiana responded. "Is she not a character?"

"I think I might grow to like her for it. Unless she proves not to like me. But we shall see, Georgie. I might be able to pass through this house and make no enemies. That would be very refreshing."

"You are being ridiculous, Kitty."

"I'm sure I am. Yes, I'm sure that I am."

We reached the door, knocked and Mr. Darcy opened it. When he did, we saw something awe-inspiring. His eyes were smiling. The sight was enough to knock us backwards.

"You look happy," Georgiana managed to utter.

"I suppose I do, don't I?" he said, his voice cracking somewhat. "I am going to be a father. I might really be so."

"Yes, you will," I said, a little wispy, "it looks good on you already."

"And what of us?" I overheard Elizabeth say over his shoulder. "Darcy, let us see our sisters. You hold them in custody by keeping them in the doorway."

Darcy moved aside and allowed us entry. Eagerly, Georgiana and I walked up to Jane and Elizabeth, who were no longer laying down, but sitting in chairs by the window. With the sun behind them, they looked radiant.

"Our sisters are going to be mothers!" I cried, as we rushed up to them and took their hands. Mr. Bingley only had time to immediately shift out of our way as we sprinted past him to get to our kinswomen. We embraced Jane and Elizabeth, giving our congratulations repeatedly.

"My *my*," Jane said, "you are too good, you both. Oh, I don't know that I have ever been so happy. Except on our wedding day, Mr. Bingley."

"No offense was taken, my love," Bingley responded, "this is an event that eclipses even our day of tying the knot. Now that I think about it, where does that phrase even come from?"

"Tying the knot is an ancient wedding tradition," Darcy answered simply, and rather instinctively, "it was an ancient Celtic practice, which dates back to the medieval era, where it literally binds couples together in matrimony by tying knots of cloth around their hands."

"You know everything, don't you?"

"I try to make it my habit."

I looked between the husbands and their wives.

"This is truly a blessed day, isn't it?" I asked, rhetorically.

"As conceited as this sounds," Elizabeth said, "I agree with you. This is the first time that I can say that being conceited is a look that I like to wear."

"And you wear it well," Georgiana assured her. "How lovely you both look. Oh, you give us such joy. You make aunts of Kitty, Mary, Lydia, and me."

"Oh," I said, amazed when hearing my one-time favorite sister's name.

"What is it, Kitty?" Jane asked.

"It's strange, but it's been so long since I thought of Lydia. And to wonder, what would she think of this now."

"Either she would think that being an aunt would be a good joke and she would die from laughter," Elizabeth inferred, "or she would be upset for not being the first one to be with child."

"I am sure that she would be happy for us," Jane said, diplomatically.

"Jane and Lizzy," I said, "do me the honor of thinking that I know what she would do. After all, we were bosom friends, weren't we?"

"Very well," Jane said, "what do you think Lydia would say?"

"I think you are both right. Lydia is more complex than she sometimes lets on. She would he happy for you both. That would be her first reaction. Her second reaction would be to laugh and say what a good joke. And then she would secretly harbor a bit of jealousy for not being the first to conceive. She is capable of having three separate reactions to the same bit of news."

"True."

Elizabeth rolled her eyes.

"And which one of us will have to write her?"

They both turned to me.

"Very well," I said, "I can take a hint."

"Well," Georgiana said, "I suppose that you both will not be able to dance at the ball at Verity Park near the end of our stay here."

"And that is the only negative aspect to our situation," Elizabeth said. "For I find dancing to be the best way of encouraging affection, even if one's partner is barely tolerable." Here she looked archly at Mr. Darcy. He rolled his eyes in turn.

"You tease me," he said.

"A wife's province."

Georgiana turned to me.

"Did we not see a similar scene downstairs?" she asked me.

"Yes, I believe we did. My goodness, it does feel like we are now part of the cycle that is conversation."

There was a knock on the door.

"Kitty and Georgie!" Mary called from the other side. "It's our turn."

Georgiana and I kissed our sisters, offered our congratulations to the happy couple once more, and then we went downstairs, for our five minutes was over.

As I came down the stairs, Lady Fitzwilliam gave me a significant look, that was masked by the others speaking in the room. I was not left to suffer under her scrutinizing eye for very long, because Colonel Fitzwilliam approached me. Georgiana seemed to marvel at being interested in speaking to everyone else, because she left my side, immediately.

"Well," Colonel Fitzwilliam said, "how did you find your sisters? Did the joys of newly found maternity render them even more beautiful than they already were?"

"The sun was shining behind them," I explained, "and the sun was jealous. Well now, twice the conception, twice the happiness."

Chapter Two

THE TORN HEART

The entire day was spent with us talking of the happy event that would soon follow by the middle of next year.

"It just occurred to me," Mr. Bingley noted as we all were sitting down. "All our dreams of going to Italy for our delayed honeymoon will now be dashed."

"Yes," Elizabeth confirmed, "I had that thought as well."

"Oh," Lord Fitzwilliam said, "were you wishing to go to Rome?"

"We very much were," Darcy acknowledged, "but not just there. We would go from there to Florence, Venice, Assisi, and perhaps even Capri."

"Oh, the Italian sky was the destination," Elizabeth said, "but now, we must be like parents and give way to thinking about someone else. And that someone is those who are growing within us."

"When they come into the world, I suppose, we would be giving them the ultimate adventure," Jane pondered, "would we not?"

"Precisely, my love," Bingley responded, "for we would be giving them life."

"Oh well," Elizabeth said, "Italy shall have to wait. After all, it's not like it's going anywhere now, is it?"

Lord Fitzwilliam turned to Mary and Enara.

"Well now," he said, "the correct response is to wish you two equal amounts of felicity."

"Thank you for my share of the compliment," Enara said, "but in truth, I fear the idea of becoming a mother, at present."

"Do you?" Arthur said.

"Ah," Lord Fitzwilliam said, leaning his head closer and becoming intrigued. "Is there trouble in paradise?"

"Give her time to explain, you rogue," Lady Fitzwilliam jested.

"My viewpoint is not permanent, I assure you," Enara said, then she turned to Arthur. "But merely selfish. I just obtained you as a husband. Therefore, it follows that I want a little more time with you before I have to share my attention with children."

"Oh, that is a relief to hear!" Mary professed. "I thought that I was strange for not wishing to run into motherhood immediately. I thought I was quite the odd creature."

"You share this sentiment as well?" Mr. Atkins asked, surprised.

"I confess that I do. After all, when you marry someone, you uncover another side of themselves that you never could have before you were so. You never fully know a person until you live with them. It's like becoming acquainted with another aspect of the person you love. It is always nice to settle down and become acquainted with that new aspect before an infant is brought into the relationship."

"You suggest that it is best to become a mother and father when you are more complete and fully comfortable in your relationship," Colonel Fitzwilliam summed up.

"I find that very sensible," Mr. Atkins supported. "Mrs. Atkins, you actually like my company? I've met quite a few couples who married, and then when the vows were finished being exchanged, the married couple wanted nothing to do with each other."

We all chuckled.

"I can attest to that practice," Lady Fitzwilliam said. "Lord Fitzwilliam, remember how we waited to have children two years into our marriage?"

"I did, and that was as good an idea as any."

"Really?" Jane asked.

"Yes, we did," Lord Fitzwilliam said, "it was all the rage to marry very young, back in our day. You must understand, in our youth, people were known for not living as long as they do nowadays. Medicine has improved greatly since we were young. Therefore, you had to marry at a young age. Remember, my dear, how everyone around us viewed us as strange when we didn't produce an heir a year into wedlock?"

"I did," Lady Fitzwilliam confirmed, "and I did not care for any of it."

"Nor did I." He waved his hand, dismissively at an invisible force that signified that he was shooing away the demons of his past. "Those fools. What did they know? Not everyone is ready to be parents so soon into marriage, just as not every marriage is the same. But no! Everyone must fit the same scale in life, and if you do anything remotely different than the status quo, they will die of shock. But we outsmarted them, didn't we, my dear?"

"Yes, we did. All those naysayers got married and had children without ever taking the time to get to know each other beforehand. The husbands and wives grew to not have anything in common, and eventually used the children as their battleground."

"Though, there sometimes was more to it than that." Lord Fitzwilliam leaned into us all, conspiratorially. "Sometimes, those couples wed, when the bride was already with child."

We all cooed.

"I cannot imagine that sort of situation," Jane gasped.

"Oh, believe it!" Elizabeth laughed. "A knobstick wedding is all too common a thing."

"Oh yes," Lady Fitzwilliam said, "and in our day, they were not uncommon. It is simply that we never talked about it. Well...not in a public manner. Although now that much time has passed, we are able to discuss things. Different times. Different times. Then again, humanity usually does tend to remain the same."

Immediately, Jane, Lizzy, Mary, and I blushed. Remembering Lydia's plight with Mr. Wickham was inevitable. And since her shame was known at Rosings Park, it surely was known at Matlock. In fact, the more that I thought of it, I was amazed that we had been so well-received as we had been. I wanted answers, and I knew just the person that I could ask about it.

~

"You are right," Colonel Fitzwilliam said as I was sitting at the desk in the music room and writing the letter to Lydia. "My parents are aware of your younger sister's actions."

"Do the servants know?" I asked, dipping my pen in the ink.

"Now that, I can assure you, is not the case. In fact..." Colonel Fitzwilliam walked up to the doorway, closed it mostly and then sat closer to me. "Let us speak lower."

"Or use ambiguous terms," I offered. "Every time that I try to be quiet, I forget—that's the product of having a voice that carries. Well, I give you permission to tell me to lower my voice if I ever fall back into resonance."

"I shall, but you are right. In such cases, ambiguity is our friend. But yes, my parents are aware of Mrs. Wickham's *situation*."

"And yet, when we came here, they had no judgment on the matter?"

"They did, initially. After all, in this world, connections are everything. And since Darcy was expected to find his marital happiness elsewhere, there was apprehension on the subject."

"And what changed it?" I asked. He rubbed his eyebrow, and there was a slight blush on his cheek. I stopped writing and was able to interpret his bashful look. "It was you, wasn't it? You helped smooth the way, as it were. You encouraged your parents to overlook our questionable connections, didn't you?"

"I did little." He blushed.

"You did something. That is much appreciated."

"Besides, my parents could never stay angry with Darcy for very long, even if they ever were. Also, my parents were very aware that Darcy was never going to marry Anne, so they were prepared for that. And since Mrs. Wickham's fate was saved, there was no lasting damage done. Though, I doubt that Darcy would have cared, one way or the other.

Especially since Darcy blamed himself for that entire situation."

"I heard that he did. Thank goodness that Darcy felt a sense of accountability because many people would not have. By having a conscience, he showed his goodness. But your parents are forgiving. I am happy for that."

I continued writing.

"What do you write?" he asked.

"A letter to Lydia," I explained. "I am informing her of our sisters' good fortune, and the news that she will be an aunt."

"Would that really make Lydia happy?"

"In truth, Colonel, I do not know. Lydia is like the rest of us: she has many parts to her, and something always remains hidden. Her reaction will be traditional, verbose, and exuberant, but the human soul is vast. Perhaps with her, there are deep waters that run underneath the shallow stream that her brain wades in."

"You still do not favor your younger sister?"

I blinked, bit my lip and then I formed my answer slowly.

"She and I were the best of friends for the longest time."

His expression altered slightly.

"You can talk about it. What still gets in the way?"

"Life, I suppose. And the fact that I realized that I was living in her shadow. She was two years younger than me, and I followed after her—and she led me into the duck pond. Well, that is not entirely true. A duck pond is charming. I allowed myself to be led into a quagmire. Has that ever happened to you? Where you realize that you allowed yourself to be led astray in so horrid a manner? To know that you are nothing but a blind follower."

"First, being a follower is not always a great evil. If life were full of leaders, and no one to follow them, then nothing would ever get done. There would be no armies, no workforce, no religion, no committees...nothing! As long as you never fall into a situation where you hurt anyone, all can be reconciled. Second, that's a part of the growing up process. Thirdly, it's a role that we all have been in, in one time or another. In the end, you seemed to escape its vicious cycle, and you came out of it, unscathed."

"Not entirely unscathed. But the lacerations I received out of it were minimal, and the wounds did heal." I leaned back and a sudden thought came to me. "But imagine what would have happened? What if I, in a fit of rash romanticism, had been like Lydia, and given into the love for a man to such a point that I would run off with him, with no confirmed prospects."

"You would not have done that."

"I know...but imagine if I had. The world would have forsaken me." I looked at him squarely. "Would you have?"

"I want to say that I wouldn't have, but you see, I am in love with you. Therefore, it would be hard for me to look at you after that."

I smiled sadly.

"I am not upset with that answer. You could have been gallant and lied to me, but you decided to be truthful, no matter how ugly it would have made you look."

"I did look ugly, didn't I?"

"I know what heartbreak can do to someone. It takes a while before rational thought and compassion can return to the torn heart."

"Yes, it does. I want to believe that I would want you to be saved from a bad fate and that I would wish you well. Maybe time would help me."

"Well, I do not believe I would ever do that. But if I ever were to slip in that way, I will ask this of you. Be my friend and help me. Be...there for me."

He leaned back in his chair.

"We really are linked, aren't we?" he asked.

"Yes, we are. Whether we like it or not."

"Then I will be your protector."

I gave him the warmest of smiles.

"Let me read you the letter to Lydia. Tell me if it is a good letter."

I did so, and when I finished, he approved of it.

⁓

As I sealed the letter, I wrote the Newcastle address on the front.

"Kitty?"

"Yes, Richard?"

"What of this other man? Is he also your protector?"

Growing somber, I lowered the letter and let it rest on the table. Breathing in deeply, I placed my hands on my lap.

"Have I vexed you?" he asked.

"No, you haven't."

"Have I made you uncomfortable?" he asked.

"Yes, you have."

"Forgive me. You don't have to tell me anything."

"But I must. Besides, we've talked about it before. I don't know why, but there is something about this moment that feels so very grave."

"I did use the word 'protector'. A man wants to be the protector of the woman that he loves. When another man also has the title, it feels strange."

"Precisely."

"I know that you adore this Lieutenant Finlay, but I must ask...do you love us in the same manner? Is it equal? Or do you love him more or less than I?"

"Richard," I sighed.

"I know, it is horrid to ask. In fact, I don't even know what I was about, for the answer would easily cause me pain."

"Whatever answer I give, what would be the point?" I asked. "No, really, what would be the point? Any answer could harm you."

"I know."

I closed my eyes, leaning back in my chair.

"I love you both equally," I professed.

Colonel Fitzwilliam placed his hand on the desk, drumming his fingers against the wood.

"Is that the truth? The real truth?"

"Yes, it is."

He sighed out.

"See?" I smiled, empathetic. "No matter what, it causes you pain."

"What pain do you think I have?"

"By me loving you as much, there is the pain of seeing me walk the halls with disappointed affections. And by me loving him as much, I might hurt your vanity. Or am I wrong?"

"You know what is so frustrating?" he blurted out. "When we first talked about this, I managed it like a gentleman—and like a true officer. I bore this all so well. And now I am reverting to a savage-like state."

"I am right, aren't I?"

"Yes, you are. And that is the most frustrating thing of all. I am frustrated that you know what's in my mind, that you understand my rashness, and am patient with it. That you can see so much into my soul and can display it in a way that maybe no other woman ever shall be. And that I am ugly under the face of your beauty."

I leaned toward him. "Why do you call yourself so?"

"You deal with me plainly and truthfully. I deal with you in a way where my heart is often retreating. Then I come back again, and I retreat again. Yes, there are rare moments where I want your heart all to myself. And then, in the next second, I respect this other man—this Finlay. I understand why he is in love with you. And maybe he retreats, like I do. But it's only a matter of time before one of us stops retreating. Where one of us finds opportunity and we can make you an offer. It's only a matter of who has the opportunity first."

"A race to the finish line," I jested. "Now it all comes down to it. Who is faster? The tortoise or the hare?"

"Which one of us is the tortoise and which one of us is the hare?"

I smirked.

"I shall never tell you that."

He groaned lightly.

"Oh, but Kitty."

"No." I was firm. "I will never tell you. I shall hold it over your head for the rest of your life, torturing you in a way that is most unbecoming, and you will have to endure it all. There! That is Kitty's revenge on you, sir! Everything that you have put me through, and now I have my reckoning."

He chuckled, then leaned forward, with his stern gaze.

"Tell me that you love me."

I ground my teeth.

"You really are incorrigible, aren't you?"

"Yes, I am. But in this moment, my more logical side is winning out. Once again, I accept your love for this Finlay character. I respect and admire him for his good taste. But I must also be evil and vain. I need to hear you say that you love me."

"And if I do, will you behave yourself?"

"Hand on my heart, I will be a good man again in the next moment."

Ah, the joys of being comfortable around an imperfect man who accepted my imperfections. We both could sit there and be as foolish as we wished, and no harm could come of it. For we were, in all manners of speaking, good people with occasional bad habits. That is what most of us in life were: good people with occasional bad habits.

I bit my lip and could not ignore my habits.

"I love you," I said simply. "Very much."

His eyes relaxed.

"Good. Now I can be a better man in this moment. And thank you."

"For what?"

"I never thought I could fall in love again. I owe you that. No matter how torn my heart now is."

Chapter Three

ATTEMPT OF AN OLIVE BRANCH

Once all well-wishes had been offered, the mothers and fathers-to-be were a little exhausted from the effusions of joy. Lady Fitzwilliam was wise to only have the others stay briefly with them, because they were content to spend the entire day removed from society and finding peace within themselves.

When appealing to the two young couples, Lady Fitzwilliam needed no explanation; their expressions said enough. She suggested that they both retreat to their own rooms and were allowed to enjoy the company of having the world all to themselves.

Bingley and Jane were profuse in their thanks.

Elizabeth was charming in her gratitude, while Darcy was more serious in his.

Both couples were able to remove their strict clothing, climb into bed and enjoy the other's company. One could wonder at what Jane and Mr. Bingley did in their moments of intimacy, but of Darcy and Elizabeth, it was more obvious. Their characters were naturally more passionate, and they pushed themselves into each other's embrace.

When the door was closed and the servants far away from their room, Mr. Darcy and Elizabeth turned to one another. Their eyes met, their spirits aroused, as Darcy rushed to Elizabeth, tore off her dress immediately, and began to remove her stays. While doing so, Elizabeth removed his jacket and waist-coat, and he fell on her as she lay bare underneath him.

Wrapping her legs around his waist, Darcy began to kiss her passionately.

"Elizabeth, you really are with child," he said harshly, between kisses.

"I am." She was breathless.

"Oh, dearest Elizabeth. What a gift you have given me."

"Ah, selfish fellow."

They held each other in their bed, too afraid that any sort of physical activity would hinder the child. Therefore, all they could do was rest in each other's embrace, finding the joy of romantic solitude. As they stared up at the canopy, their bodies glowed, wrapped in each other's arms.

"Married life continues to present new plateaus, doesn't it?" Elizabeth asked as she ran her hand through Darcy's hair.

"If one does it correctly, then yes it does."

"And if one does it incorrectly, it presents new abysses?"

"Precisely. And we do it correctly."

"Yes, we do. I daresay that I haven't polluted the shades of Pemberley yet, have I?"

"Ah, is that where your mind goes?"

"Your Aunt de Bourgh leaves quite a distinct impression. One cannot ever fully get her out of one's mind. How shameful and tedious it is, isn't it? The habit of dwelling on a terrible moment when you are in a very happy sort of place."

"Yes, I understand the sentiment. Many of us remember the provocative moments, even when they are long gone, and better days are on the horizon."

"And better days will be." Elizabeth rested her head against Mr. Darcy's chest, and she found herself unable to think more on the subject. Her mind was at work, as was a sudden desire for peace. "Darcy?"

"Yes, dearest."

"I have stumbled on the strangest notion."

"And what is that?"

"I have come upon the idea of wishing to extend an olive branch. You know very well that I didn't care a fig for when Lady Catherine objected to our match. I was content to let her rot at Rosings Park, where we were free from looking at her. Do you despise me for sounding so wicked?"

"Never. Nothing can account for how abominably she treated you. You were well-within your rights to give her a proper set-down."

"Thank you for encouraging your sordid wife," she joked. "And now I shall be serious. I suppose that it all may account for now discovering that I am growing another life within me. I don't want our new child to be born into a world where part of the family is estranged from the other."

Darcy's eyes narrowed, seeing where the conversation was headed.

"You wish to write to my aunt de Bourgh, don't you?"

"Yes," Elizabeth stated, "I do."

~

"Maybe, we ought to try and reach out to your aunt," Elizabeth began to state her claim, "informing her of our new development. Sometimes a child is the best sort of olive branch in the world. I cannot say that it will work, but I can see Lady Catherine's mind at work now. She is the sort who cannot stay quiet for long and prefers speaking more than holding a grudge. Unless I am wrong."

"You are not. Her anger of feeling scorned might fuel her for a while, but having a captive audience will always be her chief object."

"Yes, because your aunt is a natural born speaker, and not a silent one. If someone told her that she could not speak for a whole five minutes, she might explode."

Enjoying Darcy's giving way to humor, Elizabeth chuckled and tickled his chin.

"You only add fuel to my argument, and that is good. I think, if she were to hear that I was with child, her mind would initially be resentful of the fact that it wasn't Anne de Bourgh's. However, soon that would give way to knowing that she, already being a mother, would order me around with all the advice that she could bestow."

Darcy chuckled.

"Oh, you see the image that I present! Can't you see her, walking here and there, ordering me on how large the carriage should be. How often the child ought to be fed. And if the child be born a girl, how I was wrong that it was not a boy."

"Her only child is a girl."

"And that will not stop her from saying that I did not do my duty."

"Oh, that is true."

Suddenly, an idea struck Elizabeth with such force, that she shrieked 'oh' and let her head fall, forehead first, on the pillow next to Darcy's face.

"Wait," Darcy observed, "I remember that face. You're doing that 'I had a revelation that is so powerful that I have to bury my head in the pillow because it's unpleasant'."

"It's because it *is* unpleasant! It just occurred to me that I have the perfect way of drawing your aunt to Pemberley."

"And how so?"

"If we are not unfortunate, and the child does not miscarry— heaven forbid that would happen! But if all goes well, and my pregnancy goes as planned, then the best way to get her was to write to her, asking her advice on everything that I ought to do. From the food I eat, to the best exercise to take, to how to lay down when I sleep."

The implications of this were not lost on her husband.

"Oh, my word. Lizzy, if you were to do that, Lady Catherine would present herself on our doorsteps within two days after receiving the letter and then dictate your life. Elizabeth, it would drive you mad."

"Yes, it would." Elizabeth groaned under the weight of her own keen insight. "What do you do when your best idea is the very worst idea?"

"You ask me," he said, keenly.

"Oh, do I?"

"Yes, you do."

"Very well, o' proud one. What is your advice?"

"I think you have the right idea of appealing to Aunt Catherine's vanity. But I believe that neither you nor I have the ability to withstand that for very long. Mr. Bingley will soon be dashing off to Godfrey Park again, so that Jane could settle down during her time, especially close to us."

"Oh, is there now some serious talk of the matter at last?"

"There is. With every day that we have been from seeing the place, Bingley has thought of it more and more."

"And I believe that you would help encourage this as a prospect."

"I do. Also, I thought it would make you happy."

"It does. Oh, Darcy, that is precisely what I would wish. Well, with the purchase of the estate, we will need to spend quite a few days there, helping them adjust to their new life. This will give us the precise excuse to only have Aunt Catherine stay at Pemberley closer to the holidays, and for a short visit, because we would have to journey to Godfrey Park and stay there until the Bingleys are well-settled. After all, Bingley will need advice."

"And your sister and you are at a special time where you both would love to be in each other's company."

"I think I could endure your aunt's tyrannical ways for a week. Though I make no promises that she and I might not become so vexed with each other that we might proceed to kick and push each other out of the window under the slightest provocation."

Darcy kissed Lizzy's forehead.

"I know that you speak by way of a joke."

"Yes, I do, dearest. I've learned to confine my answers to her in two or three-word sentences. But I will be thinking of how good she looks when falling from a window the entire time. Of course, I respect her because she is your aunt."

"Oh, I am sure that you do."

"Yes, I am happy you are sure." Elizabeth breathed in deeply. "Well, there is nothing for it. What ought to be done cannot be done soon enough."

Wrapping one of the sheets around herself, she walked to the desk and composed the letter. As she did so, Darcy rolled over and watched her as she sat there, dipping the pen in the ink, and composing the missive, with her dark brown curls falling around her shoulders.

"You know something?" Darcy asked.

"Yes?"

"For the longest time, I always wished that you ladies were allowed to wear your hair long."

"I have often wondered about that myself. When I was a child, I wanted long hair so very much. What a joy I thought it was, to be able to grow my hair down to the top of my thighs, with it blowing in the wind, like a savage and hearty creature. But fashions even hold precedence over me. It's one of the few things that are my lord and master."

"And where do I fall in that category?"

"Never fear. The first lord and master will always be you. Oh, I lie! Fashion will always be the first."

～

When Elizabeth finished writing her letter, she read it out loud. When she finished it, Darcy approved, and it would be sent the next day.

"Well now," Elizabeth said heavily, "the deed is done."

"You are scared of the notion of seeing my aunt, aren't you? No, Elizabeth, your jokes and witticisms will not save you from me noticing that you are preparing yourself for a daunting task."

"I cannot hide from you, can I?"

"No, you cannot."

"How terrible! To be a wife and not have the skill to hide things from one's husband. What a shocking thing."

"Ladies must have their secrets, and I keep taking them from you."

"You do. I cannot forgive you."

Elizabeth stood up, walked over to him, and kissed him passionately.

"And you throw me off from our course of conversation. Once again, you use your witticisms."

"I do. Oh well, at least I can enjoy your more agreeable aunt and uncle Fitzwilliam. They make up for all the rest."

"Yes, they do. Don't they? They like you, and it was all because they were willing to like you."

"And that makes all the difference when it comes to family. When a family is prepared to like a new addition to their set, it makes everything all the easier. I am happy that they are so kind. Oh, but I do wish that we would have been able to dance at the Verity Ball. Though I may not know the Luxfords, dancing is always a good way of making a stranger find you agreeable. Oh well, we have four sisters to make us look like a novelty, and Mrs. Philips will be very good at interesting everyone. But when it comes to charming single ladies, Kitty and Georgiana will have to represent us."

"They will like that."

"I am certain that they will."

Darcy looked at Lizzy, contemplative.

"Never would I have known that they would become such friends."

"I never would either, but the more I think on it, the more it makes all the sense in the world. I am fond of Georgie."

"Even you call her that now."

"Kitty started something that is quite contagious. But yes, I am fond of Georgie, but nothing can make more sense than two single ladies always being in each other's confidence. There is a similarity of situation there, that no one else can supply. And whatever could be said of Kitty, she is nonthreatening and amiable in every aspect. That makes her a very easy sort of person to connect to. And Georgie is the precise sort of friend for Kitty—gentle, unassuming, and willing to enjoy her spirit. Yes, they quite complement each other, don't they?"

"Yes, they do," Darcy concurred. "And yet, there is one thing to worry over."

"What?"

"Well...what happens when Georgie marries? Your sister is

attractive, but your father can give her little. My sister will probably marry first. Do you think that would change their friendship?"

Lizzy's eyes widened.

"Oh, I never thought of that."

"Yes."

"Maybe they might be able to weather the change, but they are so much partners in crime, that it would alter things. When that happens, I will feel heartily sorry for Kitty. First Lydia is lost to her, and soon Georgie might be. Would Kitty be able to bear it, I wonder. I've grown to worry about her. She desires to have a place in the world—and to have some importance."

"We all do, I suppose."

"Yes, but Kitty's mission feels deeper. More intense and more confusing to find. I don't think she is meant to walk down the same path that we are."

"No, I don't think so. If that be the case, it must be so much harder for her."

"Oh, we worry too much for two people who just found out that we might be parents."

"Yes, we do. I suppose that it is the product of caring about one's family. But I just had another thought."

"What?" Elizabeth asked.

"I never thought to consider this, but I wonder if my aunt and uncle are aware that their son is in love with Kitty?"

"Oh, my word! Now that is another development. Do they know that their son is in love with my sister?"

Chapter Four

THE MOTHER-IN-LAW THAT MIGHT NEVER BE

The next day, I was changing out of my day clothes to prepare for dinner. Fortunately, Lucy—who finally was brought to being my maid here—had finished my hair earlier than expected. There was a knock on my door.

"Who is it?" Lucy asked me, for she had grown accustomed to me being able to tell who it was by someone's knock.

"I don't know," I answered her, "the knock is unfamiliar therefore it must be either the mistress or Enara. Come in!"

The door opened and Lady Fitzwilliam entered. Well, at least I knew that I was half-right.

"Lady Fitzwilliam," I extoled, a little breathless. Instinctively, I curtsied, even though there was no reason to. "I am honored that you came to see me."

"You are too formal, my dear," Lady Fitzwilliam said. "I merely came to perform the service that I said I would when you all first came."

"Service, ma'am?"

"Yes. Do you not recall that I said I would visit all you ladies individually to decide what would be your best gown to wear at Verity Hall?"

"Oh," I sighed, relieved, "yes, I remember now. When it comes to remembering announcements about such things, sadly you ought not to depend on my memory. Wait, do I give off the impression that I never remember anything that people say?"

Lady Fitzwilliam nodded her head, diplomatically. She turned to Lucy.

"You may go and be free of your duties for half an hour. Enjoy yourself and I would recommend that you get better acquainted with my servants in their quarters."

"Very good, ma'am," Lucy answered confidently, and she left us alone. When she closed the door, Lady Fitzwilliam wasted no time in presenting me with truths.

"You are intimidated by me, aren't you?" she asked suddenly. It was so shocking a confrontation that I was a little offput, initially.

"I... I," I stuttered.

"Yes?"

Oh well, there was nothing for it, was there? A lie would be seen through quickly. Or me laughing my way through our discussion would not do at all. Innocent laughter would not do for such a great woman as Lady Fitzwilliam. Thus, my lighter side was not to be born, and all I could do was tell her the truth, plain and simple.

I sighed.

"Well," I confessed, "yes, if you must know. But please, Lady Fitzwilliam, do not take offense at my words. You are an excellent host. It is merely that you are the Lady, the mistress of Matlock, and I am a country girl. You must understand that there will always be a sense of dread of not living up to any expectations that are placed on a person."

"I understand. Also, you are young, and that accounts for some senses of anxiety when meeting new people. When you reach my age, you become less phased by the grandeur of others —especially if your self-respect is set properly in its place."

"You understand me!"

"Believe it or not, I was young once too, you know."

"Yes, I do know. It is just that it's very easy to assume that no one else suffers an inner sense of dread, in the way that you do. You forget that the world does have compassion in it. I just... every time we talk, I feel that I am saying something wrong."

"If you feel that you are always wrong, then you will always be wrong."

"I do not deny that a bit of my self-awareness does depend on the reactions of others. What I mean is that the problem is not that I feel wrong, but that my feelings are a reflection of others."

"What do you mean by that, child?"

"If someone approaches me, preparing to think everything I say and do is wrong, then I feel it, and therefore, I do wrong. I fall into the trap that they have set out for me. If they come towards me, prepared to not believe in me, and think everything I do is ugly, then I feel it. What I am trying to say is that...I feed off of the encouragement of others. I need the energy of others to activate my own. Call it a weakness if you may, for you may not ever wish to covet it. But it is, nevertheless, true. When I am met with a negative attitude in the room, I have a hard time keeping my head above water, if you will pardon my colloquial speech."

"Is that what you feel?"

"Yes, it is."

"I had never thought of that before. Then again, perhaps my station in life never brought me in the company of those who dared to make me feel any such thing. But I believe I can stretch my imagination and see why other people's reactions can make a young person question their self-worth."

"When you become accustomed to knowing Elizabeth, it's very easy to think we are all like her."

"Yes. Your sister does give off a feeling of being immovable. The whole world could despise her, and it would not distress or vex her in the slightest."

"I will never know how she does it."

"As you have mentioned, we are all born a little different."

"Perhaps," I said, "if I showed you gowns, it might help me be less apprehensive."

"Very well. After all, that is why I came. Proceed. And bring out the gowns that you think would be most fitting for a home like Verity Hall."

"What sort of place is Verity?"

"I prefer our home, but Verity Hall is equally as happily situated and equally as large."

My eyes widened.

"Oh. Your message is received."

I rushed to the closet to retrieve three of my best gowns.

❧

The first I took out was the blue gown, then the pink gown, and my white one, which was one of the first ballgowns that I ever had made for me when I was fully out in society.

Lady Fitzwilliam immediately picked them up, one by one, to inspect them.

"They are all handsome, and I believe that they will do nicely. But the blue one is cut in a way that I think will flatter you the best."

She raised the gown up to me and placed it against my person.

"Yes, I think it will do handsomely. And with a few ornaments in your hair, neatly arranged, it will be suitable."

"I am happy that you approve. This gown was made from some cloth from my uncle's factory."

"Your uncle?"

"Yes. My Uncle Gardiner owns a fabric and cloth factory. He's quite successful."

Then it occurred to me of what I had done. I had mentioned my uncle, a tradesman and manufacturer, to an earl's wife. I had made our connections more known, to a lady who was not used to suffering such talk.

I felt my cheeks redden as I looked to the floor, folding my hands in front of me.

"If a man is to be a tradesman," I excused, "then my uncle is the best kind. He is quite successful. If a man or woman is born to the world of manufacturing, then their achievements must surely count for something."

"I already am aware of your connections. Do not look on the floor in shame. While I confess that I am not eager to have such relations, I will not belittle them, for your family's sake."

"Thank you, ma'am. They are, after all, my family. I have the right to be proud of them."

"I can imagine so." She looked at the gown. "Well, while I would not recommend mentioning your uncle's profession at the ball, I can say that he evidently is very skilled at choosing cloth. A man who understands silk, and muslin, always ought to be commended."

"He would be happy to hear your praises. Can I give leave to write to him of your kind words in my next letter to them?"

"You may, but that is the only thing that I will give you permission to write about me."

"Of course. Thank you for your advice."

She continued to hold up the dress. As she inspected it, she opened her mouth and continued scrutinizing it.

"I will have my servant, Vera, prepare both your blue and pink gown on the day, in case I am in error. I need you to look your very best."

"I, madam?" I was marveled. "I'm not belittling my self-worth, but what importance would I have at this ceremony?"

She laid the gown back on the bed.

"I know that you are in love with my son."

~

The horror!

I do not think in hyperbolic and exaggerated means, but realistic ones.

I was standing in the room of a powerful woman, and she was the mother of the man that I fancied. And my connections not only were questionable, in her eyes, but I had no prospects either.

I took sharp breaths, preparing myself for a weighty conversation, where everything I said could come out wrong. There is nothing very simple about facing a doting mother.

"I know that I should say that I do not," I began, my voice perhaps a little uncertain. "But that would be disrespectful to you."

"Precisely. This is my house, and I prefer gentle sincerity."

She sat down, crossing her arms over her lap, and I stood before her. Feeling like she was a judge, and I was a defendant, who had no attorney. My case was mine to defend and explain.

"Well," she continued, "are you?"

"First," I began, "your ladyship should have no fear of me. I am poor, and I have no special title to my name. Your son is aware that I am not the right choice for him. Therefore, I am no threat to you."

"But if you did have the money, the title, and the means, would you consider my son?"

"Yes," I replied heavily, "I would. For a part of me is deeply in love with him."

She looked at me narrowly.

"A part of you? What does that mean, precisely?"

"When I first met your son, I had...been recovering from a lost love, who also is in the army. Like your son, he had not the means or prospects of supporting a woman from landed gentry. I was made and shaped to be a woman of leisure. Not labor. If that man were to marry, he would need a woman who could either bring a sizeable dowry, or she was economical and could run the household herself. I would bring neither to the match, so him and I were parted.

"When I met your son, I was recovering from that loss, your son was there for me during that time, and I was determined to recover. By doing that, my heart began to expand, and I found that I had room to believe in life after losing one's first big love. But your first love can never be fully forgotten. And then, your son, the Colonel, found his way into the part of my heart that was newly free."

"Whoever this man is," Lady Fitzwilliam stated, very seriously, "my son is better."

I blinked, for I felt the potency of her maternal instincts descending upon me. When a devoted mother discovers that her son's attachment to a young woman could be rivaled by another man, it doesn't matter how much that young woman is unsuitable. Your son is the man that should be first in that young lady's affections. It only took me a couple seconds to deduce this, therefore, I knew where her perspective came from.

"He very well could be," I said, for her comfort. "However, Colonel Fitzwilliam and I both have our first loves that we cannot forget. He and I are the same."

"Yes, he has. My son is a hopeless and wonderful romantic. I don't care for when he is blamed for being a rattle. The world is pathetically stupid in that way. They demand a man to be charming, but then when he is, he is labelled as a shameless flirt. Society is of a mean understanding, in such a way that it can never make up its mind about what is offensive.

"But my son...he is something more. Even in his plainness, he is wonderful. Sometimes, you need confirmation that you were a great mother. Richard is my confirmation. Despite not being considered handsome, he deserves a lovely woman with a sizeable dowry."

"He really is regarded as plain?" I asked, uneasy with that assessment.

"You don't think he is?" she asked, light and optimistic.

"Perhaps he is, objectively, and I simply forget. Yet he is of good height, is well-built, and perhaps his features are a little irregular, but what is regular?"

"Well now, that is confirmation of your affection for him. If you don't notice his plainness, then that means that you love him blindly." She looked ahead, falling back into her memories.

"When he was a child, he was beautiful. So very much so. It should have continued into his manhood. But it didn't. The teenage years can be hard on a young person. It altered him so much, and he went through a terrible time of insecurity. By the time he reached his manhood, in full, worry lines were on his face, his skin was hardened, and the army made it worse. But when I look on him, I still see that handsome boy who clung to me when he was scared of the dark. With his older brother, I was a little insecure with my parenthood. Frederick was my firstborn, and so he was the first test of how to raise a child. When I finally had Richard, at that point, I knew how to look after a son. I knew how to be a mother, and we raised Richard

35

very well. But Richard was also born with a female heart, so perhaps, he understood me from the beginning. And so, that beauty stayed on his face, no matter what scar the army gave him."

A part of me wanted to sit down and listen to her talk about Colonel Fitzwilliam all day. After all, a mother can tell you oceans about the man you care for. However, I knew that she had other duties, and that it felt like it would be disrespectful to sit down at all. So, I just stood there and restricted myself to brief sentences.

"He loves you," I said. "I see it in the way that he talks to us women. You raised him well."

"Thank you. I trained him to think that us women were everything in the world. He believed it, wholeheartedly."

At this point, Lady Fitzwilliam still had not mentioned my unsuitability as a wife, therefore, a part of me wondered and hoped that maybe she did not look on me like a problem. For a brief moment, it seemed like maybe she didn't measure me from the size of my poverty, but by the content of my character. If that were the case, then she was quite the interesting lady. For, in our world, we are all trained to size up a person's worth by the size of their pocketbook. Therefore, for her to start by analyzing other aspects of my person was unique.

"Your ladyship?" I couldn't help but ask.

"Yes?"

"By the way that you speak, you don't seem to hate the idea of me. What I mean is that I mentioned my lack of a dowry, and you said nothing. I simply say...oh, I fear any way I put this, I might be causing offense."

"Oh, I can answer to your implications. I do not like the fact that you have little to no dowry, I am upset that you are quite poor, and my son could never marry you."

The facts of life now fell upon me once more. I had assumed too quickly, but now the reality of the matter returned me back to the scenes that always encircled my life.

"I do not wish to hurt you," she continued, "but that is the reality of the matter."

"I know," I answered, "the truth is, you have not said anything that Colonel Fitzwilliam and I have not spoken of on quite a few occasions."

"And that is what makes it harder on me, and this whole situation."

"What would your ladyship mean by that?"

"From my observation, you both speak in a way that two people could try to obtain their entire lives, and not reach. There is a connection between you both, a comfort, that is organic, and cannon be replicated. It was how it was when I met the Earl. You can walk the entire world and not establish such a bond again. Richard could have had that with you. He could have had a wife who complemented his character, eradicated his loneliness, incited his passions, and was handsome. As vain as this sounds, we are all shallow creatures. Beauty is a currency in life, especially when it comes to us women.

"Jane and Elizabeth will have lovely daughters. With your beauty, any girls my son would have might look like you, and that would be good for them. Yes, again, I am vain, but we all have our vices. The idea of having pretty grandchildren is one of those. You had it in you to actually be almost worthy of marrying my son. Not many can boast of that. And so, your presence here antagonizes me. You are like a possibility that will never happen."

Her eyes shifted from resolution to wistfulness. "Are there truly no prospects on the horizon for you? Are there no relatives that can leave you a dowry in any way? No distant relative with no children who needs to pass down their wealth?"

"I hate to disappoint you. That is the last thing that I wish to do. But I have no prospects at all. My father can only leave me, perhaps, a hundred pounds a year."

Frustrated, Lady Fitzwilliam stood up, went to the window, and looked out through the curtains.

"Your father should have done better and saved money for you all," she stated simply.

"He had every intention of fathering a son. By the time that it was rendered impossible, he felt that there was no point in saving."

"That is no excuse. Forgive my rudeness, but truth is, if he were here now, I would tell him so to his face. When you have an entailment, you have to take everything into consideration. You have to consider every outcome. Children die for a plethora of reasons. It is always unwanted and undesired. But it is so. To think that you will always have a male heir is wishful thinking, but not practical, because a man might not always be produced, or he can die.

"Your father should have taken better care of you all. Or found another way to bring more income into the household, so that when you married, he could continue to provide a dowry throughout the years. I do not say such things to offend him. I speak in practicality. When you are a parent, it is your duty to provide for your child. You must be angry that I chastise him from a distance."

"I would be if I knew that he didn't feel the same way. But, looking back on his life, I think that he wishes that he had taken more steps, more measures. Now he lives by way of regret."

"He ought to. For it has affected your life, and mine. I want grandchildren. I'm at the age where I am healthy, but anything can happen. I want to see grandchildren before I die. I want to be able to know that our future is intact. Frederick still is not married, and Richard could have been, if your father had provided for you. I could have been a grandmother by now. But I'm not. So, forgive an old woman for being angry with your father, despite that I have neither the right nor the claim to render his actions accountable to my happiness. His negligence has, accidentally, affected both our lives."

"I never thought of it that way," I considered, truly perplexed at the concept of it. "But now that I do, yes...so much of my life has been dictated and shaped by the roads that my parents could have walked down...but didn't. But your ladyship, even with their faults, I do love them."

"As you ought to. They created you, raised you, and so, there is a sense of loyalty that one must always have. It is our moral duty. I just wish that more care had been taken."

"I suppose that I do as well. If that were the case, my sisters and I could have walked through life with less cares and worries."

"And more hope. But alas, here we are..."

Sighing, she stood up and looked down at my gowns.

"Lucy is a good servant, but I will always make certain that Vera tends to you as well, to prepare you for the ball. If you cannot marry my son, at least you can help in this way."

"How can I help him? I would like to be there for him, in every way that I can, but what could I do?"

"Your two eldest sisters are married women. Their beauty is definite, but it is also unavailable. Your third eldest sister, Mrs. Atkins, is not uncomely, but she is not as handsome as you. You are the last single woman in the set, and your beauty, charm, good nature, and friendship with Georgiana, are four qualities that can enhance my son's appearance. When a man walks into a ball with a beautiful woman whose heart he won, he looks more beautiful and attractive by association. You make him desirable, and that makes him more attractive to other ladies. That's how popularity works. You *have to* be the handsomest woman in the set, because other women of wealth and inheritance will want to dance with him, consider him for a prospect, and ignore that he is a younger son."

"Very well. I will help him in every way that I can. My only problem is that that's the only thing I can do. I am sorry that I am not the heiress that you were hoping for."

"I am sorry as well. I curse your father."

She walked to the door.

"And this conversation will never be revealed," she stated, and it was a direct order.

"No, it will not," I assured her. "My parents will never know that this conversation happened. And this tale will never leave Matlock. Here it will stay."

"Very good."

She closed the door behind her when she exited.

When alone, I was able to finally breathe out with ease. All the tension released, and I felt my limbs slacken.

I was being used. How interesting!

Chapter Five

A TALK WITH TWO COUSINS

"My mother really said all that?"

The next day, Colonel Fitzwilliam and I were walking along the grounds.

"Yes, she did," I confirmed, having finished telling him the entire story. "What a determined and maternal woman."

"Should I speak to her about what she said to you?" he asked, protectively.

"Not at all," I urged him. "I shall leave it to your own discretion to decide whether or not you want to tell her that I brought you into my confidence on the matter. For that is your right. But if you do, do not do so with a negative tone, or as if you are chiding her. She did not offend me in the slightest but was generously candid. She simply wanted to confront the truth of my relationship with you. Being your mother, perhaps she does have a bit of a right to know if another woman is obtaining your heart vainly. In fact, I like that she came to talk to me."

"Do you?"

"Yes," I stressed as we walked through the lovely gardens, with a wonderful assortment of bushes on both sides of us. "First, I now know where I stand with her. There is something altogether scary about when you don't know the depths of a woman's judgment about yourself. We're such deep creatures, us ladies. Our minds, hearts, and souls are a bottomless ocean. Perhaps it is the same with you men, but with us, we fear the unknown element that is in each of us. Your mother poured her soul to me. I appreciate that. Now, I am not afraid of her. Or at least, not in the way that I was before."

"True. And yes, we men are similar in that we are the largest body of water, and you can never see the bottom of us. Even we don't know where we begin and end sometimes."

I ran my hand through the leaves in the bushes.

"You look comfortable here," he noted, smiling.

"And I feel it. Then again, places don't matter, but people do." I looked at him, smiling, and he felt the vastness of my compliment. "I will always be comfortable around you. Your mother saw that about us. And I owe her that. It would have been much easier for her to hate me, but she didn't."

"My mother. I know that everyone says that they have the greatest mother in the world, Kitty. But that does not remove my right to stake my claim like a man of spirit. My mother is a superior woman. She would walk on hot coils for any of us."

"She would. She wants you to be happy, Richard. She wishes that you were given your heiress, and the sooner the better. I understand her reasons. Besides, the second reason that I was not upset with her candor was because I am just happy that she likes me."

Colonel Fitzwilliam laughed.

"Really?"

"Yes. You may not be aware of this, but not all mothers are happy with any woman who might be interested in her son. They look on us as an intrusion. You could be a saint, and you still would not make that mother happy. She didn't scorn me for favoring you. She only despises the fact that I cannot make her dream come true."

Colonel Fitzwilliam pulled a leaf from a tree and began to twirl it in his fingers. His brow was furrowed, and I could see that the weight of his mother's desires was hanging over him.

"She knows you would be a good father," I noted. "That's all."

"I do want children." He looked at me, as a sideway glance. "We would have had many of them, wouldn't we have?"

"Probably at least four," I acknowledged, "we are a passionate sort, aren't we?"

"Oh yes. More than four, I gather. Probably seven."

"Seven?" I laughed. "Even I would not have the energy to keep up with that many."

"I'd keep up with the first four, and you could keep up with the last three."

"You dream, Richard, you dream. Oh, very well, dream away—dream until something close to your dream comes true."

"Unbelievable!" he professed.

"What is?"

"Here I am, speaking in the most vulgar way imaginable, and you take it as casually as if we are talking of the weather."

"Do you want me to talk of the weather?" I asked, poking his side with my elbow. "Surely, you would not confine me to such a mundane topic of discussion? It's sunny out, not cloudy, and the weather is brisk and cold. You know it is. I know it is. Especially since we are already walking in it. So, what more is there to say?"

"No, I would not restrict you to stating the obvious. I merely marvel at you. It is our tendency to always be falling toward the way of vulgarity that leads to my mother noticing our link."

"Yes, it does. Your mother is not wrong. But what of her dream? Does she ever talk to you about how much she wants grandchildren?"

He turned serious again.

"Yes. Oddly enough, she never talks about that to Frederick. He's the heir, but perhaps she has accepted that he still enjoys his bachelorhood."

"Ah, that's the sort of man that your brother is?"

"Yes. Frederick is aware that he has been born with the lion-share, and so he views life as one long adventure. Why interrupt it with the confinement of having a family?"

"But you view matrimony in a different light."

"Yes. I view it as one of the greatest adventures of all. To have a wife, Kitty! Ah, to have a wife! To wake up knowing that you have a woman in your life, and she's always there...and that she loves you and desires you...then to be a father! I suppose my mother has always known that about me. As such, I am her great hope."

We reached a bench along the pathway, Colonel Fitzwilliam gestured to me to sit down, and I accepted his invitation. We sat together and he handed me his leaf. Taking it, I raised it up and it was silhouetted against the sky.

"One leaf, and one man," I said.

"You talk mystically."

"I'm talking of you. There was something else that your mother mentioned that caught my attention."

"I'm not surprised. She spoke about volumes, with each sentence clearly being more intriguing than the last."

"She mentioned that you were lonely. This surprised me because you never appear as such."

He smiled gently.

"Lonely people smile the kindest."

I squinted, perplexed by this confession.

"But you? You of all people strike me as the sort who never is alone."

"You haven't seen me among the ton. Recall, I am the second son. I spent a great portion of my teenage years falling into the background, feeling trivial under the weight of my elder brother's shadow. Frederick is better-looking than I am and is the heir to Matlock. I always spent portions of my life fading into obscurity when in his presence. It wasn't until my twenties that I learned charm, and that began to bring me more into the light of company. I was close to my family, but when out in society, I could sometimes be in a room full of my peers, and it felt like I wasn't there. As if no one saw me. Do you ever have that feeling? Like when you speak, no one hears you. When you stand there, and no one sees you."

"Yes. I have felt that painful sensation. And you want to cry out, 'I am here! See me and treat me equally to how you wish to be treated!'. But you can't do that. That would be an even greater sin than being invisible. I never knew that you underwent such a frightful experience."

"Yes, I did. For the longest time, I regretted the person I was, but as time went by, I realized something."

"What?" I asked.

"It made me kinder. It made me humble in a way that, perhaps, I would not have been if I had not been taught the agonies of nonexistence. Now, whenever I meet someone, I choose to see them, to note them, because I know how it feels to be overlooked. Humility has helped me in the course of my life."

"I never thought of it in that way."

"But now that you do, it was a bane that was truly a blessing. You were made to feel insignificant. That is something that I am all too aware of. But, as painful as it is to say this, it was a trial that I needed to go through."

"It's led to me always wishing to meet new people and be open to them."

"Yes. We were humbled all our lives. It led to us connecting with the rest of humanity. Who would have thought? Our growing pains really were necessary all the while."

⁓

"Oh, poor Aunt Fitzwilliam," Georgiana said. Since she and I were close comrades, I felt that I could bring her into my confidence, and it would not be me betraying her aunt. After all, Georgiana had the right to know where I stood with her family. Besides, I was going to tell Elizabeth and Jane about it. It seemed like it would be cruel to leave Georgiana in the dark on such matters. "I had never thought that she would want grandchildren. But the more I think about it, it is a natural reaction."

"It is. You have children, they grow, they thrive, and you want to see the line continue. Especially when you are so proud on the job that you did in helping your boys reach manhood. Georgie?"

"Yes."

"I am certain that she loves her eldest son, Frederick, but does she favor Richard?"

"Oh yes. He was the baby of the family for long enough before they had their third son, Gregory."

45

"How much older is Richard to Gregory?"

"Five years older. Gregory is traveling abroad with some friends of his. When he returns, he is going to take holy orders and take over Ordling, which is Matlock's parsonage."

"What manner of men are Frederick and Gregory?"

"Oh, Frederick is not meant to be a father. Of that I can tell you."

"Really?"

"Yes. He is a good man. There's nothing vicious or harmful about him, and his looks help him in society. However, he's just not the sort to favor patience—the very patience that it takes to raise a family. He is a very independent sort of creature. Also, he is shrewd and witty. And when I say witty, I mean his wit has a cynical and caustic sort of manner. He is sharp. He is the first person to admit that he is too selfish to consider the wishes of a wife and regulate the education and raising of children."

"Well, at least he is aware of that. In the grand scheme, it is best not to follow a path in life when it's the last path for which you are suited. Catastrophe can result if you do that, and you can become the ultimate failure."

"Oh yes, time has taught me that one. Initially, I thought he was an oddity for his thought process. You must understand that I was younger back then, and I was still very singular in my idea of what our mission in life was."

"Indeed," I groaned, rolling my eyes, "the mission of life: if your parents can be attentive to your education, then be as accomplished as you can. When you are not out, you must be silent. Grow up to be handsome, which one ought to be if one possibly can. And when you are out, you must automatically know how to integrate yourself into social scenes that you weren't given enough experience in. Then when the season comes, you must scrape around for a spouse, and if you are unsuccessful, you spend the rest of the year preparing yourself for the next season, when you try it all over again. Yes, that is the routine."

"And Frederick wanted none of it. Well, since I was raised to choose that path, I found him to be a bit...funny. But then, as I grew, developed a wider acquaintance with the ways of the world, and saw that romance was quite the quagmire, I began to understand Frederick more. Because, truth is, there is more to life than just one road to walk down. Life can be so much more heart-breaking, more confusing, more unique, more fascinating...and somehow, you wouldn't change it if you could."

I gave her a gentle smile.

"You have now reconciled yourself to your past, haven't you? You now see that we weren't foolish for all our romantic missteps. That was just a part of what we were meant to undergo."

She looked at me, comprehending.

"Yes. I do see it now."

"That's good!" I stressed, energetic. "I was worried that one day you might give into that thing called 'regret'. It's an inevitable pit to fall in from time to time, but I was worried that you might stay there. I'm happy you found your way out of it."

"You don't regret anything, do you?"

"Sometimes, I do. But most of the time, I know that if I could turn back time, I would do it all over again. My mistakes and trials have worked wonders for my development. Where would I be without all those experiences? I would be boring, tedious, pedantic, and cold. To me, those are the most criminal things I could do to myself."

"Then you will understand why I am happy that you are poor."

I looked at her narrowly.

"Why?" I asked.

"If you were wealthy, then you would either be married to Lieutenant Finlay by now, or Richard. Are you really telling me that you want to be a wife just yet? Kitty, I know that you still are not."

I sat down on her bed and looked ahead at the wall.

"Yes," I admitted, "you have a point there. I could never have rejected either man if I had the means to marry one of them, but I would have come to the marriage without the experiences that I needed to be a better companion."

"Precisely. I hated that Wickham proved to be the worst

choice of husband, and was mercenary in his behavior, but that disaster forced me to lean back and reflect."

"And now you understand Frederick Fitzwilliam."

"Yes, I do."

"I suppose that I do as well."

Looking up at the canopy, I summed up the situation.

"Yes, you are right. Poor Lady Fitzwilliam. Richard is her last hope, and love has not been convenient for him."

"Yes, she is."

Chapter Six

THE HEIR OF MATLOCK

T hree days before the Verity Ball, Lord Fitzwilliam had a message. While we ate breakfast, he produced a letter from his pocket.

"I have just received some wonderful news that I think will rouse your attention and curiosity."

"Ah," Colonel Fitzwilliam said, "curiosity in a good way, or a frightful one?"

"It all depends on if you will miss being the only Fitzwilliam son at Matlock. The letter is from Frederick, and he has written to tell us to expect him to come on the day of the ball."

The table was roused with astonishment.

"Ah," Elizabeth said, "we're going to meet your eldest son? Now that is an unexpected pleasure. Unless I am wrong, and he does not enjoy coming home to our company at his house."

"Oh, Frederick will be very interested in seeing you all," Lady Fitzwilliam said. "My son always comes with stories, and regrets when he doesn't have a listener for them."

"But if he is coming the day of the ball," Mary noted, "then will he attend it? After all, when arriving home after traveling, you do not have the energy to go somewhere immediately afterwards. It has been my experience that a person wants to find their bed and rest to their heart's content."

"With anyone else, I would say such, but Frederick is a whole other matter. He is filled with youthful energy and can arrive at home after riding his horse clear across the country, sit down, bathe, then go to an engagement, and speak to everyone who is there."

"He has more energy than I do, I confess," Jane voiced.

"Well, it would be best if I read you his letter, so you get a better understanding of my heir."

He raised up the letter and read it.

> *Dear Mother, Father, and whoever else is home,*
>
> *I have returned from the races in London, and this time, I come with glad tidings. The horse I have groomed and bet on, Eurystheus, came in first place, and I can say that I returned with good fortune. Finally, I can begin to profit from my investment.*
>
> *I suppose, all profit is risk, as my friends often say. Therefore, father and mother, I am finally with a sense of victory. And what can be more fitting than returning with a ball waiting for me? This way, I can pride myself on connecting Matlock to the heroism of Eurystheus, who bore more than just himself across the finish line.*
>
> *What I also can pride myself on is receiving the handkerchief of more than one lady when I dismounted from my noble steed. For the first time in my life, I can see everyone loves a winner and wishes to be one. I'd say that I buckle under the weight of feeling such flattery, but it does help carry one over, when feeling the eventual defeat that always faces another man. Besides, we are all vain, in some form or another, and that vanity needs to be satisfied. Feeling like a hero, hoisted up on the shoulders of the crowd, I want to believe that I have made my family proud.*
>
> *Now, I shall return, limb and head intact, back to Matlock, where your son will soon be climbing the walls, ready to get back onto a horse again and find his triumph where he may.*
>
> *For the moment, life is lovely, isn't it?*
>
> *And if you read this out loud to anyone else in the family, ha!*
>
> *I cannot wait to see their faces when they have discovered that I have won. I know that Gregory is away, but Richard's face is something that I cannot wait to see.*

Your roguish son,
Frederick

When he lowered the letter, he looked at us.

"Frederick won the races?" Lady Fitzwilliam cried. "Oh, that is wonderful."

"Your older son races horses?" Enara asked.

"Yes, he does," Lord Fitzwilliam said. "Since my son was a young man, he always had a love for horses. There were times where I felt that, if I didn't take the time to check him, he would have slept in the stables with his favorite horse if he could."

"He did sleep in the stables sometimes," Colonel Fitzwilliam confessed.

"What?" Lady Fitzwilliam gasped.

"Yes, he actually did."

"He did? Why did you never say anything?"

"It was not out of any disloyalty to you, Mother, I can assure you. Or Father for that matter. There is just that unspoken rule that when your older brother does something, if you are not to be his accomplice, you are to at least keep his secrets. If I told you that I knew he was sleeping next to Eurystheus, Frederick would never let me hear the end of it."

"Oh, sibling confidence," I said, "I have been there myself."

"It's just a natural habit," Georgiana said, "sometimes, I didn't tell Mother and Father when I saw Fitz do things."

"When have I ever done anything that could be taken amiss?" Darcy asked, a little piqued.

"Do you really forget your teenage years?"

"Oh. Well, a man can't be held down by what he did at four-teen. That would just be unseemly."

"I'm not holding you to it," Georgiana chuckled. "I'm just saying that you did it."

"Well, now you all have begun your acquaintance with my eldest son, through his letter," Lord Fitzwilliam said, "what is your first impression of him?"

"Dearest," Lady Fitzwilliam said. "You know very well that they cannot speak freely about what they think."

"Precisely," Elizabeth said. "There is something very socially self-defeating about giving a true impression of a man, in the presence of his parents, while visiting them in their home."

"That means you have many thoughts on the matter," Lord Fitzwilliam said.

"Perhaps I do, but I'll never voice them. The only thing I will say is that he seems like a very interesting person."

I looked at Colonel Fitzwilliam.

"What did he mean that he couldn't wait to see your face?" I asked.

"I told him to stop racing horses," Colonel Fitzwilliam answered, "not because victory was so rare for him, but because of the danger of it. Naturally, he didn't listen. And now, when he comes, from one moment's beginning to another moment's end, he is never going to let me stop hearing of it."

When we finished eating, and before the men separated to do other things and we ladies sat down and began to work on our sewing, I managed to whisper to the Colonel.

"What is your true relationship to Frederick? Your secret is safe with me."

"Oh, it's no secret. He and I love each other, but we also love to plague each other. There is a deep loyalty there, and also sometimes, a deep sense of competition. We provoke each other. You will see."

~

And I didn't have long to wait.

Each day of our visit at Matlock comprised of being given a tour of the entire estate, dining at neighboring houses and Colonel Fitzwilliam showing me his favorite horse. When I confessed that I never learned to ride a horse, he began to show me how to groom one.

The first day, I learned to brush a horse and feed it. As the Colonel said, I had to gain a trust and mutual respect with any horse before riding it, because if I didn't, the horse wouldn't do anything. All the while, Doctor Carney would come every other day to check on Jane and Eliza. So far, their early stages of pregnancy were going well. Each day brought a fresh report of both our sisters still being healthy and there was no talk of any miscarriage. This news naturally enhanced the joys of our party.

This comfortable arrangement resulted in our time in Matlock going very well, right up until the day of the ball. Of course, despite the amusements of being thrown into such a society, the occasional boredom has no choice but to find its way in, every now and again, for one cannot spend an entire visit always being thrown into the peak of delight. There must be slow times, down times, and the moments in between the great moments, that serve as a foil to augment the greater times that one anticipates, and no amount of playing a game of Whist, Cribbage or Speculation can help the obligatory boredom that must ensue. But that is life, I suppose. And if boredom-passing-through is the only thing a person has to worry over, then one has little to complain about.

"Missus," Lucy said to me as she helped me dress that morning, "remember to eat very little today. And drink what you wish in the morning, but don't drink anything else after 1 o'clock. By the time that it is to go to the ball, you will be empty and can stay for hours without having to leave to use the Necessary Room."

"I won't," I assured her, "I don't want to be the one who forces the company to leave early. Oh, I hope all goes well today."

"Begging your pardon, Miss, but I heard that Mr. Frederick Fitzwilliam is coming home today."

"Yes, he is."

"Well, I heard some things about him from the servants."

"You have?" I asked eagerly. "What have you heard?"

"I heard that he and his brother are a little competitive."

"Oh, yes," I said, rolling my eyes, "Colonel Fitzwilliam told me of that tendency of theirs."

"Well, when brothers compete, it can either be kindhearted, or it can get serious. According to the servants, Master Frederick can be determined in his ways and means. He has a dual character of either kindness or a shrewd wickedness."

"What do you mean?"

"I don't know much, and I can't say that I was told the truth. After all, sometimes servants do like to exaggerate. I just wish to say...be careful there. Where brothers compete, many things can be their battleground. *Be careful there*."

She had to leave, to tend to Enara's dressing.

I looked at myself in the mirror.

I trusted Lucy, implicitly.

Servants usually know their masters very well. Or they could exaggerate. What was the truth?

After breakfast, we were all sitting in the drawing room, prepared to expect Frederick Fitzwilliam at any moment, and we were not left to wait long.

Very soon, we saw a rider from a window.

We all gathered ourselves in the sitting room, waiting expectantly.

We heard a confident male voice greet Mr. Wimlett gayly, and it was nice sounding. We heard him inquire about Wimlett's health, and about his family. From what I heard, Master Frederick seemed like a nice and considerate man.

At last, the door opened, and we were graced with a ball of energy. Frederick Fitzwilliam practically bounced into the room—if a person could bounce—and he came up to his mother and father, eagerly.

"Mother and Father." He smiled, kissing his mother's cheek, and shaking his father's hand. "I hope you are happy to see me."

"Of course, we are dear," Lady Fitzwilliam said, "now if you care for me, you will greet everyone in the room like a gentleman."

"Oh, come now, if you can't be yourself around family, then when can you be?"

He turned to Colonel Fitzwilliam and both men embraced.

"Little brother," Frederick uttered, amused, "still alive?"

"And still a force to be reckoned with," Colonel Fitzwilliam said. "You look fit and well. I must congratulate you on your recent triumph at the racetrack."

"And you ought to."

Colonel Fitzwilliam raised an eyebrow.

"Is this where you are about to tell me that you told me so?"

"Now why would I do that?"

"Oh, how nice of you."

Colonel Fitzwilliam turned away from him, preparing for us to be introduced.

"Told you so," Frederick cooed, over his brother's shoulder.

Colonel Fitzwilliam rolled his shoulders.

"Why am I not surprised?"

"Well, before you both get too involved in your debate and discussions," Lord Fitzwilliam said. "Introductions are involved."

Lady Fitzwilliam introduced us all to him, excepting the family with which he was already acquainted.

"Family and new friends," Master Frederick began, "how timely met." He clapped his hands together. "I trust that we shall become well-acquainted over time. But for the moment, I hope that you are like me and are excited for the ball this evening."

"You ask ladies if we are excited for a ball," Georgiana said. "Cousin, the answer is in the question."

"Then I hope to have the honor of dancing with every lady in present company. Forgive me, husbands in the set, but I trust you understand the joys of me wishing to have some very pretty partners throughout the dances."

"Well, cousin," Darcy said to him, "my apologies that two of our wives must be allowed to always be in their husband's company."

"You come with more delightful news in your wake," Mr. Bingley said, "my wife and Mrs. Darcy are with child."

Frederick's smile widened.

"Truly?"

"Yes, my dear," Lady Fitzwilliam said merrily, "since their coming, Mrs. Darcy and Mrs. Bingley discovered that they are going to be mothers."

"Well, I offer my hearty congratulations. Pemberley shall have an heir very soon, I pray. And what of you Bingley? Is Netherfield Park still the place that will be the home of the new little Bingley?"

"And that is where we have more news," Bingley added. "When we return to Pemberley, I am going to take possession of a purchase of another estate, Godfrey Park."

"Godfrey Park? I recall that estate. Doesn't it belong to the Granvilles?"

"Yes, it does. Sir Thomas Granville has had to sell the estate, out of a desire to establish himself in Bath, and he has put the estate up for purchase. I wrote three days ago to state my express desire to accept his offer and informed him to send his confirmation of my purchase to Pemberley. Hopefully, the letter will be there, waiting for me."

Frederick's eye was more discerning, and he was able to see the truth for what it was.

"You are kind in mincing your words, Bingley. I have long known that about you. But let's state the truth for what it is. A knighted man does not sell his longtime country seat for Bath out of leisure, but only out of desperation. There is no point in denying it. It's long been known in the ton, that Sir Thomas Granville has mismanaged his estate woefully. His knighthood was felt too keenly, and he expected that he had to live up to that image. Whatever my faults, my expenses are always aimed at aspiring to a talent that could give financial returns."

"Did your victory bring you profit?" I asked. By the looks of everyone around me, save Georgie, I realized that maybe I might have been importunate. "Oh, have I been vilely indiscrete?"

"On the contrary, Miss Bennet, I was hoping someone would ask me. Well, due to the odds being so much against me, I was able to earn eight hundred pounds from this race."

"You did?" Enara said. "Oh, that must be such a delight. Not only to be victorious, but also to be given such a prize."

"My dear Frederick," Lady Fitzwilliam said, "I am happy for this! Truly, I am, but I still do not want you to make it appear as if we need your earnings to run this establishment."

"Mother, I assure you that I will never allow that thought to enter anyone's head. I confess my profits for the sake of displaying that it is proper to take money from one's pocketbook, as long as you return that sum with interest. What sort of man takes from his estate without giving a little back, is what I believe. What do you say to that, Darcy?"

"I say amen to it," Darcy responded, "you know that I am quite the advocate for leaving your estate better off than how you obtained it. That's how we were raised."

"And clearly how Mr. Osmund Granville wasn't. He's known for squandering his family's fortune as much as his father. Oh well, his loss will be your gain, Bingley. And take the joy of knowing that you are saving a frivolous knight from the poorhouse."

"I confess, I purchased the estate for selfish reasons," Bingley responded, "My dear Jane deserves the best, you see. However, I am happy that I gave someone else a good turn in the process."

"You do good even without knowing it. You just might be the envy of us all."

"You flatter me, Frederick."

"We all have our skills. I am happy I know where I stand with mine. Oh, and Mother and Father, I have some very good news. My good friend, Tom Musgrave, is going to be at the Verity Ball tonight."

"Brother," Colonel Fitzwilliam said, "you have been remiss in giving us the current news of your life. We didn't even know that Tom Musgrave *still* was your friend."

"I haven't mentioned him recently?"

"Not for a year, at least," Lord Fitzwilliam observed, "we thought you had a falling out with each other. Now, this is a shocking blow." He looked at Jane and Elizabeth. "This is what happens when you become a parent. You put all your love, sweat and care into raising children, and you spend most of your life not knowing what they are about and up to something. This is what you have to look forward to."

"You just made them uncertain about being mothers, I fear," Lady Fitzwilliam said, amused while she chided him.

"Thank you for shielding us from the bitter truth, madam,"

Elizabeth responded. "But since the child already grows within us both, I suppose that it could only be determined that 'in for a penny, in for a pound'."

"True. When you start, there is no going back." Lord Fitzwilliam looked at his sons. "One day, you both will learn that same lesson."

"Oh, and that's my cue to leave," Frederick said, standing up. "Whenever a married couple says that I shall have children, I say that they do not know that I ever shall know what that feels like, they say I shall, I say that I shan't, they say I shall, we go round and round, and there's an end to it."

We all laughed at his remark, but it turned out that he really wished to leave. For, since he had been journeying since early morning, he wanted to be well-refreshed for the ball, so that he wasn't falling asleep within an hour of the ceremony.

His parents allowed this, for it did make a great deal of sense, and that was my first impression of Frederick Fitzwilliam.

"So," Colonel Fitzwilliam said while I helped him clean Artemis's coat and brush his beautiful mane and tail. The stables were well-maintained, as the rest of Matlock was, and was cleaned daily, thus it smelled like well-bred horses, and that's it. No pungent and unpleasant odors really came from the place. "You now have met my brother. And what do you think of him?"

"Well, I see that charm runs in the family."

"You found my brother charming?" Colonel Fitzwilliam questioned, raising an eyebrow as he moved some hay. This response had all the subtlety that was proper for a gentleman raised in such a fine estate as Matlock House, however, one learns to read in between the lines of a casually delivered sentence.

"Oh," I said, rolling my eyes. "I see."

"What do you see?"

"What is plain as the sky to see, and as self-evident as a bird's right to fly along the clouds...you don't want me to find anything good about your brother, do you?"

"Well, it's not that, per se…"

"But it *is that*, per se. I am not wrong, Richard, therefore, there is no need to conceal it."

He looked sheepish as he arranged the hay.

"Oh, very well. Maybe I do not like it."

"Of course, you don't. What man wants a woman to respect his brother, when he wants to always be the only man in her affections? I'd say that it must be a natural part of male instinct—to be possessive. But that's not true at all. We women are the precise same way."

"You are?"

"Oh, yes. We can be equally as possessive and be equally as vicious in our attempts to keep that attention on us. Sometimes, I wonder that the most difficult thing in the world is to be human."

"Because it is. We rationalize, then over-rationalize, and then use rationality to justify when we are being irrational. It's a very difficult business. And we make quite the mess of it all."

"Well, I shall not chide you, because maybe I would be the same way if I were in your shoes. But hear this now." I turned to him. "No. Look into my eyes so that you can see the sincerity of it."

He did as I instructed.

"I appreciate your brother's charm, but you have a more genuine character. While I'm certain your brother is not a bad sort of person, but I get the sense that there is more weight behind your flattery."

His eyes twinkled as he leaned toward me.

"That is precisely what I wanted you to tell me."

"Yes, I bet you did," I replied, equally as lit from within, "and I mean it. Mr. Wickham has been very good at teaching me to be cautious. You are one of the two men who have taught me how a man can be alluring and still be real. I appreciate that."

"My brother is said to be more handsome than me."

"No," I replied, seriously, "he's not."

He looked on me in a determined and fixed way. Then he

went up to Artemis and gave him an apple to eat. As a result, our bodies were close, and I felt the heat of his intent.

"You find me as handsome as my brother?"

"Yes, I do. There is only one man that I've ever met, who is as handsome as you. Your brother is not the other one."

"When a woman finds you handsomer than true handsomeness, which is when you know that she really cares."

"I do. And there's the end of it. Besides, you actually are handsome. This world simply has a very singular idea of what good looks are. Beauty is not a singular thing. It's plural. You are handsome, by definition. The world is just not ready to enhance its idea of what that definition is."

He took my hand and held it.

"The woman I love is going to the ball with me, only for her to be used to help me find an heiress."

"If I have good looks, I suppose that I am happy I can put them to good use."

"You have excellent looks. But for my own happiness, and not for the sake of using your beauty to make me more attractive, I request that I secure your hand for the first two dances this evening."

"You dolt!" I cried, pushing his shoulder. "I was wondering when you were going to ask me!"

He laughed and we left the stables, with me skipping along beside him.

When it was time for us to prepare for the ball, we all separated, and were tended to by a servant each. Lucy outshone herself, did my hair properly, and then put on my gown with extra care, to avoid any wrinkles occurring. Vera came in and added some trinkets to my hair to add the final touch. I got the instinct that it was Lady Fitzwilliam's doing.

True to her word, Lady Fitzwilliam did come to my room, to check on my appearance. When seeing that Lucy and Vera had done all in their power to make me look ten times better than I usually looked, she suggested me to pinch my cheeks before we arrived at Verity Hall, for the sake of making my cheeks redder. Other than that, she was satisfied with my appearance and didn't regret me wearing my blue gown in the slightest.

When the ladies were finished, we felt that we all complimented each other's looks and there was a beauty to our company. When we went down the stairs, the gentlemen greeted us eagerly, and to my surprise, Frederick Fitzwilliam approached me first, gave me the grandest of compliments, and then asked if he could secure my hand for the first two dances.

Over his shoulder, I saw Colonel Fitzwilliam give him a queer look, and the surprise was not lost on me. I was left to decline the request, explaining that his brother had already secured my hand for the first two sets.

"Oh, is that a fact?" Frederick said to his brother.

"Yes, it is, brother."

"I should have known; you move quickly." Frederick turned to me. "He acquired that skill from me."

"No, I did not, Frederick."

"Yes, you did, Richard."

"No, I did not, Frederick."

"Yes, you did, Richard."

"Did not."

"Did too."

"Boys?" Lady Fitzwilliam said. "Will you tear my nerves to shreds?"

Instinctively, Mary, Jane, Elizabeth, and I turned to each other, feeling the intensity of coincidence. Lady Fitzwilliam had said something that our mother was often known for saying. Oh well, I suppose mothers always have one thing in common: we children can be very trying on their nerves.

"Sorry, Mother," Colonel Fitzwilliam responded, lightheartedly. "Just a little sibling bickering."

"And both siblings thought alike, in this case," Frederick said, turning to me. "Well then, since you are secured for the first two dances, might I secure your hand for the next two?"

My eyes widened in awe.

"Well, Kitty," Enara said, "you will be quite busy for the first two hours of the ball. Now that is what I call beginning well."

"She will if she accepts my offer."

"You rogue," I announced, "you know, very well, that of course I must accept. Therefore, I shall."

"Oh, you oblige me."

"Women often do that to gentlemen when at balls. You shall be no more or less different than the rest of your sex, sir."

He chuckled, then he turned to Colonel Fitzwilliam.

"We got wit on our hands. This ought to be interesting."

Colonel Fitzwilliam's expression was difficult to read, and I didn't have time to ask what these two brothers were about. Ergo, all offers were accepted, we put on our cloaks, coats, the carriages were drawn, and we were a large party of fourteen traversing along to a winter ball, where no one knew what to fully expect.

Chapter Seven

THE VERITY BALL

"Behold, ladies," Lady Fitzwilliam whispered to Mary and me as we looked out of the carriage window. We had arrived at Verity Hall, the seat of the Luxfords, and we were peering at it as we drove down the lane. "Verity Hall, one of the best homes in this county."

"By George," I uttered, amazed, "it's almost as lovely as Matlock and Pemberley."

"Matlock and Pemberley have a more natural elegance," Mary added, "but yes, this is almost equally as impressive."

Verity Hall was a gorgeous and vast estate, and even in dusk, we could see the beauties of the grounds around it. Its meticulous care augmented the stones of the house, and the windows reflected the sky, giving it a majestic look.

"Even when going to a place where you are not certain if you will enjoy yourself," I said, "a lovely scene before you can help you forget your anxieties."

"What have you to worry over?" Lady Fitzwilliam asked me. "You shall find all the pleasures that can be found at such an event."

"I think I can hazard a guess of Miss Bennet's apprehensions," Mr. Atkins said, "when you are going to so very fine an establishment, there is always the fear of the unknown. That is what strikes me now."

"That was how I was feeling." I looked at Lady Fitzwilliam. "When I first came to Matlock, it was a different feeling. I knew I had friends there. But sometimes, when going to a new place, it feels like visiting into the lion's den."

"Rational thought," Lady Fitzwilliam said as she rolled her eyes. "What are you all doing being so logical before a ball? It will spoil the fun of it."

We all chuckled, and our carriage came to the front, parked, and footmen helped us.

Now that we were in front of the steps, I whispered to Mary.

"What do you think?" I asked her.

"I think that I feel very small. And you?"

"I always knew I was small. Never fear; use that revelation to your advantage."

"Oh, that's a skill that you and I learned very well."

"Are you both being insecure again?" Mr. Atkins asked us.

"Yes," Mary said, blushing. He took her hand and kissed it.

"Courage, Mrs. Atkins. You are the wife of a clerk!"

She looked at him fondly, as I went over to Georgiana, and took her hands merrily.

We all walked up the steps and very soon entered, waiting in a line of people so that we could meet our hosts.

The Luxfords were a married couple in their late fifties, and the Fitzwilliams were very familiar with them. The Luxfords also had three children: one son and two daughters. The eldest son, a Mr. Desmond Luxford, was heir of Verity Hall, and did the very best he could to show interest to all of us. Although, instinct will always prevail, and his eye turned directly on Georgiana, immediately appealing to her for the first two dances of the set. Obliged to accept, Georgiana did so with great fortitude. This made sense on two levels. First, nothing about Mr. Luxford was comely, and his general air and manner did nothing to counteract his lack of good looks. His eye was too predatorial, his gaze too intense, and his voice too weasely.

"Of course," Georgiana groaned to me as we had to move along the line, so that the family could greet the rest of the attendees.

I sighed, empathetic for her.

"Maybe he might actually like you for your character, and not your purse." She gave me a sideways glance. I realized that she didn't want to hear a falsity. "Oh, very well, you are probably very right. After all, you know the Luxfords better than I do."

"Oh, I know him all too well. While the Luxfords are not in debt, like the Granvilles, but naturally, my fifty-thousand pounds is precisely why he finds my looks superior to every woman in the room. Of course, dowries matter. However, I'm quite sure that he doesn't even know that my eyes are green. I'm just a shadow to them. My dowry is the character that they notice. Besides, I have it upon good information that he is very unruly when it comes to servant girls."

My eyes widened in hearing this news.

"Truly?"

"Yes."

I groaned inwardly.

"These ladies...please tell me that they are not being pressured? That they allow his attentions, and that his wanton ways are invited."

"According to reports, the servants are not forced. Not that I know these women..."

"Well, as long as they are unmarried, I do not judge them."

Georgiana looked at me, shocked.

"You do not?"

"No. Do I have to?"

"Well...aren't you shocked by this behavior?"

"As long as these women aren't married, then what crime have they really committed? Besides, think about this. They are working-class women who cannot always have marital prospects. Not all women can afford to wait their entire lives for the perfect husband to fall into their laps one day. Some of them need that romance in their lives. Besides, if Mr. Luxford is considered respectable and he behaves a certain way, then why should the women be considered less so?"

"Oh, I had not thought of it that way."

"You don't have a sister who ran off and lived with a man for weeks, when he had no designs to marry her. When that happens, your capacity for forgiveness and compassion for the follies and vices of others becomes wider. Or more blurred if you will."

"Perhaps not. I am just the girl who did something similar to Mrs. Wickham."

This was not the outlook that I wanted her to have when going into this evening. I held her shoulders.

"Don't you dare think of that. You were the innocent one, and don't believe any different. This is a ball. Let us have a wonderful time."

Georgiana smiled ironically.

"You can," she whispered, "I have to dance an hour with that face of his."

I laughed. In such cases, vanity was acceptable.

Eventually, we joined our group, and we were not left to socialize amongst ourselves for very long. We were joined by a rather handsome man, with fair curly hair, symmetrical features, and he had very clear skin. Truly, there was not one mark on his face that signified a scar from a pimple long past. We, all of us, had some form of mark, be it a mark of beauty, freckles, or a scar leftover from the troubling times of our youth. With him, there was nothing to indicate this.

"Frederick!" This man cried, approaching our set, "you smart creature. You brought your lovely family with you."

"I did, indeed, Tom." Both men met each other happily, and I was able to deduce that this man must be no other than the Tom Musgrave that he mentioned before. It turned out that I was correct. Tom Musgrave was indeed the man, and his reputation proceeded him. He was an independent man, who had inherited nine hundred to a thousand pounds a year, while also being given his own comfortable home.

When meeting us, he ingratiated himself into our company very well, but he mostly appealed to us ladies and Frederick more than anyone.

"So," Tom began, "I must offer my congratulations. When last I heard, Darcy and Bingley, you both were as single as I am. But you managed to capture two ideal sisters. Along with you, Mrs. Atkins. Well done, Mr. Atkins. And something must also be said for the exotic. Mrs. Philips, you are an event."

"You are too kind, sir," Enara said.

"No, he's not," Arthur Philips said, "my love, he's actually quite accurate."

"But I must not forget the single flowers that seem to be blooming," Tom Musgrave said, turning to us, "a pity that you are secured for the first two dances. Between you both, and all the husbands wishing to dance with their wives, what is a poor man to do?"

"I have a suggestion," Elizabeth offered.

"I am all ears."

"Dance with yourself."

This made his eyes raise in surprise.

"Well, I might have to, if one of the pleasures that drew me to this ball does not manifest itself in time to divert me."

"Ah," Frederick said, rolling his eyes, "you never give up, do you?"

"Never give up enjoying superior society? Of course not, friend." Realizing that we all were ignorant to what they were referring to, Mr. Musgrave decided to be kind to us, and explain.

"A ball gives us all the perfect place to meet old friends and make new acquaintances. I have done the second when meeting some of you, but nothing is comparable to doing the first. Frederick is aware of my friendship to a distinguished family, the Osbornes."

"Ah," Lord Fitzwilliam said, "that is where your mind goes."

"It is. Am I wrong to do so?" Tom turned to the rest of us and continued. "This county has the pleasure of boasting of two great families. The Luxfords, and the Osbornes. The Osbornes estate is Osborne Park. It's as handsome as this establishment. Yes, I am aware that nothing compares to Matlock and Pemberley, I know, but we all must start somewhere, mustn't we?"

"You don't need to butter me up, sir," Mr. Darcy said, "I know that you respect my home."

"It never hurts to say it. However, the Osbornes are a particularly favorite family of mine. There is Mrs. Osborne, a handsome woman, and is a widow. Her son, Lord Osborne, is a great friend to me. I will not be surprised if you ladies will not be struck by his charms."

"Would I be struck by his charms?" I whispered to Colonel Fitzwilliam.

"Not in the slightest," Colonel Fitzwilliam whispered back, "Lord Osborne barely knows how to put two words together, when he's in women's company."

"Ah."

"Also, Lord Osborne's younger sister, Miss Osborne, will be attending with her friend, a Miss Carr," Tom Musgrave informed us. "Present company excluded. Miss Osborne is one of the handsomest women in my acquaintance. You all will be enraptured by her."

"And here's our chance," Frederick uttered, "they just entered."

∽

After hearing about this 'legendary' family, our curiosity was naturally peaked. Thus, we could not resist moving closer to the line of guests who were filing in and being announced.

Making sure that I was in front of him, Colonel Fitzwilliam watched me as I glimpsed the new arrivals.

My eyes fell on Mrs. Osborne. She really was a handsome elderly woman of fifty. Clearly, she had taken good care of herself over the years, because her face had very little wrinkles, and her figure was plump and well-made.

The next was Lord Osborne, her son, heir, and inheritor of his father's title. His looks were neither handsome, nor plain, but had a comfortable in between. A man of average looks, he also had dark brown hair that was straight, and it didn't frame his face very well. There was a stiffness to his demeanor that reminded me of Mr. Darcy when we first met him at the Assembly.

The next part of the family was Miss Osborne, the younger sister. Since she had been given Tom Musgrave's most particular praise, we all were in anticipation. What we got was the opposite. When seeing her features, I was reminded of Mary King. She was not particularly gruesome in any way, but nor was she beautiful. Like Mary King, Miss Osborne was plain. Initially, I wondered what inspired Tom Musgrave to call her Jane, Lizzy, and Enara's equal. Then I naturally assumed that perhaps she was one of those women who had a natural animation to her character, and it made you forget her flawed appearance. After all, most attractive people are not always the handsomest ones in the room. Usually, attractiveness is a quality that is given to lesser creatures in the world, to give them a fighting chance. This Miss Osborne could very well be a superior creature, just by how she carried herself.

Next to her was her friend, Miss Carr, whose looks were on the same level as Miss Osborne's. She was rare in that she had red hair, which was done up very well, and I actually found worked for her face. Red hair was not considered a desired trait, but I felt that it enhanced her appearance.

Behind them was a mystery. For there were three more people to the company.

"You have us at a disadvantage, sir," Arthur Philips said to Tom Musgrave, "for there is more to the company than you informed us."

"Ah, those other few are not Osbornes, but they are worthy of being known. The first one there is Mr. Howard. He was originally Lord Osborne's tutor. Fortunately, when Lord Osborne no longer required a tutor, they did not forsake Mr. Howard. Rather, profession shifted, and he shifted from being a tutor to being a clergyman on Osborne's estate's parish."

"And is the lady, next to him, his wife?" Mary asked.

"No, she is his sister. Her name is Mrs. Blake, and she is a widow."

Next to Mrs. Blake was a little boy of about ten years old.

"And the boy?" Mr. Atkins asked. "Is that Mrs. Blake's son?"

"Yes. His name is Charles, and he is very fond of dancing."

"A little boy fond of dancing?" Elizabeth questioned. "Well, that is very novel."

"Would you mind if I bring them over to make the ladies' acquaintance?" Tom asked.

"Tom, we know that you would not have it any other way," Frederick said.

"You know me too well."

Tom Musgrave departed, went over to the Osbornes, gestured to us, and soon the Osbornes were being ushered over.

Now came the first night of many surprising introductions.

Lord Osborne's looks did not help him in the way that it ought to have. There was an air of awkwardness and coldness to his manner, securing his connection to Mr. Darcy's first arrival in Hertfordshire even further into my mind. Between the two of them, Mr. Howard was the principal speaker. He was around thirty-one years old, and he was pleasant-looking.

And then came Miss Osborne. Here came the moment of truth in discovering if she was like the modern-day Cleopatra, where her personality eclipsed her plain looks. I was very quickly disappointed. She spoke mostly with her friend, Miss Carr, and had nothing to recommend her character to any of us.

So, what could inspire Tom Musgrave to prefer her to every other woman? The answer was simple: he wanted to marry her. By the way that he sought her out and remained by her side, it became more evident with every waking minute.

"Well," Mrs. Osborne began, "we already were going to have a ball with an illustrious company, but I had no knowledge that we would get the Matlock and Pemberley families as well. You have quite raised up the festivities."

"And now we worry that we will not be able to live up to that praise," Bingley answered, "but thank you, madam."

"And I long to see your estate, Mr. Bingley. I have heard good things about your country seat, Netherfield Park."

"Oh, I am happy that you mention it. I am releasing myself from renting that establishment and have taken purchase of Godfrey Park."

"Godfrey Park?"

"Yes, madam. The Granvilles have discovered that they prefer to change their lifestyle and retire to Bath."

"And by that," Tom Musgrave uttered, "you mean that they have run their finances into the ground, and selling their estate is the only thing saving them from finding their way into debtor's prison."

"My words precisely," Frederick said.

"The fools," Lord Osborne said, but it was so random, that no one knew how to respond to it, "Sir Thomas Grandville now lost his home. I would never do that."

"No, my dear," Mrs. Osborne said, "you would not. I raised my son well, I believe."

"Yes, you did indeed, madam," Lady Fitzwilliam said, diplomatically. "You deserve admiration for that."

From over our shoulder, another family's arrival sparked interest.

"The Edwards!" The name was announced.

"Ah, the Edwards are coming as well," Georgiana said, turning around.

"Who are the Edwards?" Enara asked.

"They are quite a respectable family," Mr. Howard said, "they are a friendly set."

"There is someone with them, brother," Mrs. Blake said, "who is she?"

We looked down the line and saw this new elderly couple who greeted the Luxfords. With them were two young ladies, so I didn't know which one that Mrs. Blake was referring to.

"Emma!" Georgiana uttered, flummoxed.

"Georgie?" I asked her, confused.

"I know that lady," Georgiana explained, "that is Emma Watson!"

~

Once more, I looked at the two young ladies, and I didn't know which young lady that Georgiana was responding to.

"Emma Watson?" Tom Musgrave repeated, looking over at the Edwards. "Oh! Is that young lady with Mary Edwards the prodigal daughter of Mr. Watson, the ailing curate?"

"Don't let her hear you call her prodigal. She was a child when she left home, Mr. Musgrave, and was taken in by her aunt. I am just surprised of what brought her here."

"Oh," Frederick Fitzwilliam said, looking smug, "then I can say that, perhaps, I have the whip hand over you, and are aware of more gossip."

"You boast of being a gossip, Frederick?"

"Of course. Being a gossip is like having social currency. There is always someone who wants you in their company." He leaned into us all, conspiratorially. "I heard that Miss Watson's aunt, a Mrs. Turner, and her were very close—until she did something very foolish."

"Emma did?" Georgiana asked.

"No, her aunt was the foolish one. Her first husband, Mr. Turner, was a sensible man and a great husband. But when he died, his wife inherited everything. He should have been smarter and made sure that the aunt would settle on Miss Watson there. But that's not what happened. Her aunt fell in love with an Irish Captain, Captain O'Brien, she married him, and naturally all her fortune went to this new marriage. Being newlyweds, he did not wish to have her niece stay with them, therefore, Emma had no choice but to return home, quite penniless."

While he narrated this, I watched this young woman who was in the company of the Edwards. She had light brown hair, it was curly and framed her face very well, which was a nice oval shape. Her features were a little brown, which must have come from being out of doors very often. I preferred that skin tone, personally, though it was not at all in fashion. The pearl white skin, a lingering ideal that was inherited from the unhealthy expectations of the Elizabethan Era, was still the chief attraction that a woman could have. Personally, I preferred having a darker complexion to myself. It seemed to be augmented by the colors that I had from my clothing. And since it was the way my skin naturally was, worrying about it seemed to be quite the waste of time. I was a little brown, by natural selection. And Miss Watson's shape was a little similar to Enara's, but she was decidedly shorter and was approximately Georgiana's height.

"And so," Frederick finalized, "this is the state that Miss Watson has come to, when visiting the Edwards. Her uncle died, her aunt remarried, she was left with no inheritance to speak of, and now she is cast out on the whims of fate."

"But you mentioned home," Georgiana said. "Emma's family resides in New South Wales."

"Yes."

"Oh, then I can at least deliver that information. She is not fully home yet. Australia is her native land."

Georgiana turned to me.

"Kitty, she is an old friend of mine that I hadn't seen for years. I must go see her."

"Would she want me to come with you?" I asked, impulsively, "sometimes, another person can mar a friendly reunion. She is close to you, but I am a stranger."

"Nonsense," Georgiana said, "don't be a dunce about it."

Georgiana excused us, took my hand, and led me towards the Edwards. With every step, I felt a strange sort of anxiety. I just felt...unwanted.

When we reached Emma Watson, I placed myself behind Georgiana, so that they could meet each other first, and then I would be introduced, by and by.

"Emma?" Georgiana announced, unabashed and confidently. "Miss Emma Watson?"

Emma Watson turned to Georgiana and now I could see her closer. She had a few freckles on her face, reminding me of Mary King in one way, but that was the only similarity. Her features were quite attractive. When Emma Watson's eyes fell on Georgiana, her expression shifted to pleasant familiarity, and a smile spread across her face.

"Georgiana?"

"Yes!"

"Miss Georgiana Darcy, as I live and breathe. It is a great pleasure to see you here."

"I confess myself to being equally surprised. If surprise is what I can call you right now."

"You may call me that very much. I can barely contain my glee in knowing that you are here, to help me face the unfamiliar faces that are bound to cross my path. Oh, and look at you? You have grown into quite the handsome woman."

"You know very well that you have always been the beauty between us."

"I shall have none of that. My vanity must not reign over your consideration of yourself. I never had the chance to inquire, have you made the Edwards's acquaintance?"

"Never fear, I am well acquainted with the Edwards. How do you both do, Mr. and Mrs. Edwards? And Miss Edwards, you are looking very lovely in that gown. I never have the courage to wear a gold gown."

"Thank you," Miss Edwards responded.

"Miss Darcy," Mrs. Edwards said, "it is a delight to see you again. I heard that your brother has been recently married."

"More than that. Soon, he and Mrs. Darcy are on the road to becoming a mother and father."

"Oh," Mr. Edwards responded, merrily, "I must meet this interesting woman, for it had been long said that a truly superior woman must catch your brother's eye."

"He found a superior woman indeed," Georgiana responded, "proof of that is right next to me. Allow me to introduce you to my friend and newly acquired sister, Miss Kitty Bennet. Kitty, this is Mr. and Mrs. Edwards, their daughter, Miss Mary Edwards, and a long-lost acquaintance, Miss Emma Watson."

At last, it was time to step forward, curtsy and make myself known to a set of people who I could mean nothing to. They were kind to me, but it was very evident that I was not the object that was of any consequence to them. Mr. Edwards spoke the most to me, and he was quite kind, but the ladies were another matter. Mrs. Edwards was friendly, but she had a reserved air, and a great deal of formal civility. Her daughter, Miss Mary Edwards, was a genteel-looking girl of twenty-two years, and she inherited her mother's reserve. We would get along for the duration of the ball, but I did not foresee us ever meeting again after this interesting night.

Emma Watson was also raised to be very fine. It was evident from her air and the manner in which she walked. She was raised to be a pretty and genteel sort of creature. She also learned the sad habit of verbal economics; she didn't speak very much but stood there and was more reactive in her conversation than proactive. Despite this all, I still felt a discomfort around her, and I could not understand why that was so. The reason would continue to elude me for the entire evening.

"Now," Mr. Edwards said, "Miss Darcy, I trust that you are not alone."

"Not at all, sir. I came with my brother, sisters-in-law, newly acquired cousins, and my family from Matlock."

"Oh!" Mrs. Edwards said, "then am I to understand that Lord and Lady Fitzwilliam are among the party with any of their famous sons?"

"Two of the three are present and accounted for," I answered, attempting to not remain as a flower against the proverbial wall, "Mr. Frederick Fitzwilliam and Colonel Fitzwilliam."

When I had mentioned Frederick's name, I saw Mr. and Mrs. Edwards's faces subtly lift and shifted their gaze toward their daughter. Mary Edwards avoided this and looked at the floor.

"Well, that is good news indeed," Mrs. Edwards said.

"Tom Musgrave is also in our company," Georgiana informed them as we led them back to our family circle.

And once more, I observed the subtle shift of the Edwards's expressions again. This time, their eyes drooped and displayed a hint of vexation at hearing Mr. Musgrave's name. This gave all the indication in the world that Mr. Tom Musgrave had evidently done something to make himself not universally loved. Then again, except for Jane, who is ever universally loved?

~

When we led them over to our company, our group became even more increased. We were already a large party when we came, and now to have four more people join our number, we resulted in standing out.

Around us, other families began to abandon their conversations with themselves, and either subtly began to watch us, or they were wondering when they could find their way to ingratiate themselves into our set. Even the Luxfords sometimes would look past the new arrivals that they had to greet and spied us, a little.

When the Edwards and Miss Watson made the acquaintance of my sisters, Mr. Atkins, Enara, and Arthur, I was able to observe everyone. Partly it was because Georgiana and Emma Watson were eagerly talking among themselves, and I fell to the wayside a bit. This led to a slight annoyance even more, that I did not delve into at the moment. The Edwards were eager to endear themselves to Mr. Darcy and Lizzy, but they primarily talked to the Fitzwilliams. There was a motive to their friendliness, besides just natural goodness. The truth is that Frederick Fitzwilliam was a single man who inherited a lovely house, beautiful lands, and title. Mary Edwards was two and twenty, had a nice dowry on her own, and nothing could be better than making such a match. Therefore, when Frederick offered to secure Mary Edwards's hand for the first two dances, her parents were excited at the prospect.

Soon, our party would become even larger. Initially, Tom Musgrave was not present when we brought the Edwards over, and that probably was to their happiness. Yet, with our party's popularity increasing, it was only a matter of time before Tom Musgrave brought another family over to get them acquainted with those of us that were strangers.

"Well," Tom Musgrave said, "upon my word. You Matlock and

Pemberley folk are finding yourselves to be the most popular sort of creatures. Mr. and Mrs. Edwards, it is a delight to see you."

Neither of them responded to his gallantry. Tom directed his attention to Miss Edwards and Miss Watson.

"And Miss Edwards, you are looking as handsome as ever."

"Thank you, Mr. Musgrave," Mary Edwards said, looking at the floor again, and having no energy or animation in her voice. She clearly took no joy in his flattery. What did Tom do? Because it was very evident that his gallantry was unwanted among the Edwards.

"Bennet ladies, and Mrs. Philips," Tom Musgrave said, "my dear friends, the Tomlinsons have expressly wished for a desire to make your acquaintance."

"We welcome any friend of yours, sir," Jane replied, pleasantly. The amount of people who wished to meet us had brought a glow to her cheek and confidence. She felt the compliment of so many people wishing to be acquainted with us, that it filled her with open gaiety.

"Mrs. Bingley, you are all goodness," Tom Musgrave said, "and that will always be the most welcoming thing at a ball."

The Tomlinsons were another family who fell into the wayside of my attention, because, at this point, I was becoming overwhelmed myself.

"You look flustered, Kitty," Colonel Fitzwilliam whispered to me.

"It's because I am," I replied. "When meeting a rush of new people, I feel like I have been like a bit of jam that has been scraped over too much bread. I don't think I can remember all these people's names."

"If you ever forget, I shall whisper the names in your ear."

I smiled up at him.

"For the moment, you complete me."

He gave me a roguish grin.

"I try."

At the other side of the hallway, the line of attendees was soon coming to an end. Therefore, the last names that were being announced were hard to hear over the conversations that filled up the halls. As such, imagine my surprise when, loud and clear, I heard three names being called. Those were three names that I had not heard in so long, and never expected to hear ever again.

"Mr. Henry Crawford, Miss Mary Crawford, and Mr. William Price!"

My jaw dropped.

It couldn't be!

But could it? I turned to Jane and my sister, Mary, and the three of us all stopped attending to anything else. We each exchanged a 'did we just hear that correctly?' expression. This did not go unseen by the rest of the company. They saw our eyes shift over to the new arrivals. When I did, my eyes widened in the familiarity of seeing an old acquaintance, and my heart lifted at the sight of one of them in particular.

There, new onto the company was Miss Mary Crawford, arm in arm with a handsome naval officer, and her brother, Mr. Henry Crawford, of the estate Everingham, in Norfolk!

～

"Miss Crawford!" Jane cried, louder than expected. When hearing her name called with such animation, Mary Crawford turned her head around. When seeing Jane, her face lit up in wonder, and that only augmented her incredible beauty.

"Jane!" Mary Crawford uttered, then she saw Mary and I as well. "Mary and Kitty! Henry, look!"

To her left, Mr. Henry Crawford turned around, and he was as I remembered him. He was around five foot seven, his skin was not fair in any respect, for there was a sallowness to it, and his figure was unremarkable in every sense of the word. And when the smile came across his face, it diminished his plainness, and his charm began to come forth.

Mary Crawford said something to the third man, who was handsomer than Mr. Crawford, and I was left to assume that he was the one called William Price.

Eagerly, Jane, Mary and I walked forward to meet them, heedless of anything else around us. After all, when Lydia had eloped and we were considered the most unfortunate family in Hertford-shire, they had visited us at that time, and it lessened our sense of shame. We felt, in the eyes of the world, that we would never be fully cast down, because they did not forsake us. As a result, their generosity and compassion for us when Lydia eloped was not to be soon forgotten. Nor was it forgotten in their eyes either, as they stepped forward to greet us. When the space between us closed, Mary Crawford reached out to Jane, they grabbed hands, and she kissed Jane's cheek.

"In all my days, I never thought we might see each other again," Mary Crawford professed.

"Nor did I," Jane gasped, practically laughing with awe. "Oh, Mary, I cannot believe it."

"Believe," Mary Crawford said, in her charming manner, "for I promise, I am no wasp of paranormal smoke." Then she turned to Mary and me. "There's my other namesake and Miss Kitty. Well, you both are in the smartest of looks. You are almost as lovely as your oldest sister here. Whatever you did to yourselves, keep doing it."

"I can attest to there being a change in my life, Miss Craw-ford," Mary said, "I am a married woman. Jane is as well."

Mary Crawford smiled.

"Jane has written to me often about her unworthy beau and told me about your good fortune. You are now Mrs. Atkins, are you not?"

Mary's eyes widened, then she turned to Jane.

"You never mentioned that you told Miss Crawford about my luck."

"Indeed," I elaborated, "she never mentioned that you both correspond at all. Then again, Jane does prefer discretion."

"Yes," Mary Crawford confirmed, "life is split between those of us who keep our counsel, and the rest of us, who display all our actions to the world. Either way, you both found where your hearts lay?"

"We did, indeed," Jane confirmed.

"They must be superior men," Henry Crawford uttered, "to choose so wisely."

"They are, Mr. Crawford," Mary, our sister, said. "You must meet Mr. Atkins. He would love to make your acquaintance."

"Would he, indeed? My reputation hangs on his judgment of me."

"Nonsense!"

"Yes, I am full of that."

"Now," Mary Crawford said, "In hearing of your good fortune, it gives me the chance to introduce you to mine." She gestured to the man who was behind her, and he came forward, looking handsome in his naval attire.

"Mr. William Price," Jane professed, equally happy to see him. "Finally, I see you both together again."

"You do indeed, Mrs. Bingley," William Price said. "And now I have the pleasure of getting acquainted with your family."

"Mary, and Kitty," Mary Crawford said, "this is my fiancé, Lieutenant William Price. My dear, this is Mrs. Atkins, and Miss Bennet."

William Price bowed to us and said all the customary things that you said when you met someone. However, there was an organic tone to his manner. His words did not appear as being forced. As they stood next to each other, he and Miss Crawford had a natural elegance to their appearance, and an obvious affection for each other. As soon as we had no choice but to share them with the rest of our company, Jane offered to escort them to the rest of our group and introduce them to our family.

Despite being willing, I could discern Mary Crawford having a slight bit of apprehension to her voice.

"We shall be delighted to meet them, as long as they will not find meeting us to be tiresome," Mary Crawford uttered.

"Oh, hush," Jane assured her. "My family shall be delighted. Now come."

As we walked back to our company, Jane couldn't help but dominate Miss Crawford's attention, along with her fiancé. This was natural, since they had become close friends ever since Jane had visited the Gardiners in London, months ago, and when it was evident that Mr. Bingley might never return to Netherfield. They had been much thrown together. Socially, a friendship was formed, and their bond was of a strong nature that I would never fully know all the history of.

However, Henry Crawford knew to ingratiate himself in the most proper of places. Standing between Mary and me, he offered us his arms. Each taking one, we walked back to our company.

"So," he began, "Mrs. Atkins, I am aware that husbands must always take precedence when securing a woman's hand to dance. Therefore, promise me that you will take no slight in me immediately appealing to Miss Bennet. In any other case, seniority would be respected."

"I am not offended at all," Mary said, falling back into his preference, "for, if I had not the liberty of dancing with Mr. Atkins for the first two dances, I would burst. However, unless I am mistaken, Kitty's dance partners might also make it difficult for you."

"Truly?" Henry Crawford said, with a raised eyebrow, then he turned to me, "Is this true, Miss Bennet? Has some scoundrel decided to not give me the chance to secure the first two dances? Oh, well, I suppose I had no choice but to be beaten to it."

"First," I said, "time was not your friend. Second, you will learn to admire the man who has secured my hand for the first two dances. He is a remarkable sort of character, and believe it or not, is as charming as you."

"You both flatter me and diminish the only talent that I have. Oh well, you are a lovely creature, so I can forgive not being special, as long as you look kindly on me. Can I at least have your hand for the third dance?"

"My third and fourth dance is also secured by another."

"Your beauty is taking you further away from my pleasure. How about the fifth? Or did the Greek legend, Narcissus, come away from his reflection and secured your hand for that as well?"

"I am free for the fifth."

"Then I finally have half my joy. And now for the other half." He turned to Mary. "And what of Mrs. Atkins? Will your husband allow me the pleasure of getting to dance with you for one set? Would he forgive me?"

"He would," Mary said, then she became insecure. "*I think.*"

Henry laughed.

"Ah, those two immortal words. '*I think*'."

We reached our company and now we added another set of three more people to our number.

~

"So," Elizabeth said when Jane introduced the Crawfords and Mr. Price, "this is a chapter of my sister's life that I have never gotten the chance to see."

When looking between both women, I noted some similarities between Lizzy and Mary Crawford. Both were around the same height, had dark curly hair, dark twinkling eyes that had a hidden brilliance to them, and sometimes they wore the same arched expression that said, 'I am analyzing everything around me, and shall determine my findings during here or there'. I wonder that I never noticed these similarities before.

"Well," Mary Crawford replied to her, "hopefully that now can be redressed. According to Jane's letters, you and I always had a habit of missing each other whenever I fell into Jane's life. When I left London, that was when you came to visit her in Gracechurch Street, after coming from Kent. When my brother, sister, and I visited your family in Longbourn, you were on holiday with the Gardiners in Derbyshire." Mary Crawford looked at Mr. Darcy. "And found pleasant company there, I see."

When I looked on Mr. Darcy, Mr. Bingley, the Osbornes, and the Fitzwilliams, I saw them eyeing the Crawfords apprehensively. They looked on them with a distrust. I could not account for this, but since the Bingley sisters had once looked down at me in such a way, I did not let that affect how I looked on the Crawfords.

Whereas the Edwards, Tom Musgrave, Frederick Fitzwilliam, and Emma Watson met them innocently and with the same curiosity that I had possessed when I first made their acquaintance. The Crawfords were, in a strange way, immediately fascinating. They had a habit of becoming the center of attention wherever they went.

Therefore, Mary Edwards, Frederick and Emma Watson were

the first to ask them questions, and soon, William Price was able to gather his confidence and join the conversation.

All the while, Darcy, Bingley, Lord, and Lady Fitzwilliam were silently observing the Crawfords.

Colonel Fitzwilliam was oddly silent as well. As I neared Georgiana, I took her arm.

"Who would have believed it? We both have found old friends at this ball that's filled with new acquaintances."

"You never mentioned her before," Georgiana said.

This question startled me.

"Well," I explained, "it wasn't out of a desire to leave you ignorant, Georgie. I simply never mentioned her because no subject ever came up that connected our conversation to Miss Crawford. Nothing ever happened that reminded me of talking about her. Besides, she was more Jane's friend than mine. They met in London when Jane was staying with the Gardiners after Mr. Bingley had left Hertfordshire. I only met her once before today."

"She certainly left a favorable impression."

I marked Georgiana's words and detected a subtle anxiety to it all.

"I think you might like her," I said, "besides, you never told me about your friend, Emma Watson."

She looked at me and detected her own hypocrisy.

"Oh. Yes. There was no way to bring up my past with her, because the subject never came up organically."

"Precisely. We are the same in this moment." I squinted when I accepted the fact that there was more to this conversation than simple vexation on us both not knowing each other's history. "I feel like there is more to our discomfort than that, isn't there?"

"I do not know."

"Never fear. The great thing about the day after a ball is that we can be analytical and theoretical later."

"Precisely. For tonight, let's not be stupid. We really ought to enjoy ourselves."

"Yes, we must."

In that moment, as Frederick Fitzwilliam and Tom Musgrave

began to speak to William Price and the Crawfords, Emma Watson approached Georgiana and me.

"My goodness," she whispered to us, her cheeks red from excitement, "I usually do not get driven away by flights of first impressions, but Miss Crawford is so elegant. I must have appeared so very simple under her wit."

I smirked.

"Miss Crawford will forgive you. She is aware that variety of witty and unwitty is the spice of life."

After the Crawfords and Mr. Price charmed half of the group, and discomforted the other half, I managed to draw near the Colonel.

"Aren't they wonderful?" I asked him.

"Looks can be deceiving," Colonel Fitzwilliam whispered to me.

"Deceiving? Well, yes, I am aware of that maxim. But what does that have to do with them?"

Colonel Fitzwilliam looked down at me and his expression was shockingly unamused. In fact, he looked stern.

"They are not what they seem."

I leaned in closer.

"Richard?"

"Don't trust them. I'll speak of this later."

This statement, while brief and simple, could not be ignored so lightly. It overpowered me and I found myself looking on the Crawfords with an apprehension as well. How the scene changes at the mere hint of deception. A beautiful scene can suddenly turn ugly. However, there was another side of the situation, and that was discomfort toward the Colonel. I had been having a delightful time, in meeting new people and also gaining older friends, and now the whole scene had been distorted and smeared. Sometimes, a person wishes that they had never been enlightened.

Colonel Fitzwilliam's warning also brought clarity on why half of the company did not meet the Crawfords so very warmly. In fact, Darcy did not speak once since they had come over, and Mr. Bingley kept watching Jane as she spoke with Miss Crawford, and he seemed uncomfortable the whole time. As a result, I began to realize that there was something going on of which I was wholly ignorant.

And the more I thought about it, the more obvious that maybe I had been blind toward something. After all, I had only met the Crawfords once, and that was hardly enough to say that I knew them. Although, they had a habit of ingratiating themselves into our company, and so it was easy to assume that we knew them well. While, in fact, we never *actually* knew them at all.

Out of the corner of my eye, I saw Mr. Darcy open his mouth and that was the first time that he had spoken in quite a while.

"Mr. Henry Crawford," Mr. Darcy began.

Mr. Crawford, who had been talking with Mary and Mr. Atkins at that point, turned to Mr. Darcy.

"Yes, sir?"

"Forgive me, I just wish to make certain. You are Mr. Henry Crawford, of Everingham, Norfolk?"

"Yes, I am, sir. I inherited Everingham, out of gratitude from my family."

"As I understand it, you once were well acquainted with the Bertram family, who reside in Mansfield Park."

The smiles that were on the Crawfords' and William Price's faces were quite wiped away and were replaced by a guarded look.

"Yes, I was," Mr. Crawford responded, "though, I am wholly aware of not being a favorite amongst them."

"You're not a favorite?" Mary Edwards said. "Well, that is quite the surprise."

"You are too kind, Miss Edwards. I thank you for that."

"I still wish that I had the ability to see Everingham," our sister Mary uttered, "but it might always be a wish to know what it looks like."

"Well," Mary Crawford said, "that might be remedied. Henry has invited us to Everingham when Mr. Price and I marry. If you are willing to ever visit, I'm sure that Henry would love to invite us there at the same time and we can make a merry party of it."

"Thank you, Miss Crawford," Mr. Bingley said, a little rushed. "But we soon will establish ourselves in a new home, and Mrs. Bingley is recently with child. I would not have her travel for a great duration."

Jane smiled diplomatically, but she didn't want Mary to feel slighted.

"Mr. Bingley is correct, but once I am safe to travel over distances, I would love to accept such an invitation. Oh, Bingley, it would be a delight to see."

"Quite so, my dear," was all Bingley said in return. His lack of eagerness to accept the invitation would not go amiss to anyone who was not familiar with his character. But for those of us who were familiar with his general nature, were aware of what he truly felt.

All the attendees had come to the ball, conversation was spent, and it was time to line up for the first dance.

Chapter Eight

THE TERRIFYING TRUTH

Taking my hand, Colonel Fitzwilliam led me to the middle of the dance floor.

Darcy and Elizabeth, as well as Jane and Bingley, had to sit out the dance, but they were not alone. Eager to get even more acquainted with her friend and fiancé, Jane asked Mary Crawford and William Price to sit and talk with them about all that she wanted to know. Miss Crawford had been all too happy to oblige, because she also wanted to know about Jane's new position of being with child and her excitement at being a mother.

Georgiana joined me as she met Mr. Luxford. Henry Crawford discovered that Miss Carr had no partner and requested her hand. Mr. Atkins came next with Mary, and Enara and Arthur also followed after us. Miss Edwards went to the dance floor with Frederick Fitzwilliam. But there was one unfortunate piece of vanity that had occurred.

Mrs. Blake, Mr. Howard's sister, had her son at the ball. Little Charles, the ten-year-old eager boy, had been anticipating when the dancing would begin. He had stood by us 'boring' adults for long enough, and now he could exert himself and find all the powers of being pleased, especially since he had a partner.

"Miss Osborne has promised me that she would be my dance partner," Little Charles had whispered to me when the Luxfords had made the opening ball announcement.

"You will not be surprised at Charles's impatience," his mother, Mrs. Blake, had said. "Miss Osborne has been so very kind as to promise to dance the two dances with him."

"Oh yes! Miss Osborne and I have been engaged to dance this week. And we are to dance down every couple."

"I am amazed by you," I had professed to him. "In Hertfordshire, I never met a young boy who preferred dancing. They usually couldn't stand us girls."

"They must have been so terribly stupid," Charles had responded, "what could be more fun than dancing?"

"Never let that perspective go, young Charles," I had encouraged, "it will take you far in life. A man who loves to dance is always welcome in society."

Charles had smiled at that. So, when the first dance was ordered to begin, he was practically bouncing in his shoes, excited. This excitement was rewarded by cold inconsideration from his dance partner, Miss Osborne. She had walked to the dance floor, but not with little Charles!

Rather, she had taken Mr. Tom Musgrave's hand, and he was escorting her to the dance floor. When Charles had stood up to dance with her, it was to the sight of being slighted.

"Charles, I beg your pardon for not keeping my engagement," Miss Osborne had requested, "but I am to dance these two dances with Mr. Musgrave. I know you will excuse me, and I will certainly dance with you after tea."

Without giving little Charles another look or waiting for a response, Miss Osborne had walked back to Miss Carr and soon Tom Musgrave had approached them both.

Little Charles was mortified. Mrs. Blake immediately tried to comfort her son, but her son's little poor face was the picture of disappointment.

Miss Osborne, you witch!

～

Every now and again, a person does something so callous that you just cannot like them. I can understand many mistakes, many flaws, and acts of stupidity. But not dancing with a little boy, who you had promised to dance with, and then set down publicly, was beyond my realm of forgiveness. Miss Osborne didn't even care to comfort him. How could I like her? The answer was quite simple. I couldn't. What a disgusting woman. What a terrible woman. A repulsive and ridiculous creature! Someone pass the salt!

Immediately taking pity on little Charles, I was about to ask the Colonel if I could postpone our dance and come to Charles's rescue.

However, my good intentions were unnecessary because Emma Watson came to save the day.

Seeing the boy trying to maintain a brave face, but failing at it, Emma Watson came forward and extended her hand to him.

"I shall be very happy to dance with you, sir, if you like," she offered.

All it takes is one act of kindness to overturn callous neglect.

Since Emma Watson was actually handsomer than Miss Osborne, the advantage of this new prospect was felt keenly. Little Charles had smiled happily, looked hopefully at his mother, and had taken Miss Watson's hand eagerly.

"Thank you, ma'am," Little Charles had said, added by Mrs. Blake's words of immense gratitude for Miss Watson saving her son's happiness. Emma received these compliments modestly, and it gained her a broad stare from Miss Osborne and Miss Carr.

"Upon my word, Charles," Miss Osborne said, "you are in luck. You have got a better partner than me."

"Yes," Little Charles answered triumphantly.

Miss Osborne, just shut your mouth! There is nothing so grating on the nerves than hearing the voice of someone that you have resolved to never fully trust.

And thus was the beginning of the first dance! Since my two eldest sisters could not dance, Darcy and Bingley were accosted by the two Luxford sisters and felt the pressure of having no choice but to offer to dance with them for the first set. After all, we were in their home and at their ball. Such consideration and respect must be paid. Therefore, Jane and Elizabeth sat down, and Mary Crawford and William Price got even more acquainted with Lizzy, who seemed open to the prospect.

I faced Colonel Fitzwilliam as the music was struck up.

"We get to dance again," I acknowledged.

"And you are wearing the same gown that you wore when we first danced together at the Netherfield wedding ball."

He took my hand, and we moved along the set.

"Oh dear," I said, "I must look redundant to you."

"Is that the impression I gave?" he asked, wishing to correct the mistake, "that was not my intent."

"Oh, it was not?"

"Never in a million years. I merely mentioned it to give the feeling that we are returned to that same place, and I like it."

"Those were simpler times...despite that it was only a couple months ago."

"Precisely. Each day can feel like a year when you are not living your life to the fullest."

We were separate for a few seconds, in the dance, and then we returned to each other.

"I'm sure that you remember our topic of discussion at that first dance," I said to him.

"How could I forget? I quite talked your ears off, with my history lessons."

"Well...what lesson will I get this time? I am all anticipation. If you know any history on Ancient Greece, Rome, or Egyptian pharaohs, then that would be most welcome."

"If I have the time in our second dance, then I will be very happy to tell you about Hatshepsut, the female Egyptian Pharaoh."

"Oh, I love hearing about her."

"Oh, you already are acquainted with her?"

"Yes, I am. I loved reading about her. She dressed like the male pharaohs and became a legend."

"Well, I shall have another figure for you, who is similar. But there is something else that I wish to talk to you about."

Looking into his eyes, the dance led to us standing still, facing each other. This gave me the chance to analyze his intent, which was evident in his expression.

"You want to talk about the Crawfords."

His eyes softened.

"We have a habit of reading each other's minds too much."

"I like that we do. That means I am right?"

"Yes, you are correct."

"Well, I am happy that you wish to enlighten me on why you, and half of our company, seem to have a subtle fright when facing them. I cannot account for it. The Crawfords are the nicest people that I have ever met."

"I cannot say anything critical about Mr. William Price, because I have heard no bad reports of him. If he is a good man, then I wonder why he associates with them."

"But Richard, you have told me nothing to give me the reason to think they are anything else but wonderful company. Help me to understand."

"They lack proper morals."

"How?"

"Mr. Henry Crawford is a libertine."

"In what way?"

"He ran off with another man's wife."

When hearing this, I almost forgot my footing, and then I forgot the next dance move. Colonel Fitzwilliam had to whisper it to me. Remembering myself, I managed to move just in time before bumping my shoulder against Emma Watson's.

"I have unnerved you," Colonel Fitzwilliam realized. "Perhaps this is not the proper place for me to make you feel disorientated."

"Too late, Richard. In for a penny, in for a pound. You cannot leave me with only that statement. Is this really true?"

"Yes, it is."

"Is there evidence to this? Perhaps he has been falsely slandered."

"Oh, there is all the proof in the world. It was in the newspapers."

My eyes widened at this.

"It was?"

"Yes."

"Who was the woman?" he asked.

"A Mrs. Maria Rushworth. But her maiden name was Maria Bertram, daughter of Sir Thomas and Lady Bertram, of Mansfield Park."

"Oh! That's why Mr. Darcy commented on Mr. Crawford's relationship to that estate."

"Yes. Darcy was doing what he does very well: subtly reminding someone of their past sin, without actually saying it."

"Oh," she said. "But she was the one who was married? What inspired her to run off with Mr. Crawford?"

"From what I have heard, she fell in love with Henry Crawford when he and Miss Crawford visited Mansfield Park. All the while, she was already engaged to another man, Mr. Rushworth of Sotherton."

"Wait," I stated. "She was engaged to one man and fell in love with a completely different man."

"Yes. Henry Crawford is popular and well-known in the ton for being a tremendous flirt, and making women fall in love with him."

I pondered this. "While I admit that there are rattles and rakes aplenty in the world, no one can ultimately make anyone fall in love with them, if they are not of the inclination. Why was this woman open to receiving attentions from another man when she was already engaged to someone? What I mean is...did this woman ever love her husband?"

"It was probably an uneven match from the very beginning, with absolutely no affection on her side."

"That's what I'm wondering. And if she did fall in love with Mr. Crawford, which I would not be surprised that she did in the slightest—he has winning ways—then why did she continue to marry this Mr. Rushworth?"

"These are home questions that I cannot answer," Colonel Fitzwilliam considered, "Only Maria Bertram can, and she never will."

"Why not?"

"From what I heard, when the affair ended disastrously, her father set her up in a cottage in a different county than Mansfield Park."

"So...she was practically exiled?" I asked, astounded.

"As punishment for her actions."

"I don't know whether to applaud the Bertrams for exercising punishment, or sympathy for Maria Bertram for being banished from her family. We all need to be chastised for when we do wrong, but to not see your family for so long, if ever, is frightful."

"Yes, it is quite the conundrum. For either way, a great evil is done."

"If they just forgave her and Maria Bertram went back to Mansfield Park, she would never learn the weight of her actions and never learn any sort of shame or humility, but for her family to cast her off, it shows a harsh unforgiving nature on their part."

"Precisely," the Colonel acknowledged. "They are damned if they do, but damned if they do not."

"But how did Mr. Crawford come to have an affair with Mrs. Rushworth?"

"Well, Maria Bertram went ahead with her wedding to Mr. Rushworth, despite not caring for him. When Mr. Crawford fell back into her life, he must have charmed her again, and she quitted her house and sought out Mr. Crawford."

"So, she was the one who ultimately pursued him?" I asked, thoroughly engrossed in the subject.

"Yes. But here's the thing. He could have spurned her and told her to return home. But he did not. Immediately, he gave into temptation, enjoyed his time with her, and then she refused to leave him. This was discovered, it got into the newspapers and gazettes and soon they reaped the bitter rewards of becoming infamous. This soured them against each other, and they left each other, with no tender feelings involved."

"What was this Maria Bertram thinking? Why choose a man who did not initially choose you?" I rolled my eyes, annoyed at the question, because I knew the answer. "Of course! She was in love. Mix falling in love, while being a lady from a great escape and never learning restraint, and you've got a recipe for romantic disaster."

"Precisely. This lady never encountered repercussions to her actions before, and that might have been the ruin of her. We all need to get corrected every now and again. It teaches us limitations. Without limitations, you will destroy yourself—eventually."

"But what has Mary Crawford done throughout all this?" I asked. "After all, she did not commit the crime. That crime rests mostly in Maria Bertram, for she committed the worst betrayal. And the second crime goes to Henry Crawford, for his vanity in enticing an engaged woman and his lack of self-control and consideration of the husband. But what's Miss Crawford's crime?"

Colonel Fitzwilliam thought about it.

"Well, she is known for being very pragmatic about things, and indelicate in her words, sometimes."

"I am like that sometimes myself. Isn't that what you liked about me?"

He regarded me.

"I recall, upon good report, that she tried to persuade her brother to marry Maria Bertram."

"Well, that is only natural. After all, if her brother didn't marry her, (as he clearly decided not to), then Maria would be ruined. As she evidently became so."

"But for Miss Crawford to suggest it showed an indelicacy."

"How is she wrong for doing the same thing that Mr. Darcy did when he paid off Wickham to marry Lydia?"

He thought of that for a moment and then he saw the hypocrisy of his viewpoint.

"Oh," Colonel Fitzwilliam voiced.

"Yes. Richard, what are you telling me? Are you saying that she ought to be considered guilty by association?"

"Very well. Perhaps Miss Crawford is not to be judged by actions that she did not commit. But she evidently supports her brother, throughout this."

"Would you forsake your brother for such actions? Would you never forgive Frederick?"

"You are determined to not let me be of a shallow mentality, aren't you?"

"And you are determined to make me into the moral one. This is very interesting."

"Why do you love me?" he asked. "I am not on my best display now."

Warmth infused me. "You just had a moment of weakness. We have all been there. You've forgiven me for my bad moments, and I will forgive you for yours. This is the kind of people that we are."

"And what of Henry Crawford? What of him?"

Hearing Henry's name, I looked at him as he was dancing with his partner.

"Now that is the true conundrum. It was in the papers, and it justifies why he was so adamant not to fully go into detail of his estate when he came to visit us in Hertfordshire. Also, he seemed to know what Mr. Darcy was hinting at when he referred to Mansfield Park. Sadly, I have to acknowledge that this all may be true."

"Oh, it's true in every way. Maria Bertram's exile is all the proof that one needs."

I nodded. "Then that scares me. All this time, I thought he was a good man. I was wrong. Now I feel like the greatest fool of all."

"Don't hate yourself. Everyone gets taken in, in one form or another, eventually."

Chapter Nine

AH, TO DANCE!

When I finished dancing with Colonel Fitzwilliam, we all sat down together, and I felt restless. When Jane and Elizabeth had gone to the punch table, I joined them, and I began to explain the truth of the matter.

"I have heard the most astonishing thing," I began.

"About what?" Jane asked.

"It's about the Crawfords."

Jane did not look satisfied, but only tense. Before I could offer another word, she placed her hands on Lizzy and my right arm.

"Kitty and Lizzy," she urged, her voice at the lowest whisper ever, "this is imperative. Whatever you hear about the Crawfords, promise me this. Promise me that you will not treat them differently than any other person at this ball."

My eyes widened.

"You know," I realized, "you've known the truth all this time?"

Jane's eyes were firm.

"Yes, I do. I know the whole history."

"The whole history to what?" Elizabeth asked, then her eyes shifted to recollection of everyone's reaction to the Crawfords. "Or are we referring to a history that explains the divisive reaction everyone had when seeing them?"

"Yes," Jane said, "it's been years since that all happened. But this is a ball. Let us have a lovely time, and please," she urged us, "whatever anyone else feels about them, do not let that impact you. Do not give into other people's judgments on people who have not harmed us. Please," she begged, "do this for me.

"Mr. Darcy and my dear Charles are evidently affected by the Crawfords' reputation, and I don't want them to leave us thinking that we have forsaken them. There are parts of the story that I will tell you and it is important for you to know. I shall do so tomorrow, but for now, believe me on this, and please support me. Be kind."

When looking at her, imploring us so innocently, we were moved. Jane was truly protective of the Crawfords—Mary Crawford in particular. And no wonder for it. It was very evident that she had reached a level of attachment that ran so deep, it was equivalent to familial habit. How could we not agree? Especially when Jane had every right for us to support her in this. How many times had she shown compassion for me, shielding me from the more painful aspects of my life? It would be a shame to not stand by her in this time.

"Of course, Jane," Elizabeth supported. We all agreed to this, which was no difficulty for my part. Despite hearing such horrible things about them, I was not in the mood to be cold and cruel toward people who never harmed me or anyone around me, for that matter. It just seemed pointless at that particular time.

～

Eventually, we returned to the company and continued to immerse ourselves in the group. The Luxford daughters had now also immersed themselves in our set, so it was easy to branch off and have smaller side conversations.

"Well, Miss Watson," Mary Crawford said as she sat down with Jane, Georgiana, Emma, and me, "you have made yourself into quite the hero of the evening."

"Oh, I did little."

"Sometimes little is enough, especially in your dance partner's case."

"Not all heroic gestures are only on battlefields," Jane added.

"And Mrs. Bingley would know that, more than ever. I saw her be the hero to a little girl in London, once. Will it find its way in the papers? Of course not. Only the horrors of humanity can find their way into print and fame."

Jane blushed.

Georgiana and I had the impulse to speak at the same time, and together we said, "I think..."

We both looked at each other, surprised and everyone laughed.

"What were you going to say?" I asked her.

"I cannot remember," she replied, "what were you going to say?"

"I cannot remember either!"

This made everyone laugh again.

Then it was time to dance, and little Charles came to take Emma's hand again. Henry Crawford came to secure Mary's hand —which he did so after getting permission from Mr. Atkins—and Mr. Luxford came to dance with Georgiana.

"A ball where I am not dancing," Elizabeth whispered to me, "well, I never thought I'd see the day."

"Your child will thank you."

She drummed her hand against her stomach.

"They had better." She grinned. "They are depriving me of my favorite pastime. Now go and be blithe and bonny."

I looked into her eyes.

"You are anxious to find out what Jane has to tell us, aren't you?"

"I am sitting on pins and needles."

"I had the inkling."

I went off to dance with Colonel Fitzwilliam. When we stood facing each other again, I scrunched my nose at him, and he smiled.

"Do you know," he began, "no matter what happens between us, and whatever we do and say to each other, we always return to the same place."

"And what place is that?" I asked.

"Peaceful understanding."

"The effects of forgiving each other, in matters great and small."

"Aye, we do that."

"Richard?"

"Yes?"

"Whatever you feel for the Crawfords, I need you to understand why I will reserve judgment for now. I will enjoy this evening and not make anyone feel unwelcome. Please tell me you understand why."

"I will. Cross my heart, under way of swearing it."

I looked up at him, with him looking so handsome in his regimentals.

"Now that is the officer that I first was drawn to."

"I lost my way for a bit."

"Well, you will not be left to be confused on what to feel for very long. Tomorrow, Jane has promised that she will tell us everything. Since she and Miss Crawford are great friends, she knows the whole of the history. Until then, we can be free to determine not what to think."

"She will?"

"Yes. Would you like to be with us when she unfolds everything? I can ask her about that."

"If she would be so kind as to indulge me, then I would be delighted." He gave me a little bow.

"She will not refuse you. You know how Jane is."

"Yes, I do. Now, are you prepared for that history lesson?"

I smirked.

"Well, it's about time, is all that I can say."

"Since we've already spoken of Egyptian Pharaohs, let's talk of other figures from the same continent. Unless I am utterly mistaken, I daresay that you never heard of the historical figure, Nzinga."

"Nzinga?" I asked, scrunching my nose out of ignorance. "No, I very much am unfamiliar with that name."

"Her full name was Nzinga Mbande. She was born in 1583, and she was a queen that ruled the Ambundu Kingdoms in Ndongo and Matamba, in Africa."

"I'm learning about a queen," I asked, quite giddily. "Oh, I love hearing about those. Even the evil ones."

"Well, you will love this one. She ruled for thirty-seven years. When she was a child, she received military and political training. When she grew into a woman, she would go on to demonstrate an aptitude for defusing political crises as an ambassador to the Portuguese Empire. She later assumed power over the kingdoms after her father and brother died. Nzinga fought for the Independence and stature of her kingdoms against the Portuguese in a reign that lasted 37 years."

Yes, I was impressed. "Then, she was groomed to rule."

"Yes, she was."

"But don't you see?" I asked, amazed. "Usually when women assume the throne, it's often by a sort of default—there was no male heir to take over. But women usually were not groomed to rule from the very beginning. They usually were not taught political aspects, and they had to learn quickly when they were thrust into the reign that they were never meant to inherit. Sometimes, it even seems like they were pawns to two opposing religious sides who could not agree, no matter how similar their religion was."

Colonel Fitzwilliam laughed at that.

"But to be groomed for it, and prepared for it when the time comes," I elaborated. "Now that is what I prefer to hear about. To be on the same level of right to education—well, you can understand. I am not saying that I would be a very good lieutenant or captain, but to be given military experience since your childhood would be ideal for a monarch."

"And it served her well. Nzinga ruled during a period of rapid growth in the African slave trade and the Portuguese Empire were invading South West Africa."

"Yes, I learned of that. The Portuguese Empire was making more attempts to control the slave trade because, at that point, we still controlled parts of it. After all, the Trade began under the rule of Queen Elizabeth, so Nzinga was born around the time that much of our economy was supported by the Trade."

"Technically, it still is."

"In England and Wales, yes, but didn't Scotland abolish slavery in 1778?"

"Very good," he said, smiling at me. "Yes, they did!"

"See," I replied, "I know a thing or two. Now continue or I shall step on your foot."

"Why do you always randomly threaten me?" he asked, amused.

"Because it is such fun."

He laughed.

"No, truly," I chuckled merrily, "there is something so very diverting about threatening bodily harm to a man that you care about. Are you telling me that I do not entertain you when I do that?"

"That's the wonder of it. I love it when you do that."

I said, "I can tell that you do. So do not question my illogical behavior when it brings about so logical a conclusion."

The dance led to us standing still again while others danced around us.

"Say that you will miss me when I have to return back to my duties," he requested.

The thought of it pained me. "You know that I will."

He studied me for a moment. "You would have made quite the queen."

"It is all about someone choosing to believe in you, isn't it? That's where it all begins. You believe in me."

"I do."

"Then maybe I could have been one. Do you believe us women equal to you men?"

"Yes."

"All it takes is one. When that happens, everything can begin."

He took my hand and spun me around.

"Now we can fly," I voiced. "Over anything."

~

For the next two dances, I walked to the dance floor with Frederick Fitzwilliam. When we stood up together, he had that familiar smirk that he seems to wear very well.

"What is that look for?" I asked.

"What look?"

"Your expression. It's saying something."

"This is my natural face."

I decided that being polite and reserved did not become him. Therefore, I decided to talk to him in the way that I talked to his brother.

"Liar," I stated.

The dance started and we moved around each other as we partook in the Boulanger.

"A liar?" he echoed. "Me?"

"Yes, you. You have a motive, and since we are to dance together for the next hour, I am determined to make it out."

"You wish to know the recesses of my brain."

"Or what is in the coinage of your mind," I compiled. "Are you afraid of me knowing you?"

"You may not like what you see."

"I am braced for anything. You do not frighten me."

"Very well, you may ask me anything," He allowed.

"Why did you wish to dance with me? After all, it was evident that you only cared to when your brother showed an interest."

"I love my brother, and he loves me."

In that moment, we drew near Colonel Fitzwilliam, who was dancing with one of the Luxford sisters.

"Is that your answer to my question?" I asked.

"No. It is just an assurance that, no matter what I say, he and I are very fond of each other. It is just that I am a very competitive man."

"When I discovered that you like to racehorses, I gathered the sense that you are a man who will apply himself until he wins something."

"Well, I have to. You see, Richard is a Colonel in the army, and that, and his regimentals, naturally endear him to others. I can never live in a world where my brother is more fascinating than I am."

"Really?" I laughed. "That is what this is about? You are insecure because of Richard's charm?"

"You even call him Richard."

"And he calls me Kitty. We gave each other permission."

"Do I have your permission?"

"My permission all hangs on how you behave during our first dance. If you prove to be wonderful by the end, then you may call me Kitty by the second dance."

"Oh." He looked on me mischievously, "I intend to win that award."

We moved around another set of dancers and came back to each other.

"You are a curiosity," I said as he took my hand.

"How so?"

"I do not get the sense that your charm is natural, indiscriminate, and used to make you into a rake. You may try to make yourself look that way, but that is not so."

"Really?"

"Yes," I discerned, not knowing where my findings were coming from. I was speaking by pure instinct. "Does that come from competition as well? Richard is charming, so you must be better."

"Precisely."

"But why, I wonder. After all, you are the heir. You inherit everything, are regarded as the handsomer one, and Richard gets nothing. He can't even marry where he wants to. You can. So, what is there to be jealous over?"

"You cannot begin to understand. Yes, I have been given everything, and Richard hasn't. And yet, he smiles more than I do. He enjoys company better than I do. He has more natural talents, is organic at making women at ease with him. And when something good happens in his life, it is everything to him. When I am given something, I am already used to having it, because it was given to me already."

"Are you saying that you wonder at his natural happiness and wish to obtain that?"

"Perhaps that is the case."

"You, sir, are positively wicked."

"Perhaps I am. But I can never be in a world where he has achieved the perfect moments, and I am still chasing after them."

This man was a walking version of 'being spoiled'.

"And this is what it's like to have everything in life, I see?" I marveled. "And here I was, always jealous of your lot, who were born with everything in life. And this is what you are? Secretly unfulfilled the entire time…always pursuing that new frontier of emotional satisfaction. Your sort will never fully be happy, will you? And while that poor boy is happy when he gets a slingshot for Christmas, and you were given a holiday in Brighton, you were wondering why you weren't as happy with that holiday as that poor boy was happy with his slingshot."

He turned me and our eyes were close as we held hands.

"Do you ever realize, that maybe, you will never fully be happy?" I asked him.

When hearing that, his face turned serious.

"Have I hurt you?" I asked.

"Yes. I daresay that you have," He admitted.

I held my head up high.

"That's good. You need someone to make you unhappy, every now and again."

He tilted his head, disgruntled.

"And why is that?"

"By making you unhappy, you will appreciate that holiday in Brighton more. I did you a favor. You are very welcome."

After I said that, Frederick's face turned into that same cynical smile.

"Back to that expression?"

"You should have known," he answered, "now I understand."

"Understand what?"

"Why Richard is in love with you."

~

When the dance ended, we went back to our company, and Colonel Fitzwilliam came up to us.

"Met well by moonlight?" he asked us.

"Very well, brother," Frederick said, a little breathless, "Miss Bennet proved to be more charming than I expected. I dare say, I might ask her for a third dance."

Colonel Fitzwilliam raised an eyebrow.

"Our motives were similar. I was about to ask her to flatter me enough to secure her hand for the fifth set as well."

Both brothers looked between each other. Instinctively, I turned to look at Lord and Lady Fitzwilliam. Both parents had a 'what is happening?' look.

I looked at Mr. Darcy and Lizzy.

They both had a 'what is happening?' look.

I looked at Bingley and Jane.

They had a 'what is happening?' look.

I looked at Mary and Mr. Atkins.

They had a 'what is happening?' look.

I looked at Arthur and Enara Philips.

They had a 'what is happening?' look.

I looked at Emma Watson and the Edwards.

They had a 'what is happening?' look.

Thank goodness Tom Musgrave and the Osbornes had to separate themselves from our company to speak to the Luxfords.

Because I am quite certain that they also would have had a 'what is happening?' look.

But truly, what was happening?

Chapter Ten

DANCING WITH A LIBERTINE

The last faces I looked upon were Mr. and Miss Crawfords. Then it occurred to me...Mr. Crawford!

"Well, gentlemen," I said smoothly and carelessly, "neither of you has to worry over a choice being made, because one already has. Mr. Crawford has already reserved the fifth dance for me."

"Indeed, I have," Mr. Crawford confirmed, standing up. "My apologies, gentlemen, for impeding your happiness. However, when there are past friends to be met, one must do one's duty... and dance with them. And a welcome duty it is."

"Well then," Colonel Fitzwilliam said, "Miss Bennet, might I secure your hand for the sixth set?"

"And I for the seventh?" Frederick asked me.

I felt the heat on my neck rise with tension.

"Very well," I rushed out, quickly. "I accept."

~

"What was that?" I asked Frederick as we began our second dance together.

"Ah, I saw your cheeks turn red as we bartered for you," Frederick said, smugly.

"And I was not amused," I responded, now wholly unafraid of

unleashing full sincerity on him. "I must know. What was the point of that? You already let me provoke you to no end." Then I realized it. "That's it, isn't it? You are not used to being provoked."

"Perhaps I am not. We're in a world of flattery."

"I like flattery."

"You like it because it's always real around you. With me, I am flattered because I am the heir to Matlock. Nothing is real."

When he said that, his eyes were like steel.

"Is that how life feels to you?" I asked. "Like nothing is real?"

"If you lived in my shoes, you would see that it was."

"And with Richard, things feel real, from your perspective. They feel more real to him than they may ever feel for you."

He sighed as he turned me.

"I am not afraid of making you upset. You like it, don't you recall?"

"Yes, I do," he acknowledged, "but perhaps you may be right. I do not like that you are right."

We held hands and I twirled around.

"I suppose that it may be something more," he furthered.

"And what is that?"

"I want to know every reason for why my brother is in love with you."

The challenging smile fell from my features. What could he mean by it all?

"And what is your success?" I asked.

"He is in love with you, because he has no choice but to be."

"How could that be? Explain the theories of your mind to me. I am not afraid."

"You bewitched him, didn't you?"

I rolled my eyes.

"Let me guess. This is the part where the woman is the perpetrator to love. I am not a witch, sir."

"But how do I know that?"

"I cannot prove it to you. This is a folly that you have to confront about yourself."

"You tempted him, didn't you? You revealed the beauties of

the female spirit to such a degree that he became intimate with all you desires, didn't you?"

I was becoming very uncomfortable. "You are about to make me leave you on the dance floor."

"You would never do that."

"Would I not?"

"No, you would not."

"Why wouldn't I?"

"Because you like me," he announced.

Dear god!

Not again!

"I like you?" I repeated his words.

"Yes," Frederick responded, "you do. I can give you more in life than my brother can."

Pompous! "I don't care."

"Women say that, but that's just to pretend to be moral."

"And men say that when they are wicked and want to justify themselves. Mr. Fitzwilliam, look into my eyes. Are you looking?"

"Yes, I am."

"Good. Now listen to my voice. Are you listening?"

"I am."

"No," I said, "I do not like you. I love two men in this world, and one of them is your brother. The other is not you. It will never be you. I will walk my days, knowing full well that you could give me all that I could desire, and it still would never be you."

"Why not?" he asked, defiantly.

"Because you do not love me. Why would I love a man who clearly is only dancing with me because it gives him a strange sort of perverse pleasure—but it's not love."

His eyes shifted to joy over his own folly.

"How did you know that I was not in love with you?"

"You said it yourself: you compete with Richard. I'm the battleground. I'm not real, when it comes to a romantic idea with you. I'm just a piece of land. And that land is no one's to claim."

"Your land is not even my brother's?"

"He has to marry an heiress. I will never be his. He knows it, I know it, and now you know it. Now that you are aware of it, you have no reason to continue on in this way."

"But I do."

"And why?"

"Because I am not in love with you. But I do like you."

I shrugged. "It is a passing thing. A mere bit of enchantment passing through."

"Yes, I know it is. But it doesn't stop the sensation. If this were a world where we could charm someone and then separate, with each of us going about our lives as if we never courted, then I feel like we would have been delightful together. We would not be meant to be together for years, or even months. But we would have been a great love for a few weeks."

"And this is how you talk to the woman that your brother is in love with?"

"Richard will understand."

"No, Frederick, he will not. He will never be able to trust you again."

When hearing this, Frederick's face turned chilling, as if I had wounded him.

"I hurt you again," I said.

"Yes. But this time, it's different."

"How so?"

"It actually felt real."

My eyes widened.

"It did?"

"Yes, it did. It all felt so very real. I think..."

"Yes?" I asked, eager to egg him on.

"I think I actually felt ashamed."

I smiled.

"That is very good."

His mischievous smiled returned to his face, and I felt the tragedy coming.

"Were you just play-acting there?" I asked him.

"Perhaps I was. You should have seen the look on your face. You actually thought that I had reformed."

"You will, one day, and when you do, you will thank me."

"Richard cannot ever marry you. Therefore, why not entertain a man who could?"

"You are not in love with me. You said so yourself."

"True, I am not. But allow a man like me to have sport and be diverting to you. I am actually helping you. And my brother."

"How so?"

"By forcing you both to walk away and let each other go."

Just as he uttered that last word, I felt my spirit rise within and I felt as if I were about to force up any food that was within me. Thank goodness I had fasted most of the day because my stomach felt so overturned.

"Frederick," I said with finality, "what business is Richard's heart to you?"

"Would you believe that I am concerned for him?"

"No, I don't. I know you love him, but I just cannot believe that."

"Well, believe what you wish. You have every right to, because I am certain that I have confused you so much, that I must be quite the question mark to you."

"Your conversation is like yourself: you come from different directions. When a person keeps coming from different directions, you can never fully know to make out their character."

His eyes glinted with pleasure. "You are uniformly charming."

"See? There you are again. I want to say thank you, and that I am flattered, but I don't know what to believe whenever you speak."

"You have reason to be confused, but I will not change who I am," He declared.

"Nor will I change who I am. Now speak truly, do you really seek me out to protect your brother from the inevitable? Or is there another reason? Speak plainly to me about this. I would prefer it, Frederick. If you know how to speak plainly, that is."

"I do not know."

"Did you really just have to answer in such a way? You are avoiding any true answer. So come now. Redeem yourself by speaking sincerity to me."

"Very well. Perhaps I am doing it to protect you both."

I was dubious, but I was willing to allow him to continue.

"How so?" I questioned.

"You both keep clinging to hope. Vain hope that everything will work itself out. I know that you don't have a dowry. Everyone knows it. Just like you know he doesn't have the money to support you. Everyone knows that as well. But hope still ties away at your heels like shadows that hold you down. It might help you to fall in love with someone else. You already do, by what you have implied."

"Do you understand the human heart at all?" I asked him. "The pains of the heart cannot be alleviated and shifted about like puffs of smoke. If it were so, then the love is flimsy and looks like it is worthless. I cannot just...forget my love for your brother."

"Choose another," he advised again, "falling in love with me would help."

This conversation was becoming unpleasant. "Stop talking like that."

"It would help. After all, I am the heir."

"And you are a dedicated bachelor who does not love me. Like, yes. Love, no. You are toying with me."

"Are you saying that you do not like it?"

I thought back on my history with Mr. Dixon. This was different because Mr. Dixon's feelings for me were sincere. But still, I knew the effects of a heart feeling like they had been toyed with.

"Perhaps I would like it if I were idle and had not experienced a sincere emotion. But I have felt the real thing, and only the real thing will do," I answered.

"Even if it will all end horribly, you still will walk down that path."

"Maybe the struggle and confusion are worth it."

"It's not."

"How can you be so sure?"

"Because you can have more experiences with someone else, who can offer you something. And he can do the same. But the more you are here, the more he will dream, and you will dream. I am only saying this because it is true. Find another dream."

I looked at him and I realized something. I could easily be wrong, for we humans often map our own experiences on another person, not regarding our own possibility of being in error. But it cannot be helped.

"She hurt you, didn't she?" I asked him suddenly.

"What are you talking about?" he questioned, his tone losing its confidence.

"Her," I repeated, "the woman who you clearly fell in love with. And she broke your heart."

He looked ahead and didn't face me as we continued the dance. His silence was my triumph. In so many ways, the shrewd observer was now being observed.

"I'm right, am I not?" I furthered. "What happened? Was she chosen for another? Destined for another? Did not have the money or prestige to be respectable enough for the heir of an Earl to marry?"

"She was a servant."

This confession was overwhelming. Did I hear him correctly? Did he really just say that?

"A servant?"

"Yes. She was very beautiful. I loved her for years."

"What happened?"

"I was told to put an end to my feelings. It made sense. How pathetic it must look for the heir of Matlock to be always following after a servant girl like a lovesick child."

His eyes grew soft, remembering his faraway love that he lost. "Many wealthy men have...enjoyed the company of their female servants, but this was different. My love was real. But I was honor-bound. I did my duty. I let her go, father gave her good references and she was given a post in Blenheim Palace in Oxfordshire. She works there as a personal servant to the mistress. Every now and again, I make inquiries about her, and she does well. Like me, she isn't married. But I never dare see her again."

~

How complicated we mortals can be!

One moment, we are viewing a person as a cynical blot of mystery.

And then, the next minute, we understand them. We see into their character intimately, and we feel not only a deep affection for them, but it is something worse; we feel sorry for them. Even when they provoke us, we feel sorry for them.

"You miss her, don't you?" I asked. "You dream of her."

"Yes, I do. Even when the dream died a long time ago."

Pause.

"I provoke you, because I must, Miss Bennet. Because you have to walk away."

"I am different than you, Frederick. Maybe my path might be as well."

"We are not very different. We both love life and are always chasing after something. You are chasing after something. I see it in your eyes. You feel as if you will walk the Earth and never find it. Your path will not be different than mine. Your dream will not come true. Richard and you will have to walk away from each other and spend your lives wondering what could have been."

"If I had not already posed this question to myself, repeatedly, you would make me cry now."

"Better to cry now, than be heartbroken later. Heartbroken beyond repair."

The dance ended, and we faced each other.

"Is that really why you danced with me?" I asked after we clapped for the musicians who played.

He offered me his hand to take me off the dance floor.

"Did I dance with you because I simply wanted to? Or did I dance with you because I wanted to entice you and make you feel for me? Or did I dance with you because I want you to avoid my fate? You will never fully know."

Once we got off the dance floor, I let go of his hand.

"Frederick, will you never give me the truth?"

His smirk returned.

"Never."

When we came up to our company, Colonel Fitzwilliam met us.

"Brother," Frederick said, sounding winded, "Miss Bennet proved to be quite a more accomplished dancer than I. I withdraw my offer to dance with her, in favor of yourself, who I think will wish to stand up with her in my stead."

He bowed to us both and we were left alone.

"What was that about?" Colonel Fitzwilliam asked me, eyeing his brother. "Kitty, what did you and he talk about?"

"I'll tell you a little," I said, "but something tells me that he will want to talk about it with you."

The next dance, I stood up with Henry Crawford. To my surprise, my previous dance had taken so much out of me, that I didn't know if I could find myself amenable to intense flattery, and the idea of worthless seduction was not diverting at all. Internally, I felt exhausted.

Therefore, when Mr. Crawford began to speak with me during the dance, he began to offer all his powers of pleasing, and I responded in one way.

"Mr. Crawford," I said, "I thank you for your pretty words. But, for the first time ever, flattery doesn't help me now."

"I am displeasing you?" he questioned, his eyes narrowing in wonder, "how would you like me to speak?"

"I mean no offense. We are in the world to say pretty things, and usually I like that. But right now... I don't want a flatterer. I want a friend. I want someone who talks innocently, and not as if he wants me to be drawn in. Can you do that? Can you talk to me like we are merely good friends?"

His smile diminished as he considered that.

"It will be a challenge for me," he said, "no one has ever done that."

"Done what?"

"Asked me to be merely a friend and that is it. I have never had a woman say that to me before."

"Well, it is nice to be original."

"Miss Bennet, if I may ask, what happened? Something is evidently draining your heart. It is not healthy for you."

"Sometimes, a person cannot help themselves. Mr. Crawford, I have to ask you something."

"Yes?"

"Have you ever done something where, no matter what, you will have to walk away from someone? And that you hurt them without even knowing it."

"Oh," Henry Crawford sighed, and for the first time, his face was devoid of all charisma. It was as if a potential façade that he had fallen away from himself and he had revealed something wholly unexpected. "Yes. I can very much say that I have done that."

"You didn't mean to be a villain, but you became one," I added. I more-so said that for himself than for me. To my knowledge, I never really did anything to destroy a life, but maybe I did, and didn't notice that I had. Maybe by being in both Colonel Fitzwilliam's and Lieutenant Finlay's life, I had been offering a dream that would never come to fruition. And by loving them both at one time, being in the cusp of inconsistency, maybe I was hurting them. After all, could any of us ever fully move on that way?

"Yes," Mr. Crawford confirmed, "I have been in such a situation."

"What was that like for you?"

"Miss Bennet, by any chance, are you aware of my history? When I first met you, I suspected that you weren't, but now, I feel that you may have been enlightened."

"I have been told something of your past, but Jane has informed me that she will tell me everything tomorrow. She has a right to, you must understand. She has defended you all and wants us all to be enlightened so that we can know you better, and not know you less."

"I am aware of Mrs. Bingley's ideal virtue. You Bennets have been one of the better additions in my life. I'd say that if I had known you all long ago, if you had been in Mary's and my life sooner, things might have turned out differently for us. But I would have probably still turned out the way that I had. So, yes, Miss Bennet, I know what it feels like to be a villain."

"What is that like for you?"

"First, I learned that thing called regret, but then you harden yourself to the mistakes of your past, so that they do not hold you down in your present. We must always keep going on, or we will go mad. But I will say this for my part: my mistake helped me realize something about myself. It was something I never thought to guess or care about before."

"And what was that?"

"I liked women. I still do. And I was not content until I made them all fall in love with me."

"Why would you want to do that?"

"Because I found it diverting. Especially since I am not handsome. You don't know the horrors of being born plain. But also being indulged. And I was. I was spoiled since I was a child, and then, when I realized that I had the gift of making women ignore my ugliness and see a man worth loving, I was not content with one heart. Rather, I was content with winning them all. I viewed it as a sport."

"Mr. Crawford, didn't you see that you might have been hurting people? I am not asking this to cause you pain. But I ask you this to see if you understand—or did you learn to understand eventually?"

"For the longest time, I never caused any harm. When it came to the worst encounter of my life, I told myself that no harm could be done, because the lady was already engaged. For an engaged lady is always more agreeable than a disengaged lady. She could exert all her powers of pleasing without suspicion."

"And what happened when you realized that you were wrong? All is not safe with an engaged woman."

"And there, I took the worst step of my life. I paid the price for my error and for my refusal to see the damage that I had done by not removing myself from that woman's life. No! I just had to charm her again, make her like me, even when I should have let her go. But I could not. The desire for immediate satisfaction was too great a temptation, the idea of being in a lovely lady's company, and I did not exercise moral restraint.

"But when I look back on it, if I had been the man that I ought to have been, I would have never gone near her. Sometimes, the best thing you can give a person is distance away from yourself. Not always, but in some cases, it is so. For sometimes, when you tell yourself that you are trying to rekindle the bond you once had with them, it is out of a desire to improve their opinion of you. You are not always doing it out of a pure motive. Often, you do it out of a selfish motive. You want to make them love you because you cannot bear to be..."

"In a world where you are not loved by them," I finished his sentence.

"Precisely. When you stay in someone's life, you cannot just do it for your own satisfaction. You also have to do it for the betterment of theirs. But when you only do it for the betterment of yourself, with no thought of how it will affect them...then that is when you cause a calamity."

Mr. Crawford looked at me.

"Are you worried about what your actions will lead to, whatever those actions be?" He asked.

"I have caused no harm, as of yet. But I realize that maybe I am being selfish for keeping certain individuals in my life. I say that I am in love, but is that an excuse?"

"It is not left solely up to you. Perhaps, whoever you are in love with, is not ready to lose you."

"Was Maria Bertram ready to lose you?"

We were separated by the dance, and I met hands with Mr. Atkins.

"Having a jolly time?" Mr. Atkins asked me as he spun me around. When he saw how flustered I looked, he could tell that there was a great deal on my mind. With the rise of his cheery mood, came a quick fall, and he immediately turned empathetic.

"Kitty, what's wrong?"

"I just feel so...Mr. Atkins, I think I'm scared again."

"What has Mr. Crawford been saying to you?" he asked, protective.

"Nothing at all to hurt me, I assure you," I said to reassure him that I was not being mistreated. "I just realized something about myself."

"And what is that?"

I looked around and he saw that I was insecure about telling him things at a ball.

"When the time comes, tell Mrs. Atkins about it," he said, informing me to tell Mary. "You must let it out."

"I will," I assured him, feeling better, "you always are there for me, aren't you?"

"Clerk of the year," he said, comforting. Then we were separated, and I was returned to Mr. Crawford. When he met me again, he was more settled and ready to answer my question.

"No," Mr. Crawford confirmed, "she was not ready. She never would have been."

"I'll judge on the matter fully tomorrow," I assured him. "But for now, I don't know if I have the strength to let go."

"Talk to the Colonel," he advised.

I squinted out of fear of being found out.

"You know?"

"No one told me anything. I just observed you both together and made a deduction. Talk to him about these feelings you have, and your fears. I didn't talk to Maria Bertram. I charmed her, but I never talked to her. I bewitched her but didn't talk to her. You can talk to someone and not actually talk to them. I gave her an image, a false ideal, and a charade, but nothing of substance. Maybe if I had talked with her, in the way I am talking to you now, and spoke truths, I would have helped her understand. She would have lived her life and not chased me. However, I also wonder, if she weren't chasing me, would she have chased someone else? After all, she lived in a loveless marriage."

"She probably thought she had no choice."

"That I will not hear of. Miss Bennet, this is the one thing I do know: we all usually have a choice. We can choose something. She made the wrong choice. And so did I. We were a danger to each other. After all, sometimes, it takes two people to cause an accident."

"I don't want to cause an accident."

"Then tell yourself not to. It will hurt. But yes, you must tell yourself not to."

The dance came to an end.

Another dance had gone, and I was mentally perplexed and exhausted. We clapped for the musicians. Mr. Crawford took my hand and led me off the dance floor.

"I thank you for this conversation," he said, "I cannot help but being a selfish creature."

"We're all selfish at times, aren't we?" I queried.

"Yes, we are. To satisfy my feelings, I liked this discussion, because no woman ever asked for friendship from me. I hope that we shall always be like that in the future."

"Tell truths to me, Mr. Crawford, and no deception. And I will be your friend."

He bowed to me, fondly, and then was called away by Miss Luxford.

As I watched him depart, I wondered at him. Henry Crawford did something terrible. By rights, I ought to hate him. But that is not so. I suppose, it's because I knew the lady did something equally as awful—or more awful, because she was the one who was actually attached.

Or maybe I couldn't hate him from the simple fact: in a world of mistakes and folly, you forgive those who own to their past. It's the ones who do not own to anything that you should be the wariest of.

Chapter Eleven

FAMILY TIES

When it came to the sixth dance of the evening, Colonel Fitzwilliam was all eagerness. Despite the revelations that I had the entire evening, I was not about to implement them just yet. Therefore, when seeing him, I was determined to enjoy this one evening with him, before I had to confront other matters.

"I ask one thing of you," I implored him as we began.

"What would that be?"

"You can tell me about yourself, you can tell me a story, or you can tell me history. Just as long as you and I keep talking tonight, that's all I care for. Know that you are something I care for."

Colonel Fitzwilliam smiled at me.

"Miss Bennet—my dear Kitty, just for you."

We danced two dances after that. At that point, the rest of the evening, he had to dance with other ladies, who naturally wished for his company. Well, at least I had made Lady Fitzwilliam happy in that way.

We dined, ate, and grew more acquainted with the Edwards, the Osbornes, the Crawfords, and Miss Emma Watson.

By the time that the ball came to an end, and it was time to depart, it was around two o'clock in the morning. We were so exhausted that, when we offered our farewells to everyone, we were all half-asleep where we stood.

The Luxfords offered their kind farewells as we got into the carriage, but they were evidently exhausted as well.

Despite it being a night of many strange interactions for me, I found that I didn't regret any of it. Rather, in hindsight, I was fascinated, but my mind was lazy from wishing to sleep.

On the way home, Georgiana's head was pressed against mine as our eyes began to close.

"I've asked my brother to invite the Edwards to visit us sometime after Christmas. If they are able to come, you and Emma Watson will become better acquainted."

"I still am afraid that she will not like me."

"Give her time. And give yourself time."

"I will. How was your evening? I didn't always get the chance to ask you about all your dances and if you enjoyed every partner."

"I took no offense," Georgiana whispered, "I assure you. Like me, you were much engaged with some tugging at your elbow for attention."

"This was a very intense evening."

"Yes, it was. I never experienced a ball of so many ups and downs."

"And that was the wonder of it."

"But I was happy through it all. That I wish to stress," Georgiana said. "I am happy for that."

"You deserved it, as well as no sycophants clawing at your attention with their foppish ways."

"Yes," Georgiana sighed, "I am free of those sorts of mercenary creatures. And hopefully, I will remain so. But what of you, Kitty? In short, how were your dances? How was your evening?"

I thought on the whole of the evening, and I was still flummoxed.

I had met new people.

I had faced older acquaintances.

I had argued and interacted with a mysterious heir of Matlock, who was determined to spend his life as a puzzlement.

I had spoken with a man who ran off with another man's wife. All the while, I did not succumb to a generalization, often placed on the female sex, that when speaking with such a character, either we faint from horror, or speak in staunch maxims and outright reject them.

This all was both beyond my grasp of comprehension, but it was also fascinating.

I felt the depth of the human experience when it came to the quagmire that was love, loss, romance, and romantic hatred.

"Georgie," I whispered, "after this ball, I can safely say that I don't know if up is *up* anymore, or when down is *down*."

This observation should have confused Georgiana, but it didn't.

"Never fear," she responded, sleepily. "As long as you know when things are side to side, you are not entirely lost."

"Oh. Thank goodness for that then."

"Welcome to the other side of our family."

"So, this is what it's like?"

"It's a family. What did you expect?"

Chapter Twelve

A TALE OF TWO BROTHERS

When all arrived at Matlock, each one was taken to their room where the servants, all rushing from their beds to see to their charges, had to come, undress them, assist them in putting on their night garments, and retiring for the morning.

All immediately fell into a quick and deserved slumber, except for one person. The late morning could not wait, for he was restless. Pacing back and forth in his room had finally resulted in him being resolved.

Colonel Fitzwilliam would not be satisfied until his brother would answer for what he had done.

Therefore, he walked through the halls, with a candle in hand, and when he knocked on the door, he entered by way of a valet's permission.

When he entered the room, it was to seeing Frederick in his night-garments, with his valet wrapping his robe over his shoulders.

"Ah," Frederick said, tying the robe closed around him, "I had a feeling that I would be seeing you."

Colonel Fitzwilliam turned to Fred's valet.

"You must excuse us, George," he requested. "My brother and I wish to discuss something."

"Very good, sir," George said.

"That will be all, George," Fred informed him, "I can manage from here. You may retire and don't expect to wait on me till after ten o'clock this morning."

"Thank you, Master Frederick."

Happy with his situation, George left.

When he closed the door behind him, and the brothers were alone, Colonel Fitzwilliam turned on Frederick with a fury.

"Just what in god's name did you think you were doing this night?"

Frederick smirked.

"Don't give me that wicked grin of yours. For once, I want some answers."

"I had a feeling that we would be having this conversation, Richard," Frederick said as he walked over to his decanter and poured a cup of wine. He offered it to his brother, but the colonel made no indication of taking it. "Very well." He drank the wine himself.

"You will not avoid this discussion."

"Richard, I had no intention of doing that. I just didn't know that you were so excited to have it."

"Excited? I take no joy in this." Colonel Fitzwilliam paused. "What is it, Frederick? It can't be jealousy because you already have everything in life."

"Do I?" Frederick spat. "Do I really?"

Colonel Fitzwilliam groaned, rubbed his forehead, and turned away from him.

"Just tell me, already. Why did you want to dance with Kitty?"

"Because I knew that you wanted to." Richard laughed bitterly. "Tell me, Richard, how deep is your love for this woman?"

"Very much," Colonel Fitzwilliam answered.

"You are madly in love with her. I can tell. And I wanted to see if she was madly in love with you."

"You and your experiments."

"Where would we be without them? I do not regret what I have done, and you can set your heart at rest. Her love for you is genuine. What a pity, huh? It could be easy to move on from loving a woman if she does not love you in return. But this one does. It always makes it all the harder, doesn't it? You have no real justification for why you must eventually walk away. Breaking a heart is only diverting to those who are indifferent or narcissistic in their affections. But I know you, and sadly, you are neither of those things. I know how this is going to end."

"Do you?"

"Yes. And so do you. When you are not busy enjoying the bliss that comes from being beside the one that you would choose."

"You speak well in one moment and then horribly in the next. Can you entertain, for a moment, that I am not like you? I don't have to walk down the same path."

"No, you don't," Frederick responded, "and that's why I know how this is going to end. You are never going to marry Kitty."

~

Colonel Fitzwilliam glared at his brother, wishing to do him bodily harm.

"You don't know that."

"But I do," Frederick countered.

"You made us look like a spectacle at the ball. It looked like two brothers who were competing over the same woman."

"I confess that was selfish of me."

"Yes, I know that it was. Don't pretend that I believed that you were doing it for my welfare."

"No. I was doing it for this family. You are the one who will carry this family onward. You are the one who is meant to be a father. You have to marry a woman with wealth."

"What are you talking of?" Colonel Fitzwilliam spat. "You are the eldest. You have the wealth and the home. You are the one who ought to have the family and should. Why do you tell me that I am the one to do it?"

"I'm not meant to be a father. You know that."

"No, I don't know that. Just like I don't know what it's like to be the wealthy brother, to live a life of leisure, to have everything!

I am the one who is meant to toil and keep going forth. Why do you place the burden of having a family on me?"

"Because you are the only one to do it. I love our little brother, but he is sickly. He almost died both times he was stricken with fever, the pox almost killed him off when he was a child, and he's still fragile today. You have to confront the fact that Gregory might not make it to his twenty-fifth birthday."

"He might."

"Or he might not. I do not wish to acknowledge that, but some are not born with the health they deserve. Gregory is one of them. Sometimes I wonder why our parents even let him travel abroad, when any illness has been known to affect him."

"Even if that be the case, what of you? You are as healthy as me."

"And I can't have children."

For a brief moment, Colonel Fitzwilliam sympathized with his brother, for he knew where this was coming from.

"I know that you still think of Rosalie, and that you miss her very much," Colonel Fitzwilliam empathized, "but you could learn to love again."

"I can't!" Frederick cried desperately. "Don't you understand? I loved her for so long that I can't fall in love with another woman. The idea of it repulses me. Any other woman, to have as a wife, repulses me because no other woman is her!"

Colonel Fitzwilliam looked at the floor, not interrupting. He recalled his early youth, coming home from university and seeing his brother always secretly going to the servant's headquarters, to spend time with the first and great love of his life. Rarely do people marry their first loves, and his brother was one of them.

But it was not because Frederick had found a better woman—it was because he could never fully release her from his heart. For some people, love hits them in such a heavy fashion, that they never fully recover from the loss of it. And when the stroke of heartbreak falls down upon them, they never can forgive anyone for not being that first love. It leads to them becoming a jaded character, tainted from the love that is gone, and shriveling into a lesser ideal version of themselves.

Frederick Fitzwilliam was such a person. He walked through life with a grin on his face, to mask that he had become a shadow of his former self. Almost like that of a wraith, a substance without full form, determined to spend their life in idleness, and using charm to mask their feeling of nonexistence.

Others move on, and either fall in love and marry elsewhere, or they remain single all their life, but use their past experiences to enhance themselves. Colonel Fitzwilliam hoped and expected his brother to become such a person. Their parents did as well. But that was not the case. Frederick retreated into the recesses of his past, the memories of happier times, when Rosalie was beside him. He kept the memories always with him, and it marred any future that he could potentially have.

Everyone else's love and romances provoked him.

Every woman who was not Rosalie antagonized him.

And he would never know happiness.

"I cannot have a child," Frederick voiced, at last. "Unless that child comes from her. Rosalie was everything to me."

"I know."

"Just like Kitty has the potential to be everything to you. You will fall into her embrace, and then, when reality comes knocking upon your door, you will have to separate. Every woman that crosses your path will not live up to the memory of her. You will measure those other women by an impossible standard—a standard that you had no right to place on them."

Frederick looked directly at Colonel Fitzwilliam.

"And it will make it that much harder to move on and want a family. It's time for you to entertain the possibility that you and I are similar. I am your future, Richard. Whether you like it or not. That's why I urge you now to spend a little more time with Kitty, and then let her go. She can't fully release you because she feels the same. Therefore, it's time that you be strong enough for you both. Let her go, give her the chance to love somewhere else. And give yourself the chance of not falling so far in love that you can't crawl out of the hole that you dug yourself into."

"I..."

"You what?"

"I can't, Frederick. I can't walk away from her just yet. Not when I feel like there might be a chance."

"A chance for what? I could give you money from my inheritance, then Darcy can, then Lady Catherine can, but it still won't be enough. You are clinging, brother."

"If you were in my place, wouldn't you cling? What would you have done if Rosalie were here?"

Despite himself, Frederick's confidence gave way, and his eyes grew misty from sorrow and sadness.

"If you say that I am like you," Colonel Fitzwilliam continued, "don't pretend that you would allow her to be sent away again. Don't tell me that you wouldn't run to her?"

"Don't," Frederick wept, "don't say her name now. Please! I couldn't bear it!"

"Frederick," Colonel Fitzwilliam said, walking to his brother. But Frederick, determined to be stoic, moved away from him and hid his emotions against the wall.

"There is nothing you can say," Frederick stated, his voice shaky, "take my advice or not. The choice is yours. Just leave me now. Leave me alone to think of her. And never say her name again."

Seeing that his brother was overcome, there was nothing that could be done. He walked to the door, and each felt a little heavier.

"Goodnight, brother," was all Colonel Fitzwilliam could muster up, before he closed the door behind him, leaving his brother to his happy memories of the woman he once loved. Rosalie would never die, for Frederick kept her stored in his mind.

Chapter Thirteen

THE FACTS OF LIFE

The next day, I rose earlier than most of the household. After all, the day after a ball is usually confined to a day of leisure or visitors coming to talk of the previous day's events.

When I woke up, Lucy had not come to my room, and I did not feel inclined to ring the bell and summon her. Therefore, I poured some water in the pitcher, drank it, and then I sat down and wrote the general overview of the ball's previous events in my diary. The more I wrote, the more the evening felt more like a 'Midwinter Night's Dream', more than it was a reality. The winter had indeed come, but it was rather at the beginning as opposed to the middle. But some titles are too beautiful to abandon. It's like the equivalent of when people say Florence, but the city is really pronounced Firenze.

When I finished my entry, I wondered at the events of the evening, and I considered all that had unfolded.

We really had encountered the Crawfords again!

I had danced four times with the Colonel, heedless of how that would look in the eyes of the other attendees.

I had my heart and resolve broken by the heir of Matlock.

And I had to face the fact that Georgiana had re-met a child-hood friend who I now had to befriend myself.

Georgiana!

That was a matter that I had to confront, while I still had my dander up.

After finishing my entry and observing all that I had catalogued in my life, I wondered at it. When I thought of all the journals and entries that I had written, chronicling my life, I wondered what the point of it was? I was neither the Mistress of Pemberley, Matlock, or Netherfield Park. I was not even the wife of a certain Lieutenant. Therefore, who would wish to know of me?

When I stored my diary safely away, I put my slippers on, crept out of the room and silently made my way to Georgiana's bedroom door.

I tried to knock gently, but I had to still make myself known.

"Who is there?" I heard Georgiana say from the other side.

"It's me," I said, "Kitty."

"Oh," Georgiana said, then I heard her unlocking the door and her tired face appeared on the other side.

"Oh, did I wake you?" I asked her.

"We're both in luck; I literally woke up three minutes ago."

"Can I come in?" I asked, "before Vera comes in to tend to you."

Georgiana moved aside so that I could come in.

"I wished to speak to you as well."

When the door closed, I sat on her bed, and she laid down.

"I'm awake, but my body isn't," she explained.

"I can well believe it," I said, leaning against the bedpost. "First the mind wakes up, the eyes wake with it, but it can take the body twenty minutes to comply." I looked at her. "Your skin glows."

"So does yours."

"Mine?" I asked.

"Yes, yours. You had a good time the other night."

"So did you, it is apparent."

"To wish for love at a ball can either we wise, or a bit of folly. I've learned to go into such nights with no expectation of falling in love. Once I learned to do that, I have learned the true joys of a night of dancing."

"Even when dancing with Mr. Luxford?"

"Even when dancing with Mr. Luxford."

"The night was made even more pleasant when meeting old friends. You and this Emma Watson must have been close."

"We were much thrown together when I met her when her aunt and uncle Turner brought her into town. She was one of the few girls who understood that my initial shyness was not pride or haughtiness. She understood me."

"Then I shall do my best to like her," I said, "but truth is, I was scared of her when we first met."

Georgiana looked quizzically at me. This was not the comment that she expected. But rather, she did not shy away from me either.

"Why?" she asked curiously.

"Well, you must understand that it is a bit of folly in its own right."

"How so?"

"We all like to think that we are special in some way. Of course, I always knew that you must have friends from your past. Having friends is quite a lovely addition to life. However, when you become friends with someone, and an older friend from their past emerges, you get a little—well, to put it frankly, you become scared."

She rolled to her side. "Explain further."

"Well, you realize that maybe, that older friend will return, and you will no longer be the main confidante anymore. I realize now that maybe I clung too hard to our friendship. I placed too much of my identity in it, because when this Emma Watson returned into your life, I felt like I was losing ground. Maybe it's good that I saw you both like that. Maybe I now have to learn independence again."

"Oh, Kitty!" Georgiana said, rolling her eyes, "you need not worry. That is a natural reaction, and it will soon pass."

Her lightness of tone made me raise my eyebrows as an immense weight was released from me.

"It will?" I asked.

"Oh yes. I have been in your place before. Where you meet someone, you feel a great bond to them, then you find out that they had another bond before you—and that connection is one that you cannot touch. Oh, yes! I've been there before. Does it feel like your chest has tightened and you feel cold inside, and a little nervous?"

"Yes!" I cried, relieved.

"Yes, and you also feel uncertain about everything?"

"Yes!"

"That's what happens when you make a friend, who has a history of close friendship with another. I confess, I am happy to see Emma Watson again. It's been years. But that's the thing; it's been years. I wish to reestablish our friendship, but there will be a little of a distance between us now. When you see her, do not shy away from her, but be willing to let her into our circle. I was once in your predicament, and I did not do that. I was uncomfortable when a friend of mine introduced me to an older friend of hers. It led to me being awkward and soon, neither of them wanted anything to do with me eventually. Also, Emma shall barely be in my life for very long. She is bound for Australia soon."

"Australia?"

"Yes. She was born there and was shipped to England to be raised by her aunt and uncle Turner. Now that her aunt has remarried, she has to return home, without a dowry or very few pounds to her name."

"Yes, the poor girl," I realized, now switching from feeling any sort of envy to now feeling pity for her. "She must feel so lost now."

"She does. She loved her aunt Turner, and now she is dashed against the whims of chance. Well, at least she has a home to go to. Not everyone can say that can they?"

"No, in that circumstance, I suppose that they can't. But to uproot oneself from Croydon to New South Wales, will definitely be a bit of a shock."

"Yes, it will. Therefore, for Emma and me, it was just an old friend who was passing through."

"Now I feel sheepish."

"You don't have to. Your reaction is very common, and I shared it as well at the ball."

I raised an eyebrow, skeptical.

"How and when?"

"When the Crawfords came. Especially Miss Crawford."

"Mary Crawford? What of her?"

"Well, when I first saw you all, you ran to her like you were drowning amidst an ocean and she was a rescue boat."

"Believe me, we have cause to be like that around her. Georgie, when Lydia eloped with...you know who."

We both rolled our eyes in memory of Mr. Wickham.

"Well, when Lydia ran off, we were a lost family. Truly, you've seen our mother. Rather than adhere to being discreet and keeping the matter quiet, the whole house flew into hysterics, most of Hertfordshire was aware of our situation, or a portion of it, and even Mr. Collins sent us a letter saying, 'who would connect themselves with such a family'. Lady Catherine was also aware of it. Well, when we were the subject of the village's pity or scorn, the Crawfords came with their half-sister, Mrs. Grant. I wish she were there last night; you would have loved her. Well, when they came, new life was brought into Jane's step, they escorted us to Meryton, to show everyone that we were not forsaken by great people in society. They helped save our reputation. It helped us never suffer under being rejected by others around us. It lessened the pain."

"How did it do that, considering Mr. Crawford's history?"

"They never advertised what estate they belonged to, so I guess no one made the connection that he was the same Mr. Henry Crawford who was in the gossip columns a few years ago. Also, many of us never saw the Crawfords before, so we had no point of reference. I am happy for that. I can't wait for Jane to wake up, so that she can tell us all about it. Apparently, she knew the truth the entire time, and she didn't tell us."

"I wonder why not."

"That's what I am looking forward to hearing. But until then, you never needed to worry about Miss Crawford being close to me. I adored her, in the short time that I knew her, but she is Jane's friend."

Georgiana smiled.

"I see that we've both been a little foolish for no reason."

"Yes, and that makes me happy. Mistakes love company."

Chapter Fourteen

JANE, THE VALIANT

After speaking with Georgiana for a little longer, I returned to my room, where Lucy was waiting for me.

"You slipped out early, didn't you?" Lucy asked.

"No need to worry over my virtue. I did nothing that was nefarious."

"I'm sure you did not, Kitty. Almost no one is awake early enough to cause any wrongdoing. Besides, when you are a servant, you stop caring about your master or mistress's virtue anyway."

"Truly?" I asked, excited.

"Oh, yes. When you work in a great house, you begin to stop caring very quickly. It's the best way to survive working in these great houses."

"You've seen some things, have you?"

"I'll never tell you."

"That's probably as it should be."

She dressed me easily, put up my hair in a simple way, and I went downstairs to breakfast. When I did so, everyone else in the house was awake to dine, but the Earl and Lady of the house.

"You must excuse my parents' absence," Frederick Fitzwilliam said as we all sat down to eat, "but they've reached the age where they have the right to be indulged. After a ball, they always sleep very late, have their breakfast brought to them in their rooms, and don't emerge to public till two o'clock in the afternoon. I find it better not to interrupt that custom."

"I agree," Mr. Darcy said, as the servants began to place the food on our plates. "If I am ever forced to undertake hosting a ball, I would do the same thing at my house."

"You're going to avoid hosting a ball as long as you can, won't you?" Elizabeth asked, amused.

"Oh, very much."

"Well, as terrible as this sounds, sometimes, I wish that we could adopt that habit even on days where there was no ball the night before," Lizzy said, squeezing Darcy's hand fondly.

"Now that is a happy thought," Jane added. "Sometimes, one wants the peace of solitude."

"And that is the one beauty of living a modest life," Mr. Atkins boasted. "There is often very little to always stand on ceremony about."

"You never know, Atkins," Arthur Philips said, "my mother delivered many a party and elaborate visit in her house. You might be forced to do the same one day."

"Me, an elegant hostess?" our sister Mary said, chuckling. "Now that is a test that I wonder if I could rise to."

"You will," Jane complimented her, "we all have the ability to rise to challenges that we must face."

"Speaking of challenges," Frederick said in between bites, "I marvel at you, Mrs. Bingley."

"At me, sir? I have committed no remarkable feats of late."

"You are too modest, I am sure. But I refer to your challenge at befriending the Crawfords, even when their history sometimes trails behind such a family."

We all froze, our forks halfway to our mouths. Jane and Frederick were not ignorant of everyone's sudden attention toward themselves.

"Frederick?" Colonel Fitzwilliam said, wiping his mouth, "you are being too forward, don't you think?"

"Yes, sir," Mr. Bingley added.

"My apologies," Frederick responded, as unaffected as ever,

"but I was of the suspicion that I was helping Mrs. Bingley. For, as I understood it, this is a story that you wished to talk about."

Jane gave him a 'how did you know that?' look, but it was not vicious. After all, Jane was incapable of distributing a vicious look. Then her eyes changed to subtle gratitude.

"Yes, Mr. Fitzwilliam, I did actually wish to speak about it. In truth, I had no means or way of knowing how to begin the conversation, so I suppose that you have helped me a great deal."

"I try to be accommodating," he replied, with that sardonic grin of his. One could never know if he was mocking her, or if that was his habit, and he was helping her on.

Jane placed her fork gently on her plate and breathed in deeply.

"I am of the belief that you all are aware of the Crawfords history. That Mr. Henry Crawford ran off with Mr. Rushworth's wife, of Wimpole Street, while he was courting another woman from Mrs. Rushworth's family, a Miss Fanny Price. Or is any of this novel to you all?"

I felt my eyes raise in alarm.

"While he was courting another woman?" I asked, startled.

"I confess," Elizabeth added, "I didn't know that side of the matter."

"Nor did I," Enara commented.

This was echoed by everyone in the company.

"Well," Jane continued, "that is another part of the story. Miss Fanny Price is the niece of Sir Thomas Bertram, of Mansfield Park. Maria Bertram is Sir Thomas's daughter."

"So," Elizabeth clarified, "Maria Bertram and Fanny Price are cousins."

"Yes. While Maria Bertram was engaged to Mr. Rushworth, she fell in love with Mr. Henry Crawford, but he abandoned any designs that it seemed he might have on her. He left Mansfield Park, she married Mr. Rushworth, while still loving Mr. Crawford."

"Wait," my sister, Mary, observed, "she fell in love with someone else, but still went through with the marriage to a man that she did not love?"

"Precisely. And that was the root of all problems. And Mr. Crawford's unrelenting rakish manner was the beginning of his downfall. I do not say this without consideration of his feelings. He is aware of this flaw to his character, and would willingly talk about it, if it was proper to allow us to confront such matters. He would not despise me for talking about his past. He is not running from it. Not anymore."

"And yet, he is not here to speak of such matters," Mr. Darcy said, "and when he approached us last night, it was as if he pretended like his history did not exist."

"Precisely," Mr. Bingley added. "My love, he presented himself without any sense of shame. Neither of them did."

"Let Jane speak," Elizabeth supported, "we offer her leave to explain."

"Thank you, Lizzy," Jane said, her courage not wavering under the doubts of others. "When you say, neither of them did, my love, are you referring to Mary Crawford?"

"Well," Mr. Bingley said, a little ashamed, "her brother did this horrible thing, and she seems to not be affected by him."

"What do you expect?" Jane asked, her voice losing its serenity and giving way to a more spirited way. "For her to forsake her brother, forever? If at all? I would no sooner recommend her to do that, than I would abandon my own sisters if they made such a mistake. In fact, one of them already has, and I did forgive her for it. If you cannot rely on family for forgiveness and acceptance, who can you rely upon?"

We all were silenced by this—well, some of us never cared to object.

"It is true," she continued, "that Mr. Crawford did court Miss Fanny Price, but it was after Miss Price had rejected his initial marriage proposal. He was attempting to improve her opinion of him, but they never were *actually* attached. He proved to be inconstant and unworthy of her, but not unfaithful, in that direction. His sole sin lies in not rebuking Mrs. Rushworth when she tried to pursue him again. Rather than ignoring her, he pressed his advantage and enticed her again. But ultimately, she was the one who left home, chased after him and would go with him. Feeling it impossible to reject her, he took her with him. Mr. Rushworth soon discovered his wife's plight."

"And he filed for divorce," Colonel Fitzwilliam finalized. "I recall reading this from the papers a few years ago."

"Yes."

"We saw what became of Mr. Crawford," Enara said, "but what ever became of the lady, Maria Bertram?"

"Her family would not receive her at Mansfield Park. She was sent to live in a small house in a different county, far from their home, where she would live out her days."

"Her family exiled her forever?" Arthur asked, unsettled.

"Yes."

I leaned back in my chair, still frightened at the prospect of being cast out from my own family if I had ever made such a mistake.

"While I still understand if they wanted to punish her for some time by making her feel the isolation of her actions," I said, repeating my notions from last night when Colonel Fitzwilliam told me this, "that is only natural. For we all must pay for when we do such a wrong. But surely, after a sufficient amount of time, her penance ought to end, and she return home."

"According to Miss Crawford, the family never allowed her to return. Miss Crawford heard a rumor that her aunt Norris went to stay with Maria, for she always favored her niece, but Maria Bertram will never return to Mansfield Park."

When hearing that, I felt my insides freeze.

To err was human. It was inevitable.

To be punished for your errors was also human. It was inevitable.

It was also expected, and it was well-deserved.

But to be a part of a family who had no desire to see you again after the mistake you made...that just felt like the ultimate sin to me. After all, what is family if they could not be there for you when you were at your lowest in life?

"Monstrous," I uttered, even before I knew what I was about.

"Not monstrous, Kitty," Mr. Darcy corrected me, "but well-deserved. This Maria Bertram broke one of the holiest of sacraments and made her family into a public mockery."

"And that is why, my love," Mr. Bingley added, "I worry over you having such an acquaintance. Men such as Mr. Crawford, and women such as Miss Crawford, are not to be trusted. I cannot help but ask you to consider your acquaintance with them."

Jane looked horrified.

"The right to forgive is my decision!" she voiced, not loudly or viciously, but desperately. "The right to do as the best parts of our faith give me the right to do so."

"Besides," I added, gently, to Mr. Darcy in particular, "without family to forgive us eventually, what do we have?"

"Precisely," Jane confirmed, happy to not be alone. "Without my right to forgive those who are ready to apologize for what they have done, is me committing to the upmost form of puritanism to which I cannot adhere. The side that is unrelenting, unkind, and extreme. Why are so many people upset with the idea of me wishing to believe in others? Especially when, if I didn't do that, then I would not forgive so many who are sitting at this table? And, in some circumstances, I could not forgive myself."

This last sentence was gently spoken, but because it was unlike Jane to say such things, it made us all sit there, still as statues, and look at her with pale faces.

Jane looked at Mr. Bingley.

"Do you want the whole story, dearest?" she asked him rhetorically. "The truth is that when you left Netherfield so abruptly after the ball, I was heartbroken. I went to London to escape my mother's constant pleas for your return—a return that I had to accept would never come."

Her eyes were misty. "You left me, your sisters also abandoned me, and in London, I met Miss Crawford, and she stood by me. She helped me feel less alone. And when I went to visit your sisters, Charles, they were cold to me. Then when Caroline returned the visit, she was even colder and made it very evident that she took no pleasure in seeing me. When she was about to leave, it was right at the time when Mary Crawford came for a visit. She gave Caroline a set down, criticizing her for her neglect of me. Mary Crawford stood by me when your sisters didn't care whether I lived or not. She and her sister, Mrs. Grant, took notice of my aunt and uncle, when they were proven too insignificant for your preferences."

Jane then turned in Mr. Darcy's direction, while still talking to Mr. Bingley.

"They also believed I was worthy of anything, even when some didn't think I was worthy of you marrying me."

This made Mr. Darcy look down, in shame. Mr. Bingley, too, was heavily embarrassed and mortified.

"And then, if I must follow such strict doctrines, then I would never forgive my sister, Lydia, for her situation. And by rights, I would be the very evil that you describe. Like Mary Crawford, I am the sister of a sibling who ran off in an infamous manner, without care of what her actions would lead to. And a speedy marriage was all that we could hope for, in the same way that a speedy marriage was all that Mary Crawford could hope for when her brother ran off with Maria Bertram."

"Well, that was different, my dear," Mr. Bingley interrupted.

"How was that different?" Jane asked. "Because I am me? That poses inequality, and a standard that does not fit to everyone. I cannot permit that. Besides, my mistake is Mary's, in one large way."

"How so?" Mary, our sister, asked.

"I caused Lydia's predicament."

"Mrs. Bingley," Mr. Atkins protested, "that is simply not true."

"It is. Because I knew what Mr. Wickham was, and I did not do anything to prevent our contact with him. I stood back and let him be as he was, under the belief that he would better himself, when all evidence proved to be the reverse. I blinded myself, in the same way that Mary Crawford blinded herself to her brother's flaws. We both believed these men to be harmless, and we could have prevented it if we just bothered to exert ourselves more and warn those who we saw were being manipulated. The only solace she and I have is that, no matter what we did, her brother and my sister would have done what they wanted, no matter what we said. But we still should have tried—that is what counts."

"You are not alone in that mistake," Elizabeth said, "for recall, I made it as well."

"Yes, and you deserved to be forgiven. As do I. As does Mary Crawford."

I looked down at my plate, remembering when I had yelled at Jane and Elizabeth for not revealing the truth about Mr. Wickham to our family. If they had, they could have prevented the calamity from occurring. But Jane was right, perhaps. No matter what they did, father *was* father and Lydia *was* Lydia. He would have believed that Lydia was not worth the trouble of Wickham choosing her, and Lydia would have complained until father gave in. We never would fully know what would have happened if another path would have been taken.

"But what of this Henry Crawford," Arthur Philips asked Jane. "He did something horrible. How does that make you feel?"

"I do not condone his past, nor make excuses for it," Jane said, "but I have talked with him. He does not hide from his past, nor lie about it, in the style that Wickham did. He freely admitted the man that he was. He and Maria Bertram were guilty. But since he freely confesses to his mistake, then I choose to believe that he can come back to being something better than he once was. I choose to forgive, the way that I have forgiven all of you. The way that I have forgiven myself."

We all felt so naked and ashamed under the weight of her virtue and understanding. Whatever supposed 'flaws' that Jane thought she had to her character, was trivial compared to the rest of us.

"Let me choose my friends as I will, when I know that they are no more or less human than the rest of us," she stated, standing up. "I feel this conversation has made me overtired, and I have more than myself to think of now. I shall rest and let you think of what I have said."

"I'll go with you," Elizabeth said, standing up as well and taking her arm.

Bingley stood up, recklessly, and watched his wife and sister-in-law exit.

When they had done so, Frederick looked at us all, amused.

"Well, I daresay that Mrs. Bingley is much more fascinating than I initially thought."

~

As we all sat back down again, Mr. Bingley was anxious. Restless. Mr. Darcy noticed this as he wiped his mouth with a napkin.

"Bingley, you wish to go to your wife."

"I think she might wish for time alone," Bingley said, "but yes, I do."

"Go to her. She will appreciate it."

Happy to have someone confirm his intention, Mr. Bingley all but rushed out of the room.

"Marriage!" I whispered to Colonel Fitzwilliam, who sat beside me. "One of the most beautiful sacraments in the world and also one of the most difficult."

"It is." He smiled at me. "But the journey is what makes it all worth it, in the end."

"Do you think so? I'm wondering now if the dream is worth it."

"Love gives us warmth. Marriage gives us children. Children give us immortality. With marriage, there will always be vexation, a little grief, and arguments. But nothing can be perfect all the time."

I nodded grimly.

"Still the optimist, despite all the trials we have had?" I asked.

"Always."

"Well," Frederick said from the front of the table. "This is quite the to-do! I wish mother and father could have seen this."

"It will be resolved by the end of the day," Darcy informed him. "Elizabeth will know what to do, and she will have solved any dilemmas that this situation would face. She just needs a little time."

Through it all, he would always have complete faith in Lizzy.

It was unwavering, unapologetic, and unyielding. It was admirable.

"Such belief in your wife," Frederick continued, "did my cousin stumble on the perfect spouse for himself?"

"He did," Colonel Fitzwilliam said for Darcy. "You know that he did. Therefore, brother, let us be jealous of them from either nearby or a distance, and be satisfied."

"I am never satisfied, Richard. You know that."

"You have it in you to be," I said, unafraid. "You just like being unhappy."

Frederick blinked.

"And you talk like this to me in my own home?"

"You gave her reason to," the Colonel pointed out, "besides, it is evident that you liked it."

"I suppose I did," Frederick replied, smiling cynically again.

Enara chuckled.

"You find me funny?" Frederick asked her.

"Is it wrong if I do?"

Frederick maintained his grin that said anything and everything.

"Not at all. I like having an identity."

After breakfast, we all sat down in the main parlor, listening to Georgiana play us some music, while Enara sang to accompany her.

While we were assembling, I had crossed paths with my sister, Mary. When seeing her, I remembered when I had danced with Mr. Atkins. He had discerned that I was upset, told me to talk to Mary about it, and he was perceptive to do so. However, when looking at her, I had no idea of what to say, or how to phrase it. It felt like the ball was so removed from me, so distant, that it couldn't be put into words. In fact, I felt as if, by mentioning it, I would only grow unsettled.

"What is it?" Mary asked me. She had noticed that I was looking strangely at her. I blinked and let my reflections rest in my diary. And that alone.

"Nothing," I said to her. "Sorry, I just had a start."

I sat down and listened to Georgiana and Enara give a duet.

While we sat there and watched them, beautiful in their talent, Colonel Fitzwilliam and I sat next to each other. Every now and again, I saw Frederick watching us out of the corner of my eye.

"I feel like I could know your brother for years, and still never know him," I whispered to the Colonel.

"Because you can't ever fully know him. He is mercurial. Ever-changing. That is the only form of happiness that he will ever know."

"What happened to him?"

"He fell in love."

"With the servant. He told me about that. Love killed him?"

"It saved him first. Then it broke him afterwards. Now, he is both a friend to love and an enemy of it. Both sides come out whenever the other side is dormant. My brother hates and loves himself. So, he hates and loves all of us."

"It must be hard to live such a half-life. It's almost like a cursed life."

"It is. Half of the time, I am angry with him, and the other half of the time, I feel sorry for him. Until I remember one very important thing."

"And what is that?"

"He has the house, the fortune, and can change his life whenever he wants."

We both looked at each other and stifled our chuckle.

"Yes, it's hard to feel sorry for those who have everything, isn't it?" I asked.

"Precisely. For then, pity becomes hard to distribute."

Georgiana and Enara finished playing, and we clapped for them.

As we did so, Mary offered to play, to which we all accepted, and this time, Georgiana offered to sing, for she now felt comfortable enough. We all were able to sit and listen again. While they positioned themselves, I turned to the Colonel.

"Jane is right, by the way. It is our moral duty to forgive those who seek reconciliation. Time was their penance, and they probably served it."

"I know. It's just... I'm like Darcy. We all make mistakes, but if we don't execute judgment when wrong is done, then who will? If all can't punish, based on our past sins, then what happens to the world? Evil is allowed to endure."

"Precisely," Mr. Darcy stated, behind us. We flinched because we had not noticed that he had walked near us at all. When we looked up at him, he stared down at us. "That is the universal conundrum that haunts me. I am flawed. But if I don't make decisions, hard ones, then I allow follies and vices to take hold, and I let chaos run mad. Therefore, I must judge."

"I know," I answered him, "it is a universal problem that may never be answered. However, Jane is correct in that banishment or rejection should not be attributed in so general a way. But rather, it should be considered from an individual basis, and the punishment should be in proportion to the crime that has been exerted. This situation should result in Mr. Crawford and Miss Bertram being lectured and punished for months, but not the rest of their lives. And Mary Crawford, despite having some callous opinions, is not guilty of anything at all, nor should be guilty by association."

"That, I do agree with. I admit, my resentful nature has led to me wondering how right I always am, but my right to accept or reject will always be considered before I execute it. However, I must judge, Kitty. I must."

"I know. So must Elizabeth. Both the judge and forgiver must be able to exist at the same time, surely."

"And thus, the world will always be at odds."

"We found the perfect song," Mary announced, "we can begin when you all are prepared."

"Our apologies," Colonel Fitzwilliam said. They were about to begin when Jane, Elizabeth, and Mr. Bingley entered.

⁓

When the trio walked in, we all stood up, in apt attention.

Mr. Bingley stepped forward first, to make an announcement.

"Everyone, Mrs. Darcy, and my wife have been talking and I

decided that the best thing I could do was listen. They have come up with an interesting proposal to our quandary."

"We are all ears, I can assure you," Frederick Fitzwilliam invited.

"Still the shrewd inviter, eh?" Elizabeth acknowledged.

"I'm the son of an earl; I would be a shame if I did anything else."

"Well, I welcome your attitude." She turned to Darcy. "My love, tomorrow, we return to Pemberley. I was wondering if the best way for us to determine things, and to better understand my sister's feelings would be...if we were to invite the Crawfords to Pemberley, along with Mr. William Price."

We all turned to Mr. Darcy.

"This is what you wish?" Mr. Darcy asked.

Jane stepped forward.

"Mr. Darcy, please, I ask this for myself, and I confess that I am a selfish creature for it. I want you to better understand them. If they come, you can question Mr. Crawford yourself about his past, and this will give Mary Crawford a chance for us to know her. We could, perhaps, help them recover into being the sort of people that they might have always wished to be...if they had been given a better example. They were given bad principles since they were young. Quite frankly, they turned out better than one usually would in such a circumstance. But this way, you can determine things for yourself."

"Jane is not taking the choice from you at all, or any of us, for that matter," Elizabeth supported. "Mr. Darcy, she is giving you the right to judge things for yourself. Whatever you choose, I will stand by your side. As always. But in this moment, I ask you to consider."

Frederick turned to Darcy.

"She really does understand you, doesn't she?"

Darcy half-smiled.

"Told you that she would solve it all. Mrs. Darcy and Mrs. Bingley, I need to think on this. I am not against this plan, but I need time to consider."

Jane breathed out easily.

"Thank you, sir."

Darcy pressed Elizabeth's cheek, fondly.

In that moment, Lord and Lady Fitzwilliam entered.

"Forgive our lateness," Lady Fitzwilliam said, "but the privileges of age, you know?"

"So," Lord Fitzwilliam said, "what did we miss?"

We all had to stifle our laughter.

Chapter Fifteen

HOMEWARD BOUND

The next day came, and it was time to depart. Since then, we had not discussed Jane's speech that was in defense of the Crawfords. In fact, she spent the rest of the day in bed, for her moment of strength seemed to raise her spirits, and she worried about the effect it would have on the child.

"A coarser person would have said that she was using this as an excuse to not be in our company," I said to Colonel Fitzwilliam, "after all, when you bear your soul in such a public way, often you don't want to see those people for quite some time. But that's not Jane. She may be gentle, but she's not weak."

"Often the former gets mistaken for the latter," Colonel Fitzwilliam noted, "but I know that is not the case with her."

"Precisely. She really was looking after the child."

"Oh, I am aware of such," Colonel Fitzwilliam said, "in a woman's condition such as Jane's, any bit of stress can lead to her losing her child. I've seen it before with the wives in the regiments that I have led. One time, a pregnant lady was told about her husband's passing. The next day, she lost her child."

I gasped and covered my mouth. "Horrible. What became of the poor woman?"

"Fortunately, she had family back in Shropshire, and they were eager to see her again. Her parents were alive, and they missed her. So, she was able to return there."

"Good," I said, relieved as servants were bringing our luggage down to the carriages. In such a bad time for a woman, she doesn't need to be alone. Family helps."

"Yes, it did. When last I heard of her, she is living with her sister's family, and she is doing well as an aunt to her nieces and nephews."

"She probably will never want to have any children of her own again."

"It might be best. For some of us, grief is something we don't want to risk feeling again."

"And there are others of us who are a glutton for punishment," I said, chuckling.

"Yes," he confirmed, looking on me fondly, "there are those of us who are like that."

He offered me his hand, and I shook it.

"Lord knows when we will see each other again," I noted.

"*I know*," he said, with a glint in his eye.

He was up to something. Time and experience taught me how to read his expressions well.

"What is that look for?" I asked.

"What look?"

"That look."

We were interrupted by the announcement that it was time to depart.

Getting my cloak, gloves, and bonnet on, I assembled with the rest. Along with the group, Frederick Fitzwilliam began to offer his gentler farewells. Whatever his flaws, no one could resist the strange fact that, just maybe, we all might miss him.

When he reached me, the familiar twinkle was in his eye.

"Well," he began.

"Well," I repeated.

"Yes."

"Yes."

"Stop doing that."

"Stop doing that."

He rolled his head.

"Something tells me that you are willing to part ways as friends with me," he observed.

"Perhaps I am. Despite everything."

"It's because you know, in the back of your mind, that I really do just want to help."

"Yes, I know that you do. Even when it hurts to hear it."

"Especially when it hurts to hear it," he stressed. "People like me need to exist. We are the only ones who do not fear the truth, of all things."

"Are you happy?"

His eyes lost their light.

"And I see that I hit a strange nerve there, didn't I?" I questioned him. "I said the one thing that you were hoping that no one would ask."

"I just didn't expect it."

"Any chance that you will give me an answer? Are you happy?"

He smiled but didn't answer.

"One day, you'll answer that question."

"But today is not that day."

"Come now, Mr. Fitzwilliam. You and I might never see each other again. Let's part with some sort of truth between us. After all, truth is what you admire, isn't it?"

His eyes turned shrewd again.

"I was hoping that you were stupid," he confessed.

"I have the impression of being considered that. That's the beauty of it. Since people have low expectations of me, it helps me be able to do something I like doing."

"What?"

"Surprise them. Or let them down. Take your preference of whatever it is."

"Very well. I will tell you one thing, and one thing only."

"What?"

"She was like you."

"Who was like me?"

"The woman that I loved. And who once loved me. She was like you."

My insides felt as if they were freezing. Is this what he was?

Richard's brother—and this is what he was? From the tip of my head, to the bottom of my feet, I felt the alarm and surprise awakening every nerve of uncertainty.

Colonel Fitzwilliam.

Frederick Fitzwilliam.

One man woke up my heart and made me doubt everything.

Then his brother came along, woke up my mind, and made me question everything.

Where was I to win with these two? They seemed to be born to walk into my life, confuse me, and leave with more questions to ask rather than answers to make me satisfied.

"Is she still well?" I asked. "Is she happy?"

"Wherever she is, she is happy. Life hurts us. Both of us were victims to chance."

"Then you know how I feel. And how Richard feels."

"Yes, I do."

"You must forgive me for being like her."

He turned serious again.

"In truth," he answered, "I don't think I can."

I sighed.

"I had a feeling that would be your answer."

With his suddenly changed demeanor, his mercurial habit, and his unpredictable way, his tone was soft, no louder than a whisper. But it was strong.

"Truth."

~

The time for departure was fully here, and we all were getting into our carriages. As we did so, Lady Fitzwilliam finally came to approach me.

"Did I do my duty, madam?" I asked her, only loud enough for her to hear.

"Yes, you did. The Luxford sisters are now quite taken with my dear Richard. They are not as handsome as you, but men don't always marry women for their elegance."

"If he chooses one of them, then I will be happy for him."

"Yes, you will. But you also won't."

I closed my eyes and then opened them.

"Why can't I lie with this family?"

"Because we are very good at seeing through them."

She looked down at me. Her expression was hard to read, for I daresay that even she did not know what to fully make of me. I would never be the woman who was fully loved or hated anywhere. In that moment, I realized, that I was the one who no one ever fully knew what to make of. And perhaps, I always would be.

"Well," I said, "at least you don't hate me. I shall take that for a small victory within itself, I suppose."

"Hate?" She looked at me curiously. "No, I do not feel that. I am happy to have met you, Miss Bennet."

Grateful, I smiled.

"Thank you. My time here has been one of the best parts of my life."

"I am glad for that."

With us all stored securely within our coaches, we set off, homeward bound.

After an hour and a half, we arrived back at Pemberley, much to the joy of those of us who were wishing for home—especially those who were with child.

Mrs. Reynolds was glad to see us, and Betsy and Sarah were also eager to hear about everything that went on. Mr. Darcy expressly ordered Jane and Elizabeth to spend the rest of the day in Lizzy's room, so that they could get the proper rest that they needed.

This led to the rest of us sitting down in the main parlor, composing letters to our respective families or friends.

Having been remiss in keeping everyone abreast of our comings and goings, I was writing to my parents, Georgiana was writing to Emma Watson, Darcy was writing to Sir Thomas Granville, to inform him that Bingley would begin to initiate purchase of Godfrey Park in two days' time. He also recommended that the Granvilles inform us of whenever they were prepared to take leave of the place and settle in

Bath, so that we knew when to have the Bingleys settle there.

Enara was writing to her family in New South Wales about all the comings and goings. Arthur was writing to his parents, my dear aunt and Uncle Philips.

Mr. Atkins was also composing a letter.

"Who do you write to, dear?" Mary asked as she was about to sit down to the pianoforte and play for us while we wrote. It was altogether amazing what confidence could do for a person. Since she had married Mr. Atkins, she was more pleased with herself, and that led to her talent becoming less pedantic and more organic.

"I'm writing to let your aunt and uncle know that we will be returning to Hertfordshire in two days. The letter will, hopefully, proceed us, and they will be prepared."

"You wrote to them about our arrival in your last letter."

"I know, but I worry that it may have gone astray."

"Better safe than sorry, I see."

"Yes. Very much that."

"You're a model employee, Atkins," Arthur said, "I am certain that my father wishes that I was more like you."

"He's proud of you, you dolt," Atkins replied to Arthur, kindly. "They just miss you. That's all. Other than that, they are proud of you. Besides, where in Hertfordshire could you have met your match?" He looked at Enara, who was flattered by the compliment.

"It's a pity," Darcy announced to the room, "that you both must return to Hertfordshire, but business must always come before pleasure."

"Yes, sadly it does," Mary acknowledged, "but we had delightful times in this house."

"And what of you, Mr. and Mrs. Philips?" Darcy asked, "have you enjoyed your time here?"

"Did you even need to ask?" Enara asked, cheerfully. "When we return to New South Wales, we shall have much to tell."

"Must you return at this time?" Darcy asked. "Or are your plans easy to alter?"

We all turned to Mr. Darcy.

"Well," Arthur said, looking at Enara, "when we would return to Australia, then we figured that we'd settle our married plans."

"My family is expecting us, but there is no pressing matter," Enara commented. "Out of curiosity, why do you ask that?"

"It is as much for your own safety as it is for our leisure. The voyage from England to Australia is already long, but to traverse the seas along this part of winter is not the best way to spend your holidays. Christmas is coming, and if you leave in a fortnight, you will be spending the day on the ocean among strangers. Would it not be more fitting to hold the celebration here, with family? After all, when you return to Sydney, you will not see us for perhaps years at a time."

"You are very gracious," Arthur said, charmed, "but I know what I am about, and I know that I would like to remain. However, one should never accept an offer when we have already outstayed our welcome."

Darcy ceased writing and turned to Arthur.

"You think I make the offer in a general way of obligation, don't you?"

"It's customary to ask someone to stay at the end of a visit, even when you want nothing more than to see the back of them."

"We don't want you to hate us because we cannot read between the lines of cordiality," Enara offered.

"Then it will warm your sensibilities to know that I make the offer out of selfishness, rather than out of decorum. The winter festivities are going to begin soon, Bingley must settle into his new house, and our wives are at a special time in their lives where they cannot go touring with us to Italy, like we planned.

"Since they cannot go on holiday, holiday must be brought to them. Having family for these next few weeks might help them during this time. It will make the twelve days of Christmas feel even more fulfilled. You need not spare my feelings by your rejection. But if you do reject the offer, it might disappoint Mrs. Darcy and Mrs. Bingley."

"Now that is not fair," Arthur commented, amused. "You, sir, play dirty."

Darcy smirked.

"I know."

We all laughed at that.

"I can write to my family," Enara said, "and tell them that we plan to stay in England till the end of the year and will not proceed to Sydney until after the New Year."

"Our wives will be very pleased."

Mr. Darcy...you furtive little snipe.

Just as I finished my letter, Mrs. Reynolds entered and went to Mr. Darcy.

"Sir," she said, "now that Colonel Fitzwilliam is going to be coming in two days, I was wondering if he still prefers the traditional room that he usually keeps when he stays here, or does he prefer another guestroom?"

My head shot up so quickly that it made the back of my neck ache.

"Colonel Fitzwilliam?" I gasped.

When hearing my exclamation, they all turned to me. Feeling flushed, I looked down at the floor.

"Yes," Mr. Darcy confirmed, "Colonel Fitzwilliam has a fortnight before he must return to his services. He wished to spend it in visiting us. After all, he worries that he might not be able to enjoy the season with his family. I accepted his request to pay a visit."

"He comes here," Mary observed, "right after we left him."

"That must mean that he likes us," Enara said.

"I'm sure that he does," Mary said, turning to me. Blushing, I looked away from them and back to the letter that I had just finished.

"How very thoughtful of him," was all that I could muster.

"It will be nice to see him once more," Mrs. Reynolds observed. "He used to visit quite often. The household would like to see him. And I come with another errand, sir."

Mrs. Reynolds took out two envelopes and handed them to Mr. Darcy.

"Two letters, sir, from Colonel Forster and a Lieutenant Finlay."

~

From Fitzwilliam to Finlay!

Within my bones, I felt the anxiety that comes when two balls of compassionate chaos collide in your life. At this point in my life, I had managed to be successful and keep both men separate. Whether it was by willpower or chance, neither man would meet the other. It was fragile ground on which I had walked, but now the surface was fully giving way.

Both men would now be in Derbyshire at the same time. One remained here at Pemberley, and the other at Lambton. Both were close enough for their paths to cross, and it was inevitable. I feared the day when it occurred, but I knew that it was bound to be.

I had to warn them both.

Especially Finlay. His jealousy was the more potent because his passions were the more like fire. Colonel Fitzwilliam's passions were more like water. Both were dangerous, but one was more likely to burn when discomfort ignited.

Darcy opened Colonel Forster's letter first. It requested the right to visit us. It was readily accepted, and Darcy informed us that he would invite the Colonel, Mrs. Forster, and his more immediate officers to dine with us. That naturally included Denny, Carter, Sanderson, Finlay, and a couple others.

After Darcy closed that letter, Mrs. Reynolds was looking at him.

"Is there something the matter, Reynolds?" Darcy asked her as he opened Finlay's letter.

"I was told to make Mr. Finlay's apologies, master," she said.

"Why?"

"Because he hand-delivered it. He begs forgiveness for his presumption, but he is standing outside, with his horse."

I closed my eyes, hiding away from the gaze of everyone in the room.

To be both immensely flattered as well as mortified can go hand in hand when a man is so eager to see you that he defies convention. A year ago, I would have only felt the compliment of it, but I guess that I had changed in some ways.

"Thank you, Reynolds," Darcy said, "Colonel Fitzwilliam will take his traditional room, and that will be all."

"Very good, sir."

She left to continue with her duties.

Darcy unfolded the letter and began to read:

> *Dear Mr. Darcy,*
>
> *My apologies for my eagerness to see your family and to await your return. I am aware of the presumption that I offer, and the example that I set. But when it comes to receiving friends who have left the county, I feel that what must be done cannot be done too quickly.*
>
> *I hand-deliver this missive, in hopes of being well-received, in order to...improve my image from the last time that I visited. I pray that I can make amends for the example I set on my last visit and wish to know that I can seek forgiveness for my less than proper behavior.*
>
> *I await your steward to inform me if I may be received now or be sent away directly.*
>
> *Lt. Finlay*

When he closed the letter, I felt everyone's eyes on me, despite that I didn't look upon them.

"I heard that," I said to them, referring to their silent implications.

"We meant for you to," Arthur replied, smirking.

"Kitty?" Darcy asked me. "Would us receiving him be agreeable to you?"

Finally, I looked around at them all, and lastly to him.

"Thank you for asking me," I sighed, happy that he was taking my feelings into consideration.

"I am aware that it does concern you."

"Yes," I determined. "Well, Mr. Darcy, while it is proper for us to order him to return the next day or after he scheduled a proper visit, he feels a comfort with us. And he is correct. What must be done cannot be done too quickly."

"Very well."

Darcy rung the bell, and his steward entered.

"Yes, sir?" The steward asked.

"Lieutenant Finlay is waiting outside. Have his horse sent to the stables and tended to. Then escort the Lieutenant to the breakfast room."

"Yes, sir."

With that, Darcy stood up and left the room. When he was gone, everyone was staring at me again.

"I heard that again," I noted.

"We know," they all said.

Oh dear.

Home again.

Chapter Sixteen

THE GIFT

When I finished my letter to my parents, I gave it to Mrs. Reynolds to have it sent. My hand had been shaking when I wrote the address, and I had hoped that my writing was legible. Although, I was not left to wait for long before the servant, Philadelphia, entered and told me that Mr. Darcy wanted to see me in his library.

"Thank you, Philadelphia," I said, then I stood up and left the room before I could see any of my company's looks. When I entered Mr. Darcy's study, he was not alone. Elizabeth was beside him.

"Lizzy," I said, "you are awake."

"Yes," Elizabeth said, "and I understand that you have a visitor."

I looked at her, then at Mr. Darcy.

"You woke her up so that you could tell me something together, didn't you?" I asked.

"It seemed like the logical thing to do."

"Understandable." I sat down. "Well, whatever it is, I am prepared."

"Are you?" Elizabeth asked, her eyebrow arching up in the familiar way that it usually did.

"No," I confessed, "I don't know if I am."

"Precisely. That is why Mr. Darcy, and I have decided to not greet Finlay initially."

"As we understand it," Darcy added, "it has been a couple weeks since you and he saw each other, and words were spoken bitterly. Maybe, you both need time to speak to each other, alone. We shall give you five minutes with him in the breakfast room, before we join you."

My heart both immediately turned to lead, as well as becoming light as a feather. The contradiction of temperament was not lost on me. I was both elated as well as filled with trepidation.

"Does that please you, Kitty?" Lizzy asked.

"Yes!" I cried, breathless. "I confess that I am a little terrified, but there are things that we need to speak of first, and I think I need to face him."

I stood up and kissed them both on the cheek. This unnerved Darcy only for a second.

"Thank you!" I cried. "Thank you ever so much!"

As I rushed to the door, Mr. Darcy called me over the shoulder.

"I ordered Philadelphia to remain outside of the breakfast room, in case he decides to become vulgar in any way. Call for her, and then she will bring the steward."

"Thank you," I rushed out again. "Thank you!"

As I dashed out of the room, I overheard Darcy and Elizabeth talking.

"Do you feel as if we shall be doing things like this forever?" she asked, amused.

"I hope not, for I will become weary by the time I am thirty. But... I gather the impression that we will be forced into these roles till the end of our days."

Oh, those two! They would never fully know the sort of happiness that they stumbled on—and how many of us envied the clarity that they found in their joy.

When I walked through the halls, every step felt heavy and weighted down by the expectations that can come from heading toward something that you longed to see. Finlay and I were two people who understood each other very well. Our moments of anger never would last because there was a comfort in our characters. We both knew who the other one was. Therefore, there was no fear of forgiving or being forgiven. So why was I apprehensive? I suppose that is what love is.

When I reached the breakfast room's door, I placed my hand on the knob.

Courage, Kitty! You are the fourth Bennet sister. You must not be afraid of life.

I turned the knob and entered.

When I entered, Finlay's back was toward me. He had been looking out of the window. When hearing the door open, he turned immediately, his posture straight, and his stern brow set.

But when he saw that it was me, his serious demeanor waned, giving way to his eyes softening a little. He stood there, in his regimentals, with his cloak pulled up on one side where his sword was. His traditionally long hair was tied up in the back, with a couple dark strands resting behind his ears.

Neither of us said anything, at first. Slowly, I walked up to him with my hand extended. Once we got within arms' reach of each other, he took my hand, raised it to his lips and kissed it.

"You come alone?" he asked.

"Through no impropriety on my account," I assured him. "Darcy and Elizabeth felt that I needed this moment."

"Tell me then, through all of this, do you forgive me?"

"You know that I do. I cannot help it."

He released a heavy sigh.

"Then through all my blustering, all my blindness, all my hypocrisy, and you still care for me?"

I placed my hands on both sides of his cheeks, to steady his fevered emotions as well as calm any doubts that he had within him.

"Son of Ireland, you need to stop walking through life thinking that everyone will always forsake you."

"Many people have."

"Yes. But their name is not Kitty Bennet."

"No, they are not." His eyes were filled with gratitude. "I...I...
I brought you something."

"You did?"

"Yes." He reached into his satchel bag. He opened it and
removed a present from it. Handing it to me, he was bashful.
"When I saw it, I thought of you."

"Did you?" I asked, placing the present down on a nearby
table. I removed the ribbon and cloth, then I saw it was a long
shawl. It was white with red lines running along it in a simple, but
elegant pattern. It was beautiful, and it suited me perfectly.

"This...this is wonderful!" I cried, immediately removing it
from the cloth wrapping, and draping it over my shoulders. When
I did, I twirled around. "How did you know?'"

"Know what?" he asked, happy.

"That I would like this?"

"I didn't. I just had hope."

"Well, you are quite the clever clogs!" I laughed, and then I
had a revelation. "Wait, Finlay, you didn't buy this because you
thought it would help win me over, did you?"

"Well," he faltered, "I was hoping that it would soften my
suit."

"It did, but I don't want you thinking that way. First, I want to
remind you that I do like it. So, do not regret the purchase of it. I
am just saying that, when it comes to every woman in your life, if
you try to solve the problem by buying her something, you will
quickly exhaust your income and have her expect that of you.
She'll always think that you expect to solve your arguments by a
purchase rather than sitting down and addressing the issues that
need to be discussed. This was money from your salary, and you
are a lieutenant. You cannot afford to always be buying me things
when it can be detrimental to your savings. That being said," I
walked over to the mirror and looked at myself in it. "Finlay, this
is one of the best gifts that I ever had. I love it."

He smiled, his eyes warm.

"You lecture me and then you thank me."

"I do it because I care, and you know that," I assured him.

"Yes, I do. And I am thankful for it. It shows that you do not look at me and see a purse with legs attached to it. How many wealthy men can boast of having a woman in their lives who did that?"

"I can only think of three in my acquaintance. So, well done."

His eyes grew misty.

"I missed you since you were away."

My heart was in my throat, pounding rapidly. "And I missed you."

"We must never be separate for long."

"We must be...if I am ever to be able to rise above my love for you."

"I don't want you to."

"I know that you don't, but you also know that I must."

He sighed.

"Let's not talk of this now," he urged. "Please, let us have happier words between us. You have a roaming soldier on your hands. Give him his island of peace to be on."

"Finlay, I want to give you that," I assured him, "I want to give you peace, but the way we live now, I cannot give. Even though you deserve it."

His eyes began to shift back and forth, disturbed.

"Are you to tell me that you have now formed a permanent attachment elsewhere? Kitty, is that what you are about to tell me?"

"No!" I insisted. "Not at all. I merely must warn you that the reality of our situation is about to come creeping up upon you and I want you to be prepared."

"Prepared?"

"It's the man that I formed an attachment to. Colonel Fitzwilliam. He shall be coming here in two days' time. You and he will meet. Inevitably."

~

When hearing this, the shift in demeanor was sudden and swift. Finlay's look of joy and wonderment turned serious, once more, and it was like a star faded over him.

"Truly?" he asked, his lips barely moving.

"Yes. Finlay I am sorry. I had not expected this to happen."

"Then..." he turned away, "it is a sudden decision of his then? I assume as such, by the way that you mention it."

"Yes. I just found out this morning. He wanted to surprise us and told Darcy to tell us that he would soon follow us from Matlock in two days."

"He was with you all that time, and now he wants more time with you."

"I cannot say that is the official reason."

"But it is. He and I are both the same sex, and therefore, I am at liberty to know more of what's in his mind. If I were him, I would do precisely as he has done."

"We don't have much time," I rushed out, "in fact, we are soon to be come upon by the rest of my company. He is not a harsh man, Finlay. Colonel Fitzwilliam is understanding."

Suddenly I had a thought. "When he comes, I will arrange it all so that you and he do not encounter each other—or if you do, it shall be as little as possible. I'll spend time visiting Colonel Forster's regiment on certain days, and when I am here—"

"He shall see you, and I will spend my days wondering what you both are doing."

I was silenced. Despite that he was not helping me on at all, I also understood the direction in which he had come from.

"There is no way that he and I can marry," I argued, to calm his fevered passions. "It has been discussed time and time again. But the fact remains, his feelings are what they are, yours are what yours are, and I don't want either of you to get hurt..."

"When seeing you in the arms of another man."

"I am not in anyone's arms, because I belong to no man," I stated.

"You belong to me," he said, strongly and desperately.

I sighed, feeling remorse of having to say this.

"But I don't, though, no matter how much I love you," I said. "In the eyes of sacraments and ceremonies, you know that I don't."

He was so forlorn my heart wept. "I know. But I still look at you as mine anyway. I cannot help it."

"I know. And I am flattered by it. I appreciate everything that you feel for me. But, at the end of the day, I still belong only to myself and family. I cannot be bound to ties that are not mine to be bound to."

"Is it so hard just to say you love me and me alone?" he asked.

"You don't think that I wish that was how it was. Feeling such passionate feelings for one man, then accidentally learning to feel for another, is not the blissful road that I wanted to walk down. It's not even bliss. It's an inferno."

"Then rise away from it and find the joys of being singular. I just...choose me at least, while your heart and feet are allowed to roam where they will."

"The heart cannot dictate who it feels for," I argued, "you know better than anyone. I am proof of that."

I turned away from his gaze. "I am the last woman that you needed to fall in love with. And you did anyway. Is that not testament to the randomness and indiscriminate tendencies of the heart?"

Then I realized that he was' ordering me around again. Suddenly, I found myself getting angry. "And who are you to order my feelings as if you reign supreme over them? No, I will not be dictated to in that way."

I moved away from him.

"You turn from me again," he uttered. "Kitty must never turn away from me."

"Well, I just did. I shall triumph over you at a short distance and be satisfied."

"No, Kitty. You will not turn from me again."

He moved toward me quickly and took my hand.

"Be angry with me," he uttered, "but don't ever turn your back on me."

"More orders?" I glared.

"Not an order. An urging. A plea if you will. I don't have much time with you. I don't want to spend it with you ignoring me."

"How is that worse than when we argue? I wonder if that even means that we are right to love each other."

"It does. That's what people do when they are in love. Sometimes they argue. Some couples are always in accordance with each other. Others bicker and quarrel, for that is their way of being so attached to one another. Indifference brings peace in romance, because it's an indication that both sides do not care for the other. True love brings occasional discord, because it means both parties actually care what the other one thinks."

"Is this the Irishman's definition of love?"

"Yes, it is. And I daresay that it's the definition for many people who have felt the real thing. Truly, have you ever met an American? Or Italians? Or the Welsh? Or Spanish? Perhaps we should also add Germans to that list as well. Or anyone from the baser sides of London."

I laughed. He laughed as well.

"No, I haven't," I answered. "I would be amenable to the experience of meeting them, though. I think I would like them all."

"You have traits in common with quite a few of them. Either way, for some of us, this is love. And we have it. Can you not see the notion of knowing that another suitor to your heart being nearby would tear at me?"

I pressed my lips together. He had a point.

"Yes, I can see how it could. If I were in your place, I would be filled with jealousy and perhaps wish to claw your eyes out."

"See!" he cried, triumphant. "THAT is love. It's not logical all the time. It is fire and red. And it is only subdued by when our rational side takes over afterwards."

"Very well, you have my permission to be angry. But do not think you have the right to order my choices. Until I marry, I am my own lord and master. In fact, if I do marry, I will only be happy with you if you understand that I ought to have my say in everything as well. Take note, Lieutenant, this is the woman that you fell for. Are you still interested, or do you have the impulse to run to the hills, then jump into a river and see where that takes you?"

"I am not going anywhere," he said casually, sitting down on the chair again, feeling self-satisfied and as if he didn't have a care in the world. "What are these hills and rivers that you speak of? I don't see them anywhere."

I chuckled.

"Your blindness is flattering."

"Why thank you, my lady of Longbourn."

"You are very welcome, my Gaelic son. But still, you must understand this. I am not meant for blind obedience. Maybe I was once, but something has stirred in me and it's your fault."

"My fault?"

"You taught me the rewards of emotional and mental independence. You cannot be angry at me for learning it now, perhaps better than you expected."

He blinked and thought about it.

"I did teach you that, didn't I?" he asked.

"Yes, you did."

"One of my best lessons," He said with a smug smile.

"Perhaps it is. And I learned it so well, that I cannot go back." I raised my arms. "Therefore, this is me. And that is how it shall stand. You must never order me to do something unless we are already in agreement on the matter. But if you ask, or recommend, then I shall always hear you."

"And what of you? Women sometimes order us men around."

"If I do that, you have the right to inform me that I am being hypocritical. And I shall try to listen. See? My logic always finds me eventually...after my illogical side has had its say."

He chuckled.

"You laugh?" I asked, lightheartedly.

"Yes. Because I am happy now."

"That is good," I declared, happy.

"I feel like we will be doing this forever."

"We just might. Whoever knows, in this mad world of ours?" I sat down next to him again. He leaned closer to me so that our arms would touch. I did not shy away.

"I will always welcome you in my life," I said, "and I will understand the anxiety you feel of when I also let the Colonel in my life as well. But if it will help, I will leave you with this one promise. I do not promise this out of a guilt that you have incurred in me, but of my own free will. I do not ever think I can break either of your hearts. Therefore, I won't. While you are free and still feel an affection for me, I would never choose the Colonel. And the reverse is the same for him. Our financial situation can break your heart, but I won't do it myself."

He looked at me.

"Do you mean that?"

"Yes. I do. I find the idea of disappointing you to be one of the most atrocious things that I could do."

Feeling smug again, he smiled the familiar smile that I have seen when we humans feel that our selfishness has been satisfied and obeyed. Well, this is love! In all its infinite strangeness.

"You mean this?" he asked.

"Yes, and I commit to it. When you, or he, finally decide to move on, then I shall release either of you from my heart. The loss of your love will hurt terribly, but I will recover. Recovery is the only accomplishment that I have to my name. I know that this very well may lead to me getting neither of you for a husband, but that is worth not hurting you."

I rested my head against his shoulder, and he placed his head next to mine.

"You give me hope, woman. That is a dangerous thing."

"Yes, I do. Now take it like the medicine that it is and enjoy the maxim that I always enjoy—anything is possible."

"Yes, it is."

The door opened.

"Dear god, get away from me!" I hissed, to shield him from any set-down that Mr. Darcy would give if he saw us touching.

"Indeed," Finlay agreed. We both moved away from each other, as if we had the pox.

◦

When we stood there, expectant, Mr. Darcy entered, followed by Elizabeth.

"Mr. and Mrs. Darcy," Finlay said, bowing respectfully.

"Lieutenant Finlay," Elizabeth said, going up to him, "what a pleasure it is to see you."

"The pleasure is all mine, and I do not say that lightly. I am indebted to you both on two counts. First, for allowing me to visit in such a presumptuous manner. And second, for granting Miss Bennet and I the right to speak candidly and sincerely with each other. I owed her many apologies."

"Yes, you do," Mr. Darcy said, "and I am happy to hear that you distributed them to where it was due. Since her father is not here, I must speak in his stead." Darcy turned to me. "I am about to lecture the lieutenant, Kitty. I implore you not to interrupt me, out of loyalty to him. Sometimes a man needs to hear words from another man."

"Very well," I said, "go ahead. I do not deny that there is something sacred about a lecture between two parties of the same sex."

"Very good."

Darcy turned to Finlay.

"Will you ever speak to my sister in the way you did on your previous visit?" he asked.

"No, sir, I shall not," Finlay responded. "I do not deny that we bicker and argue together, but I will never raise my voice."

"Have you told Miss Bennet your entire history, when it comes to your own actions in alleviating your passions?"

Finlay blushed.

"I did not. At first, I worried that a young lady might not wish to hear such vulgarity. But then I did wish to but was only delayed with our discussion on another matter."

"Tell her by the end of your visit. The first step toward a true bond is unfolding everything. Only then will you be worthy to be in the presence of any woman in my family. And lastly, do you prefer green or brown tea?"

Finlay looked at me, when hearing this shocking question.

"Brown, sir."

"Very good," Elizabeth said. "I was worried when you visited before, and we never asked you about your preference. Now I know what to have our cooks prepare. Now come, Finlay, let us get you re-acquainted with the others. Kitty? Come."

I went up to Elizabeth, while Mr. Darcy gave Finlay the 'you will walk with me, and we will talk of things that *I* wish to talk about' look.

Finlay, naturally understanding the respect that was due to the Master of Pemberley in his home, succumbed to Darcy's stare of submission and both men walked ahead of us, talking as casually as one could with a man like my brother-in-law.

As we followed the gentlemen, I turned to Elizabeth.

"That was longer than five minutes," I commented.

"You were counting the minutes? That must mean that you both were not enjoying each other's company."

"I guessed the number. But it was quite the contrary. I thank you for the extra time that you gave us. It helped a lot."

"Kitty, I wish I could say that our delayed entrance was for your welfare—that Darcy and I had a wise perception that you and Finlay needed more time. But that wasn't it."

"Then what was it?"

"Darcy and I were thinking of names that we could name our child, and we lost track of time."

I raised an eyebrow.

"That was it?"

"Yes, it was."

"Might I ask what names that you came up with?"

"The list is so long that we had to write it down."

"Ah."

Chapter Seventeen

FORGIVENESS

When Finlay joined the rest of our company again, Bingley was back in attendance. While Jane and Elizabeth had rested, he had been riding among the grounds, and now he was returned, with Jane beside him.

An officer would always prove to be a diverting element to a company that was visiting on a country estate who had little to do. He spoke to us about all the goings on that the regiment had committed in our absence, and I longed to see Mrs. Warrens and the three knowing ladies again.

Finlay was invited to dine with us, which he accepted very easily, and while we ate, I had a thought. Since I was sitting next to him, we could speak without being overheard.

"I wonder about Mrs. Forster," I said, "for it just occurred to me that I have not seen her since Lydia's plight. Were you there when she learned that Lydia and Wickham had run off?"

"I didn't see her till the next morning. Colonel Forster had me look after her when he rode to Longbourn to tell you the news. Oh, Kitty, you should have seen her. She was fraught with guilt."

"Really?"

"Yes, she was. She was a little aware of Lydia being partial to Wickham, but she never saw anything to cause any alarm. Therefore, imagine her shock when she had proven to be wrong. It wasn't just the anger that comes with a friend letting her down in such a way, but also her pride was affected. She had thought that she had seen everything clearly."

"When it came to Wickham, we all thought we saw everything clearly," I said, rolling my eyes. "Except you of course."

"I had the advantage. I was able to see him, in unguarded moments between men. You could not have known what I did. We humans will always have a dual identity: the person that we really are, and the person that we make sure everyone sees. Wickham is best at showing the latter, while secretly indulging the former."

"That is Wickham's gift. Why do the evil ones always have that?"

"That sort of maliciousness comes from the stronger sides of ourselves. That strength brings confidence. Confidence brings charisma, and charisma brings charm."

"If only good always appeared as good, and bad appeared as bad, life would be simple. But we are not meant to live the simple life, are we?"

"No. Fate would not find the fun in that, I expect."

After we ate, we sat in the drawing room, listening to Georgiana play and Elizabeth sang with her. They were quite the ideal set to stand up together. For Elizabeth, who may not have the perfect singing voice—whatever that is—was very sweet to listen to, and Georgiana played masterfully.

Afterwards, the others sat down to a game of cards while Finlay and I were allowed to sit on the other side of the room, playing a game of backgammon.

Now that we were away from them, we could speak on more private matters. Matters that I had long wanted to discuss.

"Now," I said as I rolled the dice, "My brother mentioned that there was something that you wanted to tell me, but you hadn't mentioned it yet."

"It was something that he advised me on before you all left for Matlock. I feared telling you, not out of cowardice, but to protect you."

"That is very kind, but that excuse could also be attributed to not telling someone something, because you don't want to hurt your image in their eyes." He looked at me critically. "Come now, dear friend, are you absolutely certain that, whatever you are about to tell me, you also might have done it to protect yourself?"

He sighed and looked down at the backgammon board.

"The game is never fair with you," he commented.

"And why so?"

"You know what I'm thinking. Always, you know what I'm thinking."

"It's not cheating," I pursued, "but the fault is yours. You unveiled your soul to me, and so now I know the words that they often cry out. You know what's inside of me as well, so there is an evenhandedness to it all. No matter what you say, the game is fair."

"Yes, it is. Very well, maybe I was trying to protect myself. I didn't want you to see me like this."

"I won't know what the 'this' is, until you expose all. Now speak your words up sharp, dearest, or I will be upset with you for holding me in suspense."

All my words, as well as his, up until that point, had been spoken in jest and friendly amusement, but now shame fell across his features. This made me even more curious to know the beginning, middle, and end of his confession.

"Kitty, I wronged you."

"I know," I said, before even knowing the truth. He looked at me queerly, so I thought it helpful to explain. "It was your eyes. It wore guilt like it was a new gown."

He half-smiled.

"It was in the worst sort of guilt that your brother, Mr. Darcy, knew of even before I said anything. Then again, a man can always tell with another man. It's like we are born knowing the tendencies and habits of each other."

"Well, that is a credit to your sex. We women sometimes can explain each other's habits, but we are so very different, that it is always hard to be sure what each of us is thinking. We can give you guesses, but only we know the recesses of our own minds, individually."

"My mother always told me that the mind of humans is vast,

but the mind of a woman is like that of a universe; you can live for an eternity and never see every anomaly in it. Well, my instincts were so shallow that Mr. Darcy dissembled them. Kitty?"

"Yes?"

"You say that you love me. Please...forgive me."

"Forgive you for what?"

"I have...erred."

"We all err. You must be specific."

"Kitty, I was angry with you for falling in love with another man, despite that you had the right to. I left you with no assurance of my return. You had the right to move along with your affections. But my pride was hurt, and I felt wronged."

"Yes, I remember living the event very well," I said. My voice had a hint of cynicism in it, but it was so subtle that I do not believe he detected it.

"Well, it was even more unfair to you because—what you must understand is that you awoke passions in me that I hadn't felt in years. Also, we men are possessed with such feverish appetites already."

I was becoming aware of what he was hinting at, but I decided to let him finish. After all, Finlay always needed time to bear his soul.

"Before I met you, I sometimes would go to London, along with other officers. For there, in the more questionable areas, is where a man can seek pleasurable company. All the time that I was in Hertfordshire, I never visited such establishments. In all the time that I was in your society, I never felt the desire to ever go anywhere for my happiness. But when I left Hertfordshire, with no hope of seeing you again... I—well, I..."

"Would visit houses in town and pay for women's company," I said, so matter-of-factly, that it startled him.

"You don't sound shocked."

"It's because I'm not. You think that I don't know what officers do when they are in town?"

"How long have you known?"

"For many months. Don't you recall all the time that I spent with Samantha, the washerwoman? A washerwoman knows the dirty laundry of all the officers, and I say that in more ways than just one. And if she didn't tell me, then think of the other company that I had. Mrs. Warrens, Mrs. Barrett, Mrs. Hawkins, and Mrs. O'Connor. Their husbands always remained home, and it wasn't just because of their age. It was because they had wives, whereas many of you younger officers are still single. Their husbands didn't need to go to London for such diversions, but you all did. If Samantha had not told me, then Mrs. Barrett told me of this fact afterwards. I have known what you all do in town for many a day now."

"Then...you were aware that I might become one of those men when I left you?"

"Yes. I didn't ever really dwell on this fact because it was so much of a common sort of revelation. Besides, we women are the ones who are pressured to come to a marriage as a maid. You all are allowed to have a reputation, and still make a good match. If we have a reputation, we are meant to be avoided. That is the only unfair part of it. For a long time, I accepted this reality, but now I am seeing the cruelty of it."

"I can only assume that it's because the proof of the act is seen in you, but not in ourselves."

"What do you mean?"

"When a woman is intimate, she can become with child. When we men are intimate, there is no sign of it."

"There's more to it than that, and you know it."

"Yes. There is. Forgive me, I was giving a superficial excuse."

"There may be some proof to your findings, for yes, there is evidence in the act through us. But that would denote that intimacy is evil, and I do not believe it is."

He looked at me fondly.

"You don't?"

"No, I do not. I refuse to. There must be something beautiful about it, or else my parents would not have had me or my sisters. If it created us, and if it created yourself, then there must be a divinity to the act."

"I never thought of it in that way. You have converted me.

When I was with those women, I was happy when it happened, but I felt ashamed afterwards."

"You have been told to feel ashamed. I had much rather you pay for a woman's service, rather than be a villain and attack a woman because you are...frustrated. This way, you help a woman who was not given the best chances in life, and you cause no harm."

"Then...you do not hate me for what I have done?"

"Not for that, no. If you had been courting me, or we had been married, then yes, I would despise you now. If we were courting, I would sever all ties with you."

"You would?"

"Oh yes. Potential spinsterhood would not frighten me from making that decision. I love you, but I want the same sort of faith-fulness. I would forgive you for your indiscretion, of course. We are all human. But I would never forget. My ability to forget such things only goes so far. But you and I are not married, we are not engaged, and at the time, we were not even in any sort of courtship. You were free. You broke no vow, and your conscience is clear on that score."

He breathed out, completely relieved.

"Oh, Kitty," he sighed, "dearest Kitty! You don't know how happy you have made me. It feels like a great weight has been lifted from my shoulders and my mind. Your forgiveness means so very much."

"Oh, why does it?" I said, happy to know that I would now fully carry my other point through. "You see I said that I forgave you on *one* score. But now I am angry with you on a completely other note."

His tone grew heavier again.

"You are?"

"Of course. There is one aspect that you are missing."

He closed his eyes.

"Oh, yes. I see it now. How careless of me to overlook it."

"The problem was not that you enjoyed those ladies' company. No. It was that you did it, and then acted like my actions were the ultimate crime, when I never betrayed you either. And then, you had to be coerced into telling me about it, by my brother-in-law."

I rolled the dice, and I moved over his piece, winning the spot.

"I would apologize," he said, "but nothing will make up for that, will it?"

"No. But try anyway."

"In all the days that we know each other, whether we end up choosing each other as man and wife or not, I will never spare you of the truth. I will unveil myself to you, from this day forth."

"And do you understand? That if you do something, I am no more or less evil, no more or less right, than you are when you do something similar, or something worse than what I have done. I need you to see that."

"I do," he confessed, "that was where the guilt was the heaviest. While you were away, there were nights that I spent awake, unable to sleep as I considered what I did."

"Good," I stressed, unafraid of sounding indelicate. Sounding delicate was never a virtue that I ever possessed. I talked with a direct and unsubtle fist. "I am glad of it. I did not want you to fall asleep, without a care in the world. If you did, it meant that you had no consideration of how your actions affect others. The propensity to feel guilt over one's actions is a good trait to have. You had better have it, or I am wrong to love you."

"I was born feeling guilty."

"Why is that?"

"Don't know. It's just my way. Therefore, you need never worry on that score. From thenceforth, I will also consider your actions in proportion to mine. If I do wrong, when you do the same, I will not hold your actions as weightier than mine. We will be equal in both our virtues and our follies."

"That is how it should be."

He gave me a significant look.

"What?"

"It's just...you make me always wish to be a better man."

"Do I?" I asked, in awe of him.

"Yes. Kitty?"

"Yes?"

"While the regiment is in Lambton, do not go away again. Please, try and stay with me."

"I will try. If I am called away, it is only because family wills me to go somewhere that I do not wish to. But when it comes to my own personal freedom, I shall stay. I'll be with you."

"Good."

We finished the game. To my surprise, I had won.

Finlay's visit came to an end.

We all saw him to the door, where his horse was brought to the front, and he mounted it.

"I promise," he said to us, "I shall inform Colonel Forster that you welcome our coming tomorrow evening." He turned to Mary and Mr. Atkins. "Mr. and Mrs. Atkins, it was a pleasure to see you once more, and I regret that we shall miss you at the dinner party tomorrow evening." He turned to me. "Miss Bennet, I shall tell Mrs. Warrens and the three knowing women that you shall soon visit." He looked at the entire company. "Mr. Darcy, Mrs. Darcy, and company, thank you for receiving me like that of a friend. I look forward to tomorrow's dinner."

After one last significant look toward me, he rode off, down the road and back to Lambton.

Chapter Eighteen

SISTERLY COMMUNION

That evening was Mary's last night with us.

Thus, in our nightgowns, we all were laying on Elizabeth's bed.

Usually, she slept with Mr. Darcy in his room, but since this was Mary's last moments with us, she invited us all to spend more time with her before we all retired.

Since the bed was not large enough for six women to lay with their heads against the pillows, it was only Jane and Elizabeth who sat such a way. Mary, Georgiana, Enara, and I laid in different directions on the bed, with our bodies overlapping.

Due to the latest romantic episode being mine, they had no choice but to ask me about it, and I was not against telling them everything.

Once we got to the part where I told them about Finlay admitting his guilt to me about his hypocritical behavior, Enara sighed.

"Ah, the evil-handed dealings of life."

"Where men can and women can't," Elizabeth noted.

"I would prefer us not to commit such acts before we marry," Jane said. "There seems to be such a greater pleasure in knowing that your spouse is the first to share every form of intimacy with you."

"It would be proper if both sides committed to that edict. But as Kitty pointed out, it is a habit placed on us, but they do not have to adhere to it."

"Precisely," Mary said, "I may not have been Mr. Atkins's first kiss, but I was his first in every other respect. As such, we both came to the match with a sense of equality."

"But did that equality breed ignorance for both of your parts?" Enara asked her. "Mr. Philips came to the match with experience, and that helped me, for surely I did not know what to do when the wedding night occurred. It was pleasant to have a more experienced person help me. In that regard, when a man has a history, it can recommend him. He can come to the match with his oats already sewn and with a sense of satisfaction. Then again, Mr. Atkins is a very different sort of man. You and he are probably the sort where complete ignorance was the ultimate romance."

"It was because we could explore it all together. Mind you, yes, my husband is a different sort of person. There is none other like him."

We cooed at her.

"Oh, shut it," she said, covering her face. "I realize now, just how much I gave away. I am heartily ashamed of myself now."

"You are amongst your sisters and your cousin," I said, "if you cannot talk to us about it, then who can you speak with?"

"I should not even be talking of this at all."

"It is not unholy to unveil yourself to the women in your family, Mary," Elizabeth advised, "that is what we are here for. To share experiences, and both give and receive advice."

"Yes, I suppose you are right. For me, ignorance did work, but for other marriages, maybe experience did help the marriage along."

"And that is the wonder of it," I continued, looking up at the ceiling. "Of course, I have accepted that the path to love is not a singular one."

"Little by little, I am learning that there are many different paths to take," Georgiana supported.

"Precisely, Georgie. But that is the trouble of it all. If both sides come innocent, there is equality in the ignorance. But if only one is allowed to come to the match untouched and virtuous, while the other is allowed to come to the match with experience, then is that fair? Should either both sides be allowed to come with a history—a reputation—or no side should. But to be a lady, we must be the maid. Or we come tainted."

"That is the way of life," Enara said. "We either come innocent or we are unfit." She breathed in heavily. "And that is the world's view of fair. Unless your name is Arthur Philips."

We all turned to her.

"What does that mean?"

Enara did not meet our gaze.

"I tell you this in strict confidence."

"We will hear you," Jane assured her. "And we will respect your secrets."

"I did not marry Arthur inexperienced."

Georgiana looked at her, with her eyes wide.

"You didn't?"

"No, I did not. I had courted a man before him, and...in the heat of the affection, we kissed a few times. Very passionate kisses, and I allowed him to lay his hands upon me. Intimately."

"Was that the whole of it?" I asked.

"Yes. But when I met Arthur, it was like being hit with a thunderbolt. I held nothing back. On our wedding night, it was not our first time."

"But you married him," Georgiana stressed, "therefore, that is still all well."

"But if she had not, what then?" I asked. "Would Enara be ridiculed for it? She just might. That is what I wonder over. I just wish...that life was fair."

"A fact I learned that was a universal truth," Elizabeth said, "is that life rarely ever is that. But we sojourn on, doing the best we can in this mad world. And when we stumble, and the world comes down on us, we must do our best to weather it, dust ourselves off, find friendly shores and rebuild ourselves."

"And when we can't?" I asked her. "What then?"

"We always find another path," she said, "we just have to spend more time sometimes looking for it. Believe me. Endurance is a trait that we all have."

~

When it was time to go to bed, Elizabeth whispered in my ear that she wanted me to linger behind when everyone else retired to their rooms. With their candles in hand, they all departed, and I made it look like I innocently was fidgeting with my candle-holder. When all were gone, I turned to Lizzy.

"What do you hold me back for?" I asked. "For advice or for a lecture?"

"Both," she said, smoothing out the blanket that lay over her. She looked at me, warily. "You asked a lot of questions tonight."

"I thought they were questions that ought to be asked."

"They were interesting because of your predicament."

"My predicament?"

"Kitty, you have two men in love with you. And you are in love with them. I know that you don't want to have such a plural heart, but you do, and there's nothing for it."

"No, there isn't. Try as I might."

"But I cannot help but wonder if these questions you asked— did you ask them out of curiosity, or because of something you did, and you are looking for forgiveness. Or you are planning to do it, and you are looking for absolution."

My heart beat harder, from the feeling of being misunderstood. Surely, she did not think that I would toy with two men at one time. That would hurt both men.

"Lizzy, you think that I have given my virtue to either of these men?"

"Hate me for asking, but I must know. If you have, I will be upset, but we would need to plan on what to do next."

"You can set your worries to rest," I assured her, "I was not speaking of myself in any way. I have done nothing more than embrace each man's hand, from time to time—you have seen the extent of that yourself. But no more than that, and sometimes, resting my head upon their shoulder. I will not hate myself for that."

"You mean this?"

"Yes. I swear, I am a maid. You can inspect me if you like!"

"Kitty, there is no reason to get upset."

"You still don't trust me."

"I do trust you. It's love that is hard to trust."

"What do you mean?"

"Love is complicated. It makes us forget ourselves. I would know. I kissed Mr. Darcy quite often before we wed."

"You did?" I asked, amazed. My elder sister, who I thought, by all accounts was filled with self-control, had even given her affections before the wedding band was placed on her ring finger.

"Yes, I did."

"But it makes no difference. We all knew that you were going to get married. So, there was no harm."

"That is how I justified it. However, your feelings can lead to you falling into the same moments of weakness that I had. I don't want you to undergo that, and then find yourself abandoned the next day."

I sat down on the bed.

"Elizabeth, thank you for worrying over me. However, I have no intention of letting my love for them get that far. If it did, I would welcome you all doing everything in your power to save me from myself, but it is not this day. This day, I am as I always was. If handholding is still not a crime."

"It is not," Elizabeth said with a grin, "I am glad of that. Kitty, I know that you will not think of it now, but in the future, do your best not to fall into temptation. And if you do, please come to us. Let us help you find your way back to the right way."

"I do not see myself falling into the wrong sort of way. Even though I do not believe women are evil if they do."

"Nor do I, Kitty. But while we are in the world, I want you to walk through it and always think of us. Promise me that you will come to me if you ever find yourself falling into the ways of temptation? Kitty, give me that."

"I will."

"Good. Because Mr. Darcy also cares about your welfare, and he deserves you to care about him."

Despite that I had never thought of it in that light, that was a true observation, and it did affect me.

"I will not do anything to make you all ashamed of me. I would hate myself if I did."

She looked content at last. This was very good. She could not afford to be stressed by anything that I did. It could hurt the child within her.

I kissed her goodnight and went to my room.

I sat in bed, but I could not fall asleep.

In the heat of the moment, could I give into the temptation and let my emotions get the better of me?

I told myself that I wouldn't. For the prospect of seeing Lizzy, Jane, and Mr. Darcy be disappointed in me would be too much for me to bear.

Lydia and I had grown up to be similar in many ways.

But we had one defining difference: guilt and remorse could reach me. I felt them stir within my stomach every now and again. That was the chief thing that saved me from the worse sorts of folly. I was aware that there was always something worth fearing: repercussion.

But, under the scene of the twilight sky, when faced with the man you love...can you always control yourself?

Because, at the end of it all—whether we accept it or not—we are human. We will stumble, inevitably. And when we did, we can sometimes stumble in a big way.

I feared myself.

But I also was aware that I was all I had, when the moon rose, and my passions were awake.

Chapter Nineteen

THE FORGOTTEN FRIEND

T he next morning presented the first departure of our company.

Mary and Mr. Atkins's honeymoon had now come to an end, and they were needed to return to Hertfordshire where Mr. Atkins could maintain his duties as clerk.

Thus, we all gathered to see them depart after an early breakfast. Hugs were exchanged, and Mr. Atkins looked up at Pemberley, with a bittersweet look in his eye.

"Mr. Darcy, I could not have asked for a finer gift than to come to Pemberley for our honeymoon. I knew that the Bennets would accept me into their family, but this has only made me feel even more like I have been accepted. That is no small matter to me."

"Treat my new sister well," Darcy said, gesturing to Mary, "and we will always treat you as such."

"Oh, Mr. Darcy," Mary blushed. "That is too kind."

"I have my moments."

Mary turned to Mr. Bingley.

"Mr. Bingley, I hope you and Jane will make Godfrey into a delightful home, and we cannot wait to hear of the happiness you find in it."

"We will be, Mary," Jane said, kissing her on the cheek, "thank you."

"Sister and new brother," Mr. Bingley said, "we wish you a speedy journey, and when you can be spared of your duties, Mr. Atkins, kindly inform me, so that we can receive you both at our new home once we are settled."

"We shall," Mr. Atkins said.

Mary came up to me and kissed me on the cheek.

"You will be happy," I said. "I can see it in your eyes."

"Yes, I will be," Mary said, "and you? What are you looking for?"

"I don't know," I answered truthfully, "and that will not break my heart."

"No, I don't think it will. But believe me when I say this, Kitty. I want you to be as happy as the rest of us."

"I will be," I said, "I'm just not meant to be like the rest of you just yet. Don't worry about me, Mary. I will find my way."

"I didn't worry about you once, and I was wrong to do that. This is me caring now."

"I appreciate it. But now we are on two different paths, and you have more to care about. Take care of that husband of yours. He will want that."

"I know that you wrote to our mother and father, but is there anything else that you need to say?"

"I said everything already. Tell Aunt and Uncle Philips that we had a delightful time. And do me a favor."

"What?"

"Tell Mr. Dixon that I want him to find peace. I'm sure that he will, but still, tell him such."

"I will."

They got into the carriage, and before the door closed, Arthur went up to Atkins.

"Tell my mother and father that I love them," he requested. "No matter where I go."

"They know," Atkins assured him. "But I will tell them none-theless."

The carriage door closed, and they were off.

"I wish that I could be the son that they wanted," Arthur said to Mr. Bingley as the coach rode down the road and soon disappeared along the trees on Pemberley's estate. "But I was too much of a roaming badger."

"They know, Arthur," Bingley assured him, "not all sons and daughters are meant to stay home. If we all did, exploration would never happen, and we would never learn how big the world is."

"We don't always do right by natives when we travel to their lands," Arthur said, "but that is one thing about my parents that I always take with me and that is one thing that I can say for myself... I am a harmless roaming badger. Not everyone can say that when they leave these shores to travel to new horizons."

"Come," Elizabeth ordered, "let us go in and admit that we miss those two already."

"Very good, dearest," Darcy said, happy to go inside and each tend to our individual activities.

~

When we sat down to our dinner, we all discussed what would be done afterwards, and it would be games of cards. Once the details for the party had been discussed, Darcy turned to other matters.

"Everyone," he announced, "there is another topic to discuss."

We all turned to him, expectant.

Looking at Bingley, who nodded to him, Darcy continued.

"At the Verity Ball, as we all know, we made the acquaintance of three individuals: Mr. Henry Crawford, Miss Mary Crawford, and her fiancée, Mr. William Price. No doubt, we all are aware of the complexities of their past."

When hearing their names, we all sat up in attention. This was more interesting than we expected.

"Well, Mrs. Bingley," he said to Jane, "Elizabeth and I have been talking. I came to realize that perhaps you are right. We all have judged these people without giving them the chance to explain themselves. I cannot guarantee that they will accept, but Mrs. Darcy and I have written an invitation for them to visit Pemberley.

"Right now, they are visiting the Osbornes and when they

finish, they might not have any fixed plans. For the Osbornes told me that they were returning home afterwards, with no other engagements on the horizon. If they do not, and they accept our invitation, we shall soon receive them in a fortnight. If they cannot attend, then we can offer an invitation at another time. But perhaps, Mrs. Bingley, it was right not to be hasty in our judgments."

Jane smiled as Mr. Bingley took her hand.

"Mr. Darcy," Jane said, "you are very generous and patient with me. Thank you for comprehending my desire to…"

"Be considerate," Enara finished her sentence for her, and Jane chuckled at it.

"Well, yes. If they do accept, and you all meet them, then I think their visit might interest us all, at the very least. Mary and Mr. Price, in their hearts, are good people. And they will prove to be diverting at least. And at this time of the year, what are we humans if we do not open our hearts to others?"

"True," Bingley said, "Christmas is coming soon. And I would do best to remember that." He kissed Jane's hand. "I wonder if I am worthy of you sometimes."

"You are, I can assure you," Jane said.

Now we had something else to look forward to. The Crawfords and William Price, a naval officer, was coming to Pemberley.

That night, I dressed with care, wearing my white muslin gown, and soon our company saw the arrival of carriages down the lane once more.

We all sat in the drawing room, waiting to receive our guests.

We overheard the steward and others usher the officers inside, taking their things, and soon they were brought in.

How marvelous and pleasant an old acquaintance is to see. Some people are possessed with the natural skill at putting people at ease. Such was the case when seeing old friends from quainter times.

"Upon my word," Colonel Forster said as he entered, with

his wife on his arm. Behind him was Denny, Captain Carter, Finlay, Sanderson, Chamberlain, and a couple others. "I never thought I would have the pleasure of being invited to such a place."

"Colonel Forster," Elizabeth greeted, "Mrs. Forster! It is a pleasure to see you all again."

"Welcome to Pemberley, officers, and Mrs. Forster," Darcy said as they all bowed.

"The pleasure is all ours, I can assure you," Mrs. Forster said, "like my dearest says, this was an unexpected pleasure."

I had to tear my eyes away from Finlay, who locked eyes with mine when he entered, and focus on the rest of the company.

Elizabeth introduced the rest of the company to Georgiana, Enara and Arthur Philips. When allowed to speak, Denny rubbed his hands together, eagerly.

"Ladies of Longbourn," he said, "imagine our surprise when we discovered that we would have the opportunity to be stationed at Lambton. It was Finlay who informed us that you Bennet sisters had found the fortune to be here in Derbyshire."

"Oh, did you?" I asked Finlay, with a raised eyebrow.

"I thought it my duty to enlighten my fellow comrades in arms," Finlay responded.

"And that filled our hearts, didn't it, Sanderson?" Captain Carter asked.

"It—it did—did," Sanderson said. "In—indeed, we were over—overjoyed at the prospect of it."

"We were indeed," Colonel Forster said, "for when we left Hertfordshire, we quite despaired of never being in your company. Therefore, imagine our good fortune in discovering that England is not large enough for us to never see your lot again."

"Our apologies that you could not see us as four in number," Elizabeth augmented, "Mary and her husband, Mr. Atkins, had to return to Hertfordshire. They left just this morning."

"How unfortunate," Denny said, "I was always fond of Atkins as well."

"My cousin would have been a great addition to our party,"

Finlay said, "I didn't get the chance to speak to him enough while he was here. I didn't do well by my cousin."

"Mr. Atkins knows that you care," I assured him. "Believe me, some words are not always said, but they are meant."

Finlay smiled at me.

We all got reacquainted very briefly before dinner was announced.

To my unhappiness, I was not seated next to Finlay, but instead was placed by Mrs. Forster. I was not upset by this for very long, because I had long wanted to speak to Mrs. Forster for quite some time.

"How have you been since we last saw each other?" I asked her casually as we placed the napkins on our laps.

"I have been exceptionally well. Colonel Forster and I have been preparing to have a child for quite some time now. As I understand it, your sisters have been more successful than I."

"Never fear," I assured her, "with some women, it takes more time than others, but that does not indicate that anything is wrong."

"I am not," she assured me, "my mother and father didn't have their first child until a couple years into their marriage. I am not fretting over the matter, I assure you."

"Good. You look remarkably well, I must say."

"Oh, thank you. Your dress is very becoming."

"Thank you. Happy to see you all again, I dressed with care."

"It is nice where there are such friends to be met."

If we kept going at this rate, I would never get on. There were things that I wished to know, and I would never get anywhere if we were only being kind to each other.

"Mrs. Forster," I said, softer and quieter, "I know that it has been quite a long time, and things had become resolved, but I still wish to offer my apologies. I am sorry for the trouble that my sister, Lydia, had caused you."

"It is not your fault," she said, "but rather it was ours. I should have paid more attention when she began to speak so warmly of Wickham. Believe me when I can tell you, Miss Bennet, that if I had thought there was any veracity to the matter, then I would have told Colonel Forster, and we would not have let the problem escalate to such a degree."

"It is not your fault either, Mrs. Forster. Lydia would have done what she did, no matter what obstacles were placed before her. It all would have ended this way."

"I suppose that it would. Well! That is a great load of grief that is removed from my mind. For so long, I do not deny, that I dreaded seeing you all again."

"You did?"

"Yes. Well, Miss Bennet, you cannot imagine what it was like for me. I was the one who stressed that I wanted your sister as a companion. It was that which led to her eloping with Wickham, who was not to be trusted." She rolled her eyes. "And Wickham! There was another antagonizing aspect there. I seem to have been doomed to blindness. I thought Wickham to be a good man, and how wrong I was there as well."

"He deceived us all."

"My husband and I wish that we had been keener, more attentive. But it was carelessness. That was our crime. We did not believe that anything would happen. After all, Wickham showed no interest in your sister. Well, no more or less interest than how he talked to any other woman."

I looked at her.

"You know the truth, don't you? You know that he ran off with her just to satisfy his appetites, and that was it. He never intended to marry her."

"Yes," she admitted, "I know. We all know, in one form or another. But you have friends with us. We do not wash dirty linens in the street, especially when it comes to our friends' business. You have our confidence and our silence."

"Thank you." Across the table, I glimpsed Finlay as he looked on me. For a second, we looked at each other, but his attention was seized when Colonel Forster asked him to contribute to a story that he was telling the table. "Do you know, when you invited Lydia to Brighton with you, as your particular friend, I was quite jealous of her."

Mrs. Forster looked at me, apprehensive.

"You were? Oh, Miss Bennet, I meant no offense at all. I had never intended to slight you."

"No need to feel as if I harbor any ill feelings toward you," I assured her, "I more so say it for my own peace of mind as opposed to the disquiet of yours. It's been many months now that I not only do not regret not going to Brighton, but I am fortunate for that. I already underwent much blame for Lydia's plight. But if I had gone with you all, and Lydia had eloped, the punishment would have been more severe on me. Besides, things happened at home that I needed to face. By not inviting me, you may have accidentally saved my soul, somewhat."

"Well," Mrs. Forster said, "as humbling as it is that my lack of company helped you, I am glad that I could be of service."

"I did not mean to offend."

"No, I deserved it. I should have kept my eyes open, and I didn't. Your sister was almost ruined because of it, and you all by association. All because I didn't see matters for what they were. Colonel Forster and I felt so guilty, for so long, because we felt like we were the means through which it all came about. Believe me, Miss Bennet, I am heartily sorry for standing by and allowing Wickham and Lydia to carry on as they did. Our indifference to the situations that we were amongst was another crime to it."

"I feel like you take it too much upon yourself, but sometimes, taking responsibility, whether we ought to or not, does lead to us enhancing our character. Nothing is more rewarding than taking claim for a mistake."

"Rewarding?"

"You lose your pride at the moment, but you win yourself back by the end of it."

"Well, that is very wise."

I gave her an impish grin. "I have my moments."

We were interrupted as the rest of the group was laughing at something Colonel Forster said, and we felt that we had been left out of a stimulating discourse.

The second course came, and we became more attentive as we ate.

The evening passed with a round of cards, so all the topics

that were discussed were general ones. This left Finlay and I little to no time to speak in any sort of intimate fashion, but I was content with looking fondly at him, every now and again, from across the room.

In one particular moment, we turned to each other at the same time and our expressions were arrested by the other. From the locks of his hair, down to the bottom of his boot, I was able to take in every detail of his person. Through it all, there was not one aspect of his person that escaped my notice, and I reveled in it. By the logic of my mind, to the passions of my heart, I could know him anywhere, even if we had met for the first time. He was a marvel of a man! And for a brief moment, I told myself that I was his lady.

When it came to the end of the evening, as they were all standing up to leave, I was able to accost Finlay, who was eager to request when we might see each other again.

"I cannot come tomorrow or the day after," he said, "for I must spend the day training the new recruits that have signed on. But might I call on you in three days' time? Would that suit you?"

"It would. And I will make certain that when you come, the Colonel will be kind and make his presence not known. I think he would prefer it that way as well."

"Well," he said, his countenance losing its luster, "I shall be content with that."

Quickly, I pinched his arm.

"You had better be. I will never turn away a kind friend."

"He is kind?"

"He understands me. In the same way that you do. How can I not be grateful to such enlightenment?"

He smiled.

"I see that you could not. Nor should I ask you to."

"There you are," I said, "enlightenment. I am proud of you."

The officers and Mrs. Forster took their leave of us and rode to Lambton, the small and quaint village that proved to be large enough for them all.

Chapter Twenty

WHAT A PIECE OF WORK IS MAN

I raced to Georgiana's room, knocked on her door and burst in. Betsy was there to do her hair.

"What is the meaning of your losing your breath over?" Betsy asked as I raced up to them and plopped down on Georgiana's bed.

"Everything. Colonel Fitzwilliam comes here today."

Georgiana looked happily at me.

"You look full of spirits. That makes me happy."

"Does it?"

"Yes. After yesterday, I thought that you had preferred Lieutenant Finlay above all things. But seeing you excited now shows me that you still hold Richard in high esteem. Since he's my cousin, I naturally cannot help but prefer him for your domestic joy."

"Well, that makes sense," I said, going up to the mirror and looking at us both in it. "And yes, I am excited to see the Colonel again after so soon of leaving him, but it's because he is good company. And there is something else."

"What?"

"I woke up today and I had a resolution."

"What would that be?"

I fixed a strand of my hair.

"That there is nothing to fret over because there is nothing I can do. This whole situation is out of my hands, and all I can do is my best to keep peace and help both men maintain their inner sense of security."

I studied my reflection. "I will tell the truth, but I will do my best to keep them from disrespecting each other. However, my anxiety over the matter won't help it. It will cause only more problems. They both need my confidence now, and not my confusion. Frederick Fitzwilliam confused me enough." I looked at Georgiana. "Georgie, do me a favor."

"What?"

"If I ever do forget that, and I begin to become distraught or frantic, please slap me."

"I've never slapped anyone before. I couldn't do it, and yet, I imagine it would be a fascinating experience."

"For the one who is slapping, perhaps so," Betsy said, "but the one who is getting slapped, not so much."

When we went down to breakfast, Mr. Darcy and Mr. Bingley both said that they would not be present to meet the Colonel when he arrived. They had gone out to Godfrey Park to have the steward and housekeeper arrange for the Bingleys to settle into the place by Saint Andrew's Day.

Since Elizabeth had settled into her role as the mistress of Pemberley with the greatest of ease, he trusted that she could entertain Colonel Fitzwilliam by then.

"He comes to see you," Lizzy whispered to me as she arranged for what we should eat once the Colonel arrived. "Soon after he is settled comfortably, I will allow you a walk along the grounds, but Georgiana, Enara, and Arthur will be your chaperones."

She saw into the recesses of my mind, along with the Colonel's. I did need to speak to him, and the sooner the better.

"I hope we don't bore them," I said, referring to Enara, Arthur, and Georgie.

"I'm sure that they would keep a safe distance. If I were them, I would."

I scoffed.

"Don't you remember what it was like before you and Darcy married?"

"Yes, and I'm quite certain that we probably were as aloof about how we looked as you are with Colonel Fitzwilliam now."

She smiled at me.

"Good luck with all that."

"Thank you. I very well might need it."

Soon we saw the familiar form of a particular Colonel riding down the road toward Pemberley, with a large haversack slung over his shoulder. From the window, I saw him, with Georgiana and Enara staring at him over my shoulder.

We all couldn't help but giggle.

"He couldn't even wait a week before he joined us again," Enara pointed out, "being lovesick is a timeless ache, isn't it?"

"It does have a habit of driving us mad from time to time," I voiced, "and I can't help but run mad with it. I was hoping Richard and Finlay would be stronger than me."

"We all have a tendency to be as human as the rest."

"Yes. I have to remember that about them."

When he rode up to the front of the house, I was seized by my rashness.

"Do you think that I would be wrong to run out and see him?"

"You won't if we all go with you," Georgiana supported. Their camaraderie fortified me, and we all rushed down the steps, passed Arthur, who grabbed Enara's arm.

"Dearest, what do you do?" he asked.

"Colonel Fitzwilliam is here," Enara replied, hastily, "and three is the perfect number to make it look like general enthusiasm."

He looked at her, confused, as she ran after us. We all emerged from the front door, and we stood at the top steps just as Colonel Fitzwilliam dismounted and a groundskeeper took his horse from him.

When seeing us, his eyes lit up and he removed his hat.

"You are happy to see the man who followed after your company like I was a lost journeyman," he said, "and then you look at me as if you haven't seen me in years. If this is not a tremendous welcoming, then I don't know what is."

"We haven't been away from you for more than a week, and

you can't be without us," Georgiana greeted him, laughing. "Richard, I cannot believe your eagerness."

"Every now and again, I can surprise you," he said, coming up to us. "Would Mrs. Reynolds put up with my company being thrust on her?"

"She misses you, so you know the answer to that."

"Come," I finally said at last, "you must not leave her in suspense, cousin."

"Suspense," he said, "cousin Kitty, we don't call each other that enough, now do we?"

"No, we don't. We are always lacking in some sort of protocol, don't we?"

"Yes. Never fear, we shall find our way back again."

Once more, his eyes were filled with that familiar gentleness that became him. It said: 'I adore you, but I shall do nothing about it. Now enough. Enough for now'.

"Come," Georgiana said, "let us bring you inside and greet you properly."

"Yes. This is Pemberley, and I have to keep to the rules."

We walked inside and Arthur was standing there, awaiting us.

"Very few could stir the ladies to not wait for a new arrival in the drawing room," Arthur said. "Welcome back to our company, Colonel."

Both gentlemen greeted each other, friendly, and then we walked to the drawing room, where Lizzy and Jane were awaiting us.

As we did, Arthur moved alongside Enara, speaking to her in confidence.

"Would you run that quickly to greet me?" he asked, a little bitterly.

"My love, you must let me be a proper friend to your cousin. Since your family likes me, I'm going to do what I can to keep it so. Believe me, when you are a new bride, there is nothing more relieving than having a family who likes you. I'm not going to lose that for my life."

She kissed his hand and Arthur had to see the logic of that.

When we met Elizabeth and Jane in the drawing room, Lizzy had no choice but to play on the Colonel's obsessive need to see us.

"Colonel," she said, "it's a pleasure to see you again. I swear, it is as if we only saw you a week ago. Oh wait!"

We all laughed.

"I deserve your laughter," Colonel Fitzwilliam said, not offended in the slightest, "in fact, I am happy that I was not met with worse when I arrived."

"Jokes are made at your expense, only because we are aware that you have the skill to withstand it," Jane offered, to be kind to him.

"Well, if a man can lead soldiers into battle, he better be able to see his actions defined as they ought to be. Mrs. Darcy and Mrs. Bingley, thank you so much for entertaining the eccentricities of this wayward soldier."

"You are most welcome," Elizabeth responded. "We have arranged for a nice meal for you, and when you are done, I assumed that maybe you wished to see to your horse. This will be adequate, because Kitty, along with Mr. and Mrs. Philips, might enjoy seeing my husband's assortment of stallions."

"I would be delighted," Colonel Fitzwilliam said.

As we walked to the dining room, once more I was near Arthur and Enara. They didn't notice me behind them as they were whispering to each other.

"I never expressed interest in visiting the stables," Arthur whispered to her.

"Just play along. There is romance to be found here."

"Out of curiosity, which man do you favor for Kitty?"

"I don't know. Each time, I decide on one man for her, the other one does something to strengthen his suit."

"This is a very confusing matter."

"I know."

We all sat down to eat together.

After we ate, Enara, Georgiana, Arthur, and I did indeed make our way to the stables, escorted by Colonel Fitzwilliam.

Being ever so kind to me, the three of them remained ahead,

with Georgiana telling them of the first mare she ever was given, while Colonel Fitzwilliam and I lagged.

Rather than begin with pleasantries, I realized that it was proper just to get to the heart of the matter. For, with the men in my life, improper always seemed to be the *most* proper.

"You couldn't help yourself, could you?" I inquired.

He gave me an arched look.

"Why, Kitty, I do not know what you are talking about."

"We haven't been away from you for a week before you come upon us again. You know what you are about, sir. Do not bother to deny it. I will haunt you like a harpy the entire time if you do not own to it."

"Very well. I wanted to see you."

"This is most inconvenient. I am supposed to be using this time to recover from my affection for you."

"Oh, that was your plan?"

"Yes, it was. I may not have said as much, however, I flatter myself that you sensed my intentions."

"Perhaps I did."

I moved ahead of him, turned around and walked backwards so that I could face him.

"Come now, old friend," I said, "unveil yourself to me. I never have held back what was in the recesses of my mind. Therefore, do me the courtesy of knowing what is in yours."

"Very well. With you, I have no choice but to be open, don't I?"

"Discretion and concealment do not become us. We tried it once, remember? And it led to us confounding each other. I would have it that we did not hurt each other again."

"That makes you better than me," he said, sighing as he pulled up his glove, which had been slipping from his hand.

"Are you about to hurt me?" I asked.

"Yes, I am."

I stopped walking and looked worried.

"How so?" I asked. "Did we not part as friends?"

"We must keep walking, or I will look as if I killed your cat."

Obeying, I continued to walk along, but I was no more or less wary of what he might say.

"You were right to begin to release me from your sentiments," he continued, "for I know everything."

"Everything?"

"From what my mother said to you, to the ball, and how my brother spoke to you. My family has forced you to endure many verbal and mental trials, and I apologize for that. One thing about my brother is that, every now and again, he stumbles on wisdom. He was right to be wary at us attaching ourselves to each other. The demon."

"Yes, Frederick is that. I do not wish to offend your family."

"I am not offended. For all his merits, I have called him worse, and he deserves it. Despite the better sides of himself."

"So far, you have not hurt me."

"I do. Just not in the manner that you think."

"How so?"

"This should be a time of recovery for you. To rise above the dilemma that has been placed on you. And yet, I cannot abide it. The idea of you moving away from your love for me is not something which I welcome. I am not ready to release you just yet."

"Richard...is your selfish wickedness emerging again?"

"Well, yes, if you must know. I still pray for a miracle that may never come. I cannot forsake the idea of you going too far away from me and not longing to see me. So, no, I do not want to release you from my feelings. Kitty, I will not suffer it."

I sighed.

"And now here we are." I looked at him, trying to hide the bitterness I felt. "Do you know what is so very hard? That no matter how much that action of yours can hinder my recovery, I cannot be angry with you. I cannot help but ignore every advice that is given to us, I find logic to be my enemy, and I am willing to sacrifice the peace in my heart, and just give into your way of thinking."

"This is what you feel?"

"Yes, if you must know. I wish I knew how to release you and set you down for pushing your company on me. I really ought to."

"But you cannot," he concluded, evidently self-satisfied.

"No, I cannot. Richard, I despise the power you have over me."

"Do you?"

"Well, yes, if you must know. You could act purely out of your own selfishness, and I would still find you charming. I would praise your flaws. I would willingly blind myself to the harm they can cause. In these moments, I realize just how young and irresponsible that I am."

"And why is that?"

"When you don't know how to say no to someone, then you are not in the most mature place to be. I cannot say no to you, and that bothers me."

"It does not bother me at all, but rather, my own weakness and wickedness are things I find myself to adhere to. I am selfish in my love for you. I do not like the notion of you not being at my side, I dream of nights we could spend together—in my bed."

My heart skipped a beat. All the time that we had known each other, we expressed our preference for each other, but never had we voiced the desires of the flesh.

I was human, so naturally, I had thought of that.

Colonel Fitzwilliam was human, therefore, he naturally thought of it.

Finlay was human, so of course, he had thought of it. To the point where he needed to go to London to satisfy his appetites.

In the depths of the night, I imagined being held by both men separately. But this was the first time those desires were voiced in such a way.

"And," Colonel Fitzwilliam continued, "I do not want to release you yet, Kitty. I will have you in my life, even when I am causing damage. I will dream of you in my bed, in my arms. With your body pressed against mine. That is my dream, and I will not release you from it."

"I should be angry with you."

"But you are not."

"You knew the answer even before I said it."

"Precisely. You and I are of one mind. Sometimes, our weaker sides get the better of us."

"I was hoping that I was getting stronger. That I was learning to improve."

"And now here I come, dragging you down. And what is sad, Kitty, is that I know that I should have never come. I know that I am confusing you by keeping myself in your life. But here I am, unable to do the right thing." He looked at me narrowly. "It would be easier if you could find yourself able to hate me, wouldn't it?"

"Yes. It would be." I smiled at him. "I do not like being so easily within your power. But I suppose, if I were to be in any other man's power, it would be harder. At least it is with you. No matter what, dear Richard, I will always be happy when you grace us with your presence."

He offered me his arm, and I took it.

"We are each other's blessing and each other's bane, aren't we?" I asked him.

"That's what love is."

"Pure Inferno?"

"Yes. Pure inferno."

Now where have I heard this argument before?

When we reached the stables, we saw some magnificent horses that were there. When going, I was beginning to wonder why we never toured the stables before. Each horse was spectacular, and the care that was given to them was interesting.

Even Enara and Arthur, who was not inclined to come before, quickly began to marvel at the stallions and marcs that were in each stall. As Georgiana had some stablemen pull some of them out, Enara confessed that she had never mastered the idea of riding. Arthur and Georgiana encouraged her to take up the activity since they were going to remain longer in Derbyshire.

While they were enjoying themselves, Colonel Fitzwilliam took me over to his new horse. It turned out that he had two stallions. The one I had become acquainted with before had broken its tendon in his leg. This new one was named Leonidas, and he was a magnificent black horse. Stunning to a fold.

"Do you miss your other horse?" I asked Colonel Fitzwilliam as I patted Leonidas along its neck.

"Oh, I do. But he deserved a rest in green pastures. After all, he had borne me through many a danger." A stable hand gave Colonel Fitzwilliam a bag of apples, and he began to feed Leonidas. "But Leonidas here, is proving to be quite the impressive substitute."

"I always marvel at how sturdy and brave warhorses have to be."

"Especially since we use them to convey us to our own conflicts."

"Richard, I don't mean to sound critical or condescending, but do you ever wonder that we are not correct for making them endure that? Using them on farms and for transport is one thing, for when doing so, we often care for them as much as we care for ourselves, and they are not put in danger over it. But where there are conflicts on the rise, after all, battles and wars are not their province, but ours. Why should we put them through that?"

"You ask a question that not many people ask themselves."

"Do you ever ask that?"

"I do, but I admit that I did not consider such compassion to animals when I was your age. To me, they were a function, worthy of care, consideration, and kindness, but that was it. It took me a while to overcome a mentality that many of my kind are born into."

"What mentality is that?"

"The 'I am man, all animals are meant to serve me' concept. We are all raised to think in that manner. It wasn't until I read the words of William Wilberforce that I began to see things in a different light."

"Well, your logic was a natural one. Until him, not many people questioned those animals deserved such care and compassion."

"It reminds one of how much of our lives are shaped by the prejudices that we are taught when we are young," he observed.

"Oh yes," I said, rolling my eyes. I took an apple from the bag and fed it to Leonidas. He took it gently and I felt the velvety texture of his muzzle. "No child can grow up without the world tainting all their virtues in some way. It's not fair. For we are not even given a chance to be better from the very beginning. There is always some wrong idea that mars our education, if we are given one."

"Even the effects of education can be detrimental, because often history does not tell the full story. You ever hear the story of the Indian woman, Pocahontas?"

"Oh yes! When I first heard of her, I was fascinated."

"I don't care what anyone says here. Until we get her actual story of what happened to her, we don't know the full story."

"You don't believe the stories of John Smith's and John Rolfe's exploits with her?"

"Never believe explorers who are going to a new land to hide what they are really doing. They say what the royalty needs to hear to keep funding them. That's one bit of advice that I cannot stress enough, Kitty. I've learned never to order you around, but please, listen to me on this. When it comes to history, until you are well aware of both sides' account to things, always assume that there is something you are not being told. There is always something not being told."

"You would make a suspicious woman out of me," I said, teasingly.

"No, I am making you informed. Never blindly follow anyone who has an agenda that they wish you to follow, that you never actually see. That's how you make the biggest mistake of your life."

"Did age make you this wise?" I asked. "I don't deny that you are right, in this case."

"Not as much age as experience. I've blindly followed people before, never questioned anything, and just went along with the wills of others. Sometimes, that is the right thing to do, but most of the time, I resulted in being the largest fool in England. I don't want you to have to walk the path that I did."

"Still protecting me, eh?" I asked.

"Always," he assured me.

"Well, I am not the sort to not appreciate a slice of wonderful advice when it's given to me in the proper way." He was on one side of the horse, and I was on the other. I reached my hand over Leonidas's back, and he took it. "Thank you for coming. Maybe I did need you here."

He smiled.

As I removed my hand from his, I placed it on Leonidas's shoulder.

Suddenly, an idea came to me.

"Richard, can you teach me how to look after a horse?"

This sudden change in tone and subject startled him temporarily. But soon, his thoughts shifted, and he was happy.

"I would like that. Why this sudden interest?"

"I don't know. But for some reason, I just realized the sort of woman that I am."

"And what does that mean?"

"I never learned to acquire talent, but I can learn practicality. Learning how to look after horses might help me in life. I could be of use. I want to have a little bit of purpose. I think you would find me to be an apt pupil. Horses are not like books of study; they don't bore me. Besides, you were already educating me at Matlock. Just continue the lessons."

He chuckled.

"Well, I won't be here for more than a fortnight. You must set up a portion of each day for my lessons."

Suddenly, I remembered what I had to tell him. He was still quite ignorant on the current situation. Now I could not refrain from telling him any longer. He must know!

"Richard," I said, "I can perhaps give you mornings, or every other day in afternoons. The other portion of my days will be spent in going to Lambton or expecting visits here...from Lieutenant Finlay."

I told Colonel Fitzwilliam everything about the current situation. I knew there was nothing to fear, because the Colonel would understand, and he did.

When I finished, he was compassionate.

"All this time, you have teetered between Finlay and my company," he observed, "and now, both worlds have collided in upon you."

"Yes. For the first instance, you both occupy the same space and time."

"My coming has made it more complicated. Kitty, I am sorry."

"It's not your fault. You did not know. I will not have you despise yourself, or him, just because of how the situation has presented itself."

"Would it be easier for you if I left Pemberley?"

"If it will make you happy, then do so. I know the awkwardness that this situation can present. However, Richard, you ought not to be driven away just because there is someone here who it might be awkward to meet. Let us just organize it all so that you and he will rarely ever see each other. If you never meet, that might be a nice bit of luck."

Colonel Fitzwilliam considered this.

"Thank you. I do not believe in retreating for such reasons. I promise you this; I will do everything in my power to refuse to let any verbal or physical altercations present themselves. If avoiding each other will help, then I see the logic of me sharing your company with his."

I pulled at a strand of his hair.

"I knew that you would understand. Give me a chance to believe in you, and you always will."

Soon, we were come upon by Georgiana.

"You both," she urged, "forgive me, but I have stalled enough. I have run out of ways to occupy our cousins and give us all leave to return to the house."

We sighed. Poor Georgiana. She knew what she had been used for.

Once the Colonel was situated, he and I returned to the stables, and he began to show me how to tend to Leonidas. It was actually quite stimulating. We continued our lessons that had begun at Matlock, but this time, it was more in depth. He was also teaching me how to tend to a horse's health, what to look out for when it was running, and how to clean its hooves. There were always stablemen nearby, so we were never alone.

We maintained this attitude until a servant informed us that Darcy and Bingley had returned.

When we went in, we met everyone briefly, before I was ordered to go and dress for dinner.

Before we sat down to eat, there was merriment when Mr. Bingley delivered his news.

"The transition for the move is now underway and should be completed by the end of the week," Bingley announced to Jane. "My love, very soon, we shall be near neighbors to Pemberley and soon you shall be mistress to Godfrey Park!"

Chapter Twenty-One

A COLONEL & A LIEUTENANT

The next day, Lieutenant Finlay woke up well before his officers—which was his tradition. One of his habits was always to be awake and prepared before any of the officers ever roused from their beds.

This was one of the reasons for which Colonel Forster always abided Finlay's stoic demeanor in the past; the man was a superlative lieutenant who cared for his fellow officers.

While he was walking through the quarters, he was monitoring—it was a subtle way in which he made certain that no officers were entertaining female company in the quarters.

For the saying may have gone 'boys will be boys', but Finlay was not in the mood to have the officers be judged under a generalization, give into the tedious reputation of ruining an innocent girl's virtue—a standard and belief that often is tied down to a regiment whenever they arrive in a new place.

When they were in Hertfordshire, Wickham's wickedness led to them suffering under giving the regiment a lasting impression of a collection of men who came, upset the lives of all the young women in a county, and then left with chaos in their wake. He didn't want to leave any maids being manipulated and then abandoned anymore.

Therefore, when he was satisfied that there was no foul

behavior committed, he would return back to his quarters, have a proper bath and then would begin the day.

Soon training began and he was sent to prepare a special guard unit, to increase their firing speed, when he was called away by Captain Carter.

When taken away from his duties, Carter did his best to explain a situation that he wasn't knowledgeable about himself.

"I'll maintain the training," Carter said, "but I don't know why you are being sent to the Colonel's study."

"Am I in trouble?" Finlay asked. "When last I looked, I didn't do anything worthy of punishment."

"I heard nothing about that, however, I do not believe that you did anything. There was another officer with him, from a different regiment, but I am ignorant as to the rest."

Carter looked at Finlay.

"You feel as if you are a student at school and as if you are being sent to the Headmaster's library, don't you?"

"That's precisely how I feel. Very well, it is best to get on with it." He handed the training over to Carter and went to the Colonel's headquarters. When he entered, it was to see Colonel Forster leaning over his desk, talking with a colonel. The Colonel's back was to Finlay, so when the stranger turned to him, Finlay wondered at being summoned.

"Ah," Colonel Forster said, "Finlay!"

"Carter told me that I was summoned, sir. Is something wrong?"

"No. You were simply called because introductions were requested on the Colonel's part here."

Finlay turned to the officer, and he took in his frame, his dark brown hair, his regular and somewhat plain features, as well as the fact that they both had a similar build. The man had a kind face, and yet Finlay had a strange sense of foreboding. There was something about the man that gave him a feeling of dread.

"Finlay," Colonel Forster said, "allow me to introduce Colonel Fitzwilliam of the 43rd Calvary son of the Earl of Matlock. He only recently arrived and is staying with his cousin, Mr. Darcy, of Pemberley."

Finlay's expression turned to a subtle dread.

Now it was happening!

Everything that Kitty managed to avoid.

All that fate had done to spare him from, and it was presented thus.

Even time usually had been his friend and always kept both gentlemen apart.

But now, all of that had been thwarted, dashed against the rocks, and come undone, because of one Colonel's will. After all, he had been the one to seek out Finlay. This Colonel had intentionally done what he did not expect: go out of his way to meet him.

"Colonel Fitzwilliam," Colonel Forster said, "this is my lieutenant, Finlay."

Both men stared at each other for a few seconds before Colonel Fitzwilliam was the first to remember himself.

"Sir," Colonel Fitzwilliam said, bowing to Finlay.

"Good day, sir," Lieutenant Finlay said, bowing as well, and trying to maintain his composure. "Rarely am I in the company of an earl."

"Alas, you are still not. I am but a younger son, and that title shall go to my brother when the time comes. I will remain like you, merely an officer."

Colonel Fitzwilliam turned to Colonel Forster.

"Colonel Forster, would you be so kind as to grant me a private audience with your lieutenant?"

Colonel Forster agreed to this, informed Finlay and Fitzwilliam that Finlay could only be spared for no more than half an hour before he returned to his duties. Fitzwilliam agreed to this, and the Colonel left them alone.

There they were.

Both men standing, face to face, at last.

And with one look, it became very evident to each that they were aware of the other's history, of their mutual love for Kitty, and that they were too combative men who vied for the same lady's hand.

How was this to end?

~

"Well," Colonel Fitzwilliam began, realizing that since he was the one to begin this confrontation, he ought to try and regulate it, "you are Lieutenant Finlay."

"I am indeed, sir. And you are Colonel Fitzwilliam. Forgive me, but I am of the impression that perhaps you and I are well aware of each other."

"Your impressions speak true. We are two men in love with the same worthy woman. How does that make you feel?"

Finlay looked surprised and perturbed.

"What is it?" Colonel Fitzwilliam asked.

"Forgive me, but I simply did not think you would care for my opinion. After all, in the eyes of the world, you are of more consequence than me."

"Oh, none of that," Colonel Fitzwilliam said, swiping the air with his hand, dismissively. "I am the son of an earl, but what of it? At the end of the day, we are two men, two officers under his majesty's service, and I want to believe that we can think well of each other."

"I want to, sir," Finlay said eagerly, "believe me, I wish that I had the power to not greet you with such apprehensions and dread. Yet, I feel it, nonetheless."

Finlay walked to the other side of the room, with his hands clasped behind his back as he looked out of the window.

"Colonel, I speak as I do now, not out of disrespect, but so that you shall know me better. Do you know what is bizarre?" Finlay asked.

"What?"

"I had hoped you were something horrible. That you were a rude man, base, vulgar, or rakish. A man must tell himself these things when he is not the only one in a woman's heart."

"I will not deny that I regretted your ability to find your way into her heart as well. We tell ourselves what we must, until the reality has no choice but to knock on our door."

"As you do with me now. You are not a villain, are you, Colonel?"

"I never met a person who wasn't. But I want to believe that I control all my demons. Can you say such for yourself, Lieutenant?"

"Normally I do control my baser nature, but it does present itself from time to time. Especially where love is involved. Colonel, before we go any further, I want to expressly inform you that I do love Kitty. I implore you to think nothing rattle or rakish about me. I must appear to you as being rash in romance, but my feelings are steady. This is no weak or flimsy inclination. It is merely that..."

"You have not the means, money, or security to marry her yet."

"Well, yes. That is the main conundrum, in my situation. You speak like a familiar. Kitty informed me that we are similar in that way."

"Yes, we are. And thus, it leads to us having to question what will happen now? Well, I know the answer."

"Do you?"

"Nothing."

"Nothing?"

"Yes. That is the answer. Neither of us is ready to offer ourselves to her, while wishing her to be devoted to us. In that way, we are *not* in control of our demons."

"Yes, I suppose, in that way, I am not the best creature in the world."

"Neither am I."

~

Fitzwilliam analyzed Finlay's character, and the more he observed him, the more he was able to assess that Finlay's love for Kitty was as profound as his. What was even worse for him to experience was the fact that Finlay had a stronger claim to Kitty.

First, he was Kitty's first grand love, having access to her emotions long before Colonel Fitzwilliam ever came into her life. The effect of a first true affection leaves a mark on the soul that is hard to replace.

Second, Finlay was different than the Colonel. Both men loved Kitty Bennet on an equal and sincere level. Yet, he suspected that Finlay's love for Kitty was like the rocks beneath; there was a heavy weight to it. Kitty, being a woman of eager sensibility, would have no choice but to feel the sensation of that, and willingly carry that 'weight' around with her, for the rest of her life.

"Colonel," Finlay said, "I must ask this, sir, despite knowing that I am being very impertinent. Do you despise me?"

"How can I? We just met."

"You and I both know that our situation is a strange one. It's a tale as old as time, but it is strange, nevertheless. A natural resentment is to be expected. Forgive my baseness."

"You do not offend me, because this is something that you and I need to address. I came here, today, expressly to make your acquaintance. I did this for the desire to inform you of our situation, and what we must do in the future. We are men of the King's service, and I will expect us both to act like it. You and I love the same woman, and there is nothing for it. I do not want her to suffer from some archaic rivalry that occurs when two people have the same love interest. We are officers, and we must be seen as perfect, and as shining examples for the officers that we command. We... I would like it if we respected each other."

Now it was Finlay's turn to dissemble Colonel Fitzwilliam's character.

Not only had all ugly images of the Colonel escaped his mind, but rather he had to accept that his rival was a worthy sort of character, an amiable man, and that Kitty had no choice but to let him into her heart. Especially after Finlay's absence from her life left Kitty with a profound sense of loss. If anyone were to enter her life and fill it up, it would be this gentleman. Truly!

There is nothing so very antagonizing like having no choice but to respect the person who your instincts wanted you to despise. Sometimes it is much easier to go through life despising someone, no matter how irrational it is. Logic, reason, and impartiality has no choice but to eventually have its way.

"Sir," Lieutenant Finlay said at last, "I am honored that you respected me enough to consider the pains this may have on me and did not think it your place to order me away from Kitty's side."

"You worried that I was a tyrant."

"In the eyes of this society, you are my superior in more ways than one. Forgive me for making generalizations, but it is very easy to assume that you will be met with someone who orders you from your love's side. Especially if both men prefer the same woman. We men can be reduced to our savage instincts to chase the other man away."

"Yes, we cannot help but be the animals that we are, sometimes."

"I wish to make it very evident that I meant no offense in my assumption. I know I ought to have regarded you as a gentleman immediately."

"I wish you had, but I understand why you did not. I've seen quite a few men be in the predicament we are in now. I told myself that I would never put myself in their situation, but here we are. But from what I have seen before, with those other occurrences, the situation unfolded in the precise way that you predicted. One thought themselves superior to the other. They bullied them into avoiding the lady. Injustice ensued on one side, pride on the other, and then the eventual quarrel and fight in a tavern. Yes, the predicament is rote and tedious."

"And I don't want to go through that. I have accepted that, if Kitty were to love another, you are a gentleman."

"She adores you. As much as that hurts to say."

"And she cannot let go of you. As much as that hurts to say it. You offer a mutual respect for each other, and I will take it. That's a lot, coming from me."

"And that is a lot. Coming from me."

"I'm sorry that our predicament makes it impossible for us to be comrades. Under a happier star, I would have wanted to loyally serve under you."

"And I would have known that I would have had a devoted lieutenant."

"But in the meantime, sir, what do we do now? We shall often wish to be in her company, but I don't want us to antagonize each other."

"And that was the main reason for my coming. I will be here for but a fortnight before I return to my regiment. I am aware that a lot can happen within a fortnight. Especially when three lovers are involved. Kitty plans to visit some of her older friends in the regiment. Would it be easier if, when one wishes to visit her, the other makes themselves scarce and find other things to occupy their time? It was her idea, and she is right. Of course, we have to spend our time with her equally, where one is not given more days than the other. That is the closest to fair that I can muster up."

"It is a proper arrangement. If the officers are invited to dine at Pemberley again, while you are still in the county, then I will make my excuses."

"Thank you," Colonel Fitzwilliam replied, grateful, "that would mean a great deal to me."

"It is all I can give, for I have nothing else to sell you."

Colonel Fitzwilliam stood up.

"Well, this could have gone worse."

"Yes, sir. It could have."

Both men bowed to each other.

"With any luck," Finlay finalized, "we will not tax each other, and be in each other's company for as little as possible."

"Hopefully, fortune will be on our side."

Both men parted ways, happy that they had reached a mutual respect, while equally dissatisfied that they could no longer despise the other.

Chapter Twenty-Two
LIKE KIN & LIKE KIND

Happily, Jane, Lizzy, Enara, Georgiana, and I rode in our carriage to Lambton.

"Unbelievable," I realized. "Our Aunt Gardiner was raised here, and yet I am so unfamiliar with the place that she was brought up."

"This place also has a wonderful claim on my heart," Elizabeth informed me.

"How so?"

"It is the place that we stayed in when Mr. Darcy paid us a visit when we were journeying throughout Derbyshire."

"Oh, I had forgotten about that."

As we drove into town, we passed an inn and Elizabeth informed us that it was the precise place they stayed in when Mr. Darcy called on them and the Gardiners, and Georgiana had met them for the first time.

"I was so nervous," Georgiana professed, "when I first met you and the Gardiners, I wanted to jump out of my shoes. Also, the fact that I was still fatigued from traveling also weighed me down."

When we reached the officers' headquarters at the lodge, we were happy to speak with the Colonel and Mrs. Forster again. However, for Enara and Georgiana, there were new acquaintances to be met.

"Kitty, and Mrs. Darcy and Mrs. Bingley!" Mrs. Warrens cried. When she and the other three knowing women entered, with their husbands at their sides, I ran across the room to greet them, with my arms outstretched. We all met so very happily, and really were a merry party.

"You missed us," Mrs. O'Connor cried. "If that is not the sight of a woman who has been without her friends for long enough, I don't know what is."

"You don't know what it's like to see you lot again," I declared, giddy.

"Well," Mrs. Barrett said, "if Mrs. Forster had thought to do the wise thing and brought you with us to Brighton, instead of Mrs. Wickham, then we would have had a longer acquaintance."

"Don't talk like that," Mrs. Hawkins chided her.

"I speak as you do."

"Yes, but what I mean is do not speak like that in public. Wait till we are behind closed doors and there is no one to overhear."

"Why should I care for what anyone else thinks, pray?"

"You sound like my mother," I said, laughing.

"I do? Oh dear." That was enough to make her sensitive toward her resonance. Then again, there is something to be said for people sometimes bringing the truth to light in so public a manner. Sometimes, things need to be confronted.

"Well," I assured them, "be as you wish. Only let me introduce you to my sister-in-law and cousin."

"Would they think themselves too highly to speak to us?" Mr. O'Connor asked.

"Never fear. One of them is from New South Wales."

"Oh," Mr. Warrens acknowledged, "that's good. They are willing to talk to anyone who is respectable."

I turned to Georgiana and Enara.

"Come," I pressed. "I would like you to get to know more friends of mine."

Enara and Georgiana came over and soon made their acquaintance. Mrs. Warrens and the other three knowing women were of the age where they understood conversation and how to execute it properly. Soon, Enara and Georgiana grew comfortable around them.

Jane and Lizzy were also happy to see them again and we spoke as if nothing had changed. To them, we were still the ladies of Longbourn, and to us, they were still the four knowing women who were the soldiers' wives.

"Oh, you should have been there when we heard that the young Miss Lydia Bennet had run off with that perfidious Wickham," Mrs. Warrens said while we all sat in their living quarters. They had invited us in, and though the room was small, we all could fit in it. Tea was set around to all, and the wives had no impulse to check their subject matter. And it made sense. They never were in a scene or situation where they needed to hold their tongue, so they were happy to finally tell us all they had felt on that fateful day: that day where one fallen sister threatened to disrupt Longbourn forever.

"Mrs. Wickham may be an amiable girl," Mrs. Barrett said, "but her behavior shows that sometimes a good-humored disposition can easily lead to empty headedness. Oh, forgive me, Mrs. Darcy, Mrs. Bingley, and Kitty, but I have to speak my mind. Lydia would not see reason, no matter how much we tried to warn her."

"Warn her?" Elizabeth asked, squinting. "You knew about her infatuation with Wickham?"

"Knew it, marked it, and forewarned it," Mrs. O'Connor elaborated. "At first, we just thought it was mere infatuation. Nothing serious, you know. After all, many girls shared a similar fancy to him, but usually, once they realized that he was full of hot air, and no more, then usually they relinquished any designs on him, and were smart enough to look elsewhere."

"We thought the same would occur with Lydia," Mrs. Hawkins said.

"It seemed natural," Mrs. Warrens added.

"Terribly natural," Mrs. Barrett said.

"Natural as can be," Mrs. O'Connor concurred. "But that's not what happened."

"Not what happened at all," Mrs. Warrens uttered.

"Quite the contrary, sadly," Mrs. Barrett sighed, shaking her head.

"Lydia went in the other direction," Mrs. Hawkins continued.

Elizabeth gave Georgiana a sympathetic eye, and I leaned into her.

"Is this talk hurting you?" I whispered.

"At another time, it would have been," Georgiana whispered back, "but rather, I am actually very interested in what they have to say. Let them talk, and don't discourage them." She turned to Elizabeth and subtly nodded a 'I am well, do not disturb' expression.

"She really believed his charm to be sincere, despite that he never did much to encourage her," Mrs. Warrens uttered.

"So, we tried to warn her," Mrs. Hawkins said.

"That Mr. Wickham did not especially care for her at all," Mrs. Barrett said.

"But she wouldn't listen to us," Mrs. O'Connor said.

"No, she would have her own way and believe as she will," Mrs. Warrens compiled. "Well, I remember what it was like being that age. All the mistakes that you make. That is why it is always best to have a mother around to watch everything, and then to have a father around to scare the pernicious suitor off."

"That was the only thing that I do not blame Lydia for," Mrs. Hawkins said, "she had none of that. Even if Mr. Bennet were there, I do not see him as the man who would challenge such a man as Wickham. Forgive me, dears! Or am I mistaken?"

Jane, Lizzy, and I looked at each other.

"Well," Jane voiced at last, "however he once was, I am quite certain that he has greatly improved since Lydia's situation. He cares for our welfare more now."

"We speak vulgarly," Mrs. O'Connor said, "we must do better."

"Yes, we will do better," Mrs. Barrett said.

"We must be more mannerly," Mrs. Hawkins said.

"We don't want to chase you off," Mrs. Warrens said, "we will be genteel from now on. How has the weather been while you were away? I hope the roads were dry."

"Yes, they were," Elizabeth responded, "exceedingly so. There were no carriages being overturned. And how has the weather been in Lambton since we were away?"

"Oh, traditional English weather for this time of year."

"People often despise the heat in the summer when it gets oppressive," Mrs. O'Connor said, "but I don't care. I miss it every winter."

We all agreed.

Suddenly, Mr. Barrett entered, we all stood, greeted him, he sat down on the other side of the room—which was not large—opened the gazette and began to read it.

Since he entered, he was able to detect an awkward silence that filled the room. The poor man! It was not his fault at all, but he evidently thought it was such. He lowered his paper.

"I suppose I should leave," he said. "My mistake for being the bad omen in the room."

"It's not your fault, Mr. Barrett," I explained, "we had been getting along charmingly—and by that, I mean that we were talking about improper things—then we decided to be proper and now we don't know what to say to each other."

"Kitty," Elizabeth chided me.

"Oh, it's not her fault," Mr. Barrett said, "rarely are things worth talking about *worth anything* when it comes to conversation that anyone cares to hear. What is proper is boring."

"Uncle Philips sounds like you," I said, happy that he defended me.

"I know. I miss that stuffy old man—I don't care what anyone says, men like him are what England is best to be made of."

"I agree," Mrs. Barrett said, "Mr. Barrett, every week, you think of something clever to say."

"Does this now give me leave to not say anything else clever for the rest of the week?"

"Sorry, my dear. But no."

He sighed—amused.

We all laughed at that.

Laughter—a family trait when it came to us Bennets.

~

While our visit was nearing its end, I looked out of the window and I saw a familiar figure popping along, down below. She was carrying a reed basket of laundry, and I don't know why I was surprised.

"Samantha!"

"Oh," Jane said, coming over to the window, "isn't that the washerwoman that you befriended?"

"Yes, it is! I must go down to see her." I turned to the others, excused myself, said that I would return in ten minutes, and rushed out of the room.

Dashing down the steps, I eventually made it out of the quarters, moved around to the side yard, and there she was.

Her back was to me as she was pinning clothes on the clothesline, along with two other washerwomen. Despite the cold air, the clothes still would dry better there than in a cellar. The sun would bleach the whites...how did I remember that?

Her height tallish, and her figure wonderfully plumb, she was precisely as I wished to remember her as.

"Samantha!" I cried.

When hearing my voice, Samantha turned around and smiled broadly.

I rushed to her, fell into her arms and she gave me a warm hug.

"Oh, my dear!" Samantha cried. "I wondered when you would find your way back to us."

We were reunited.

"Would you believe it? I never thought I'd see you all again. And here you are, all the same. Oh, let me help you."

"That's another thing I missed about you."

I helped her hang up the clothes, and we talked all the while.

"I thought," Samantha began, "that with you now being even fancier than before—with you already being a gentleman's daughter—and now being a Pemberley resident, that you would not want to be seen with the likes of me."

"First, don't underestimate me in that way," I assured her, "I no longer am puffed about by the world's whims. I've grown more robust—even though I still cough from time to time." She laughed at that. "What I mean is... I'm not as afraid of the world as I once was. Therefore, no one can tell me who I can and cannot talk to. Also, I was the one who chose to fall in love with a poor lieutenant—and the world would not consider him to be the best match. If I am brave enough for that sort of love, I'm brave enough to talk with the person who does laundry for those I respect, don't you think?"

She half-smiled at me.

"I was worried that you would not want to talk of that matter."

"Well, there is no point. After all, I am pretty much aware that you all know of how I felt."

"We knew, even before you did."

I looked pointedly at her. Was this true?

"How could that have been, I wonder?"

"It's not your fault that you and Finlay took so long to come to the point," she explained. "You both had no intention of falling in love. Since you both came to each other innocently, without art or artifice, you had no choice but to delve into a deeper meaning of love that you did not expect."

She pinned a sheet to the line. "Love crept up on you and it bit you before you even could see it pounce. What was it like for you when you discovered that you returned his affections? Here in the regiment company, we all were aware that he loved you before you felt the same. With him, it was obvious."

"How? When I first knew him, he was so solemn and serious."

"Then he stopped being so. That was the main sign."

"Oh," I realized, my eyes widening. "I suppose that it would have been, wouldn't it? How blind I was to not see it for so long."

"You are young. Don't despise yourself for not seeing what we more experienced people do."

"I missed you all. I really did."

"And we missed you." She sighed. "If only you had been invited to Brighton instead of your sister, it all could have ended up differently."

I chuckled.

"Why is that chuckle there?"

"Because you sound like the four knowing women. They mentioned such when I was visiting them."

"Makes sense. We spoke about it a great deal so often when we saw Lydia and Wickham in some corner, speaking in such terms. You must understand, we all remember when he paid particular attention to Mrs. Darcy, then when he found his way into Mary King's pocketbook, we realized that he spoke pretty words, but would choose elsewhere, in a mercenary fashion. But we told ourselves that it was prudent. Then she gets whisked away to the North by her uncle, and he thought that he could pay attention to Elizabeth again, as if she should have been grateful. And then, for him to charm and attract Lydia was when his nature truly came to light. We made excuses for Wickham enough, but between that, and the debts we heard that he left behind, we were done. How do you flirt with a lady when you were willing to continue to dote on her sister? That's just a callous maneuver. And we turned out to be right."

"And I wonder what would have happened to me if I did go?" I asked. "I believe that I would have acted better than Lydia. But then, perhaps it would just be fortune on my side. After all, I was already in love with a superior man than Wickham. And quite honestly, I don't even see how Wickham's looks are more fascinating than Finlay's. Darcy also has a superior look. It was only his proud and haughty manner that held him back from being regarded as ideal. And another man I know...well, he may not have the best looks, but his manner and art of pleasing quite make you forget. Either way, I wonder, since I had the better fortune to have fallen in love with a man who would never run off with me, with no intentions of abandoning me afterwards, I just merely had better circumstances."

"You're worried that you will never know if you would have done the right thing, or you escaped a bad fate because of the different manner of man that you and Lydia chose."

"Yes, I never thought of it before. But I wonder now."

"I do not think so."

"In what respect?"

"Well, Lydia's love was the response of the mad and chaotic love that you feel when you are a teenager. It's wild, wanton, and it can lead to you being erratic. Have you ever felt that before?"

"Yes. And the madness that came along with it."

"Well, you had already undergone it, but Lydia was in the very throes of it. Where sensibility and passion overtake any sense of control—control your sister never had—you have already recovered from. Your passion did not burn hot so quickly as hers did—like a mad flame. Yours was a smoldering sort of fire. It grew more over time. As a result, you had more time to let logic and romance balance themselves out."

"Oh!" I said, happy at the thought, "if Finlay had asked me to run off with him in Brighton, which is something that he would never do, then I would have been dubious, because I wasn't even sure of what my feelings were. I neither knew how deep my feelings had become, or if I even wanted to act on them."

"Precisely. A flame that gradually grows always has more stability than a sudden spark that doesn't have enough foundation to keep it going. Remember that."

We finished hanging up the laundry.

"Samantha?" I asked.

"Hm?"

"Did you ever give into your passions, even if just a little? I do not speak with a desire to expose you."

"I know that you don't. Besides, I'm a washerwoman; what importance am I, in the eyes of fancy gossipers? None at all. There is freedom in obscurity. I'll tell you that. Well, to answer your question, yes, I have."

"Did you ever regret it?"

"At first, I did. But then I realized something."

"What?"

"That I could look after myself. Once you are able to look after yourself, you begin to look on your past mistakes as beneficial experiences in your life. I had much rather loved, acted on it, then regretted it, than to have never had any sort of passionate experience at all."

I smiled.

"Do you ever worry, when you age, that you will be the sport of jokes?" I asked. "We're always told the horror of that fate when we do not marry."

"You can't fear the world that much, Kitty. If you do, then you will never get anything done, because you spend the time worrying. That's folly. Besides, as I said, if I keep saving, I will find some family in the regiment who will be satisfied with me looking after them and being a nurse to their family. I know where I shall end if disease doesn't get me first. Do not worry about me, Kitty. Samantha always finds her way."

I smiled wistfully.

"I really missed you. I didn't notice that I did until now, but I suppose it explains my constant attaching myself to the hired help in the Darcy household."

"Really?"

"Yes. You remember that I have a servant, Lucy. When she had days off, I would visit her friends with her. I always attributed it to my curiosity for knowing and seeing as much of the world as I could before I settled down. However, now I think it's because I was looking for the same comfort that I found with you all."

Samantha removed some lotion from a pocket in her apron and she rubbed it over her hands, to help soothe the crust that a washerwoman naturally gains from washing too much laundry and being exposed to the harsh cleansers.

"And as you recall, she saved Georgie and my life by doing what servants do best: gossip.

"The joys of being a washerwoman. We are given all sorts of dirty laundry."

Chapter Twenty-Three
TWO OFFICERS WHO ALSO WERE GENTLEMEN

Soon, it was time for us to return to Pemberley. Overall, it was quite the beneficial experience. As our carriage was brought round and we were about to mount, I saw three riders ride passed the headquarters. I recognized one figure.

"Miss Bennet!"

I turned and my eyes brightened at the familiarity. I was happy that I thought to wear the shawl he brought me. It hung over one of my shoulders.

"Finlay."

He rode up to me and watched as our driver opened the door for us.

"You are leaving?" he asked, disgruntled.

"Yes. We actually have visited for quite some time. I have no right to make my fellow company wait any longer." I lowered my voice. "Though it is pleasant to see you."

"Yes," he sighed, a little winded under the weight of knowing that I could not speak to him. Elizabeth, seeing that we needed a minute, ushered the rest of the ladies into the carriage, so that I could get in last.

Taking advantage of the opportunity, I began to engage Finlay immediately.

"We visited the four knowing women, and I got to see Samantha," I explained.

"Oh, that must have been a pleasant experience for you," he said, satisfied and actually sincere.

"It was, it was, it was," I said eagerly, to which it made him laugh. "For a moment, a brief moment, I felt as if I had fallen back in time. And that we all still were in Hertfordshire, as we always had once been."

"Those were happy days," he said, once more, his eyes sincere.

"You know what's amusing. You actually believe it."

"Why should I not?"

"Because not everyone does when they say that. But you do. That's what makes you special."

His eyes were soft again, and I could tell that he was happy. Nothing could touch him. I wish that he could always be that way.

"Can you come back again?" he asked urgently. "The day after tomorrow? Please?"

"I think I can. I wish to see you. Georgie will most likely accompany me. Just to prepare you."

"Chaperones are important things."

"Yes, they are."

His eyes shifted and he appeared more contemplative.

"Kitty..."

"Yes?"

"I understand now."

"What do you understand?"

"Why you fell in love with him as well." I felt my smile drop, my lips form into a tight line and I'm certain that my expression widened in wonder. Never was I one for dissembling or indicating anything else other than how I felt. Subtlety and artifice were not my province, and emotional display would always be the order of the day.

"You do?" I asked.

"Yes. We've met. We've spoken. Of course, it hurts that I am not the only one in your affections. But that is a matter of pride, you understand."

"Of course, I understand. Your behavior is natural. I am just happy that you now understand that."

"Yes. He is a good man. An honorable one."

"You are both honorable men. I had no choice."

"No, you didn't. I asked for forgiveness before. But I didn't know what it meant. Will you forgive me now? This time, I truly mean it."

"You know that I was always ready to forgive you. And I always will. I said I would never forsake you, Finlay. And I keep to that."

"I know."

"Kitty," Elizabeth called. "We must return now. Jane needs her rest. As do I, for that matter."

"Yes," I obeyed with alacrity. After all, you never argue with pregnant women when it comes to them needing their rest.

I big farewell to Finlay, he helped me into the carriage, gave us all a significant look, and the carriage was off. Naturally, my impulse was to turn back to him and watch him until we disappeared down the road.

When he was no longer in sight, I turned to my company. Jane and Elizabeth had been too much in the habit of not commenting on such things. However, Enara and Georgiana were not so willing to be limited to decorum. They gave me a look.

"You may say all that you wish."

"You are in love," Enara cooed. "How different you wear it than the rest of us."

~

When we returned to Pemberley, we were greeted by the kind and impressive riding of one particular Colonel Fitzwilliam. He had been riding along the grounds, on Leonidas. When he saw us coming, he rode up to our carriage and escorted us to the front door. Dismounting from his horse, he walked up to our carriage door and helped us all down.

"Darcy and Bingley will be happy to see you," Colonel Fitzwilliam said to Jane and Lizzy. "When a mother-to-be goes too far away from the husband, it can drive him to distraction."

"Have they been driving you mad since we left?" Elizabeth asked.

"So much so that I had to retreat to the stables." He smirked. "I speak in jest. They have been as tranquil as ever. Well, as tranquil as husbands can be when their wives go where they can't see them. I shall leave it to you to decide as you choose."

As he escorted us inside, I walked alongside him and looked up at his 'all-knowing' face.

"You couldn't help yourself, could you?" I asked.

"I couldn't help doing what?" He questioned by way of reply.

"You couldn't help solving the problem and saving me, could you? Finlay told me about how you spoke to him. Never fear, I do not hate chivalry. I am as tough as nails, I have learned, but I always admire a little help."

He sighed.

"Thank goodness. I do worry about being high-handed, but sometimes, you cannot do anything else but help."

"Do not fear me being disrespected for your attempts of consideration. I can save myself, occasionally, but sometimes, with a little help from one's friends, there's nothing wrong with being saved, every now and again. If you see a man who might disrespect me or disregard me, do not fear confronting him about it. Darcy did it, and he was right. You were right to clarify our situation."

"I'll always be here, no matter what," he assured me.

"I know. I appreciate that. And that is a promise."

Chapter Twenty-Four

SPARKS FLY

When we all gathered to eat, Mr. Darcy and Mr. Bingley had excellent news.

"My dear," Bingley said to Jane, "I have spoken with the steward, and we shall be able to establish ourselves at Godfrey Park by the end of the week."

"Oh, that is very good, my dear," Jane said, but there was something in her tone that I found was wanting. I couldn't detect it fully, but there was some worry in her voice.

"Jane," I considered, "is something wrong?"

"No," she said, "no, nothing is wrong at all. I am excited."

None of us believed it.

"Dearest," Bingley said, unable to ignore my instinct, "is something wrong? I would have you tell me. I will not be upset if you do."

Jane sighed.

"It is selfish," she said.

"What is?"

"Well, since Lizzy and I are both with child, together, it has led to a dependency on family, as well as the comfort of being close to them. I fear getting acquainted with a new household and having to learn to be its mistress."

"Oh, I had not thought of that."

"If I were not with child, I would be overjoyed beyond

measure, but now," she said, touching her stomach, "things have changed me a little."

"Oh," Bingley said. "Would it help if I take on many of the household duties? You may relax yourself as much as you wish, and I'll bring you to Pemberley often, to be with Lizzy."

"That would help a great deal, but there is one thought that I had." Jane turned to Elizabeth. "Lizzy, this might not make you happy, but I need something familiar to help me transition."

"I am always happy to assist you," Elizabeth said, "name what you need."

"I... if they are not against it, but I was wondering if you would accept if I took Betsy and Sarah with me to Godfrey Park?"

"Oh," Elizabeth professed, "that is all? Well, we must consult them first. However, I do not believe that they would deny you anything. And they have experience with looking after pregnant women. We can ask them today. I will miss them. Whenever you come to visit, bring them along. They seem like charms of good luck."

"Yes, their bickering just feels comfortable," Jane said.

"It's not a matter of asking them," Darcy said, "they are servants. They will go where you tell them."

Elizabeth patted his hand.

"First, a mistress goes further with her servants if she asks things rather than always goes by way of command. You are the lord and master, but with us, honey goes further than vinegar. Secondly, my dear, think of Betsy and Sarah. Now imagine ordering them like they are cattle. Would you risk it?"

"You think I fear them?" he asked, amused.

"No, but I'm only saying that out loud. What I'm really thinking is something I shall tell you later."

Darcy sighed, but he wasn't displeased. She was teasing him; he liked it.

"Besides, I am certain that Sarah and Betsy will be amenable to the scheme. They know to go where they are most needed."

Betsy and Sarah might leave Pemberley. How many servants were going to walk in and out of my life, I would never know. But it was something that I had to adapt to. As they would do the same with us. No one ever really contemplates the relationship of lady to her servant. After all, they are trained to be there, and we are trained to view them as *just* there. But every now and again, we realize that they are people, living amongst us, and there is something within them. Something under the surface, that we perhaps ought to learn about.

Once this all was settled, Darcy now could avail himself of his news. He brandished two letters that would soon appeal to us. The first was a letter from Lady Catherine de Bourgh! When hearing the name, we felt the weight of this response.

"Ah, a reply at last," Elizabeth remarked. "Should we be afraid?"

"Normally, I could understand that instinct," Darcy replied, "my aunt does incite such a reaction. She is a powerful and impressive woman. But this time, her will of iron does not aim to break us. There are some things in her letter that I could not repeat, for they were written—with venomous spirit."

"That means she gave some very cruel and cutting words toward Lizzy," Colonel Fitzwilliam whispered to me. "They cannot be repeated."

"Ah."

"But there is the other half of her letter which I can relate," Darcy said, "I trust that she will understand if I read it aloud."

Darcy raised up the letter and began:

> '... now that I have finished speaking the truth of how I feel with the current developments and family that now occupies Pemberley's great halls, I am not against attempting to improve things.
> The new Mrs. Darcy finds herself with child—well, her ignorance on the matter is understandable and can be tempered and overcome by my superior knowledge and expertise on the subject. Having raised a successful daughter myself, who is greater than anything that Hertfordshire could produce...'

We all either rolled our eyes or placed our faces in our palms, frustrated with the great lady's arrogance.

'I shall be happy to administer all my advice to the new mothers to be. But since I deserve the respect for which I am owed, I demand for you all to come to Rosings Park for the Christmas holidays. This way, I can begin to apply my teachings to the humbly-brought-up ladies of Longbourn.

YOU all will attend.

And any guests that you may have at Pemberley may be allowed to visit as well, provided that they are respectable enough.'

Darcy continued to read the letter and when it ended, Elizabeth gave her witty response.

"She only offended me five times throughout that letter. She is improving."

When Darcy closed the letter, it was to see Bingley a little vexed.

"We are to have our wives travel to Kent during their condition. Is that wise?"

"Never fear, dearest," Jane assured him, "our mother traveled in carriages when she was more along than Lizzy and me, and she produced us all successfully."

"Well, I had hoped to spend our first Christmas as husband and wife here in Derbyshire." Bingley turned to Darcy. "But I realize that this is important to your family."

"It is," Darcy responded, "despite my aunt's bitter words, I would like to establish a peace again."

"Then I will welcome being in your company."

"Thank you, Bingley."

"Strength in numbers, you know."

"Oh, believe me, I know."

"Well," I sighed, "it is confirmed. Lady Catherine really doesn't like us."

"She is a woman who's plans I completely disturbed and destroyed by marrying her nephew," Elizabeth said, "I am the only horror here. The rest of you are simply guilty by association."

"But that will not be allowed," Darcy assured her, "when I write back to my aunt, I will make it very evident that I will not tolerate any cruel words spoken to you or anyone else in the company. That I promise you."

"And Mr. Darcy always keeps his promises," Elizabeth noted, with love in her eyes.

"Yes, he does," he said, smiling a little.

"And will she suffer the son of an attorney?" Arthur Philips asked.

"Oh, she will. But be prepared for a lecture. That is just her habit."

"So, I am learning."

Darcy looked around at the rest of the room.

"Very well, it is settled. We are going to Rosings Park for Christmas."

"I wonder what holiday that would be like," I whispered to Colonel Fitzwilliam.

"It is going to be an event that is either brilliant or ghastly." He was giddy. "I can't wait to see."

So, now our doom was decided; very soon, we were going to face Lady Catherine de Bourgh—the woman who never wanted us to exist in her life.

~

Now it came time for the second letter.

"I have received a reply to our letter from Mr. Henry Crawford and his sister." When he spoke such, all of us dropped our knife and fork, and were eager to learn of its contents. "Jane, brave heart, the letter is as you wish for it to be. My only surprise is how eager they are to not only agree, but they also are willing to visit in a week's time, as I hoped."

Mr. Darcy read the letter, and it really was an eager letter, probably written by Mary Crawford. Happy that Jane and I had not forsaken her at all, she appeared to be willing and desirous to see us promptly. I sensed that there might be a reason for this, but we would not know until they came.

A wonderful surprise was that they would be a company of four. Mary begged our forgiveness for including an addition to the party, but Jane and I were not upset. For Henry Crawford and the rest were going to London to retrieve their half-sister, Mrs. Grant, who was a widow.

"Oh, that is delightful," Jane cried. "We get to see Mrs. Grant again."

"That is a perfect present for the season," I said, turning to Elizabeth, Georgiana, and Enara. "Mrs. Grant is a large ball of comfort. She has a way of making herself agreeable to everyone. And she is curious about other places. She would like to hear about Australia."

"Oh, then that gives me importance," Enara said, "one enjoys that."

When Darcy finished reading the letter, he had already told his valet, Jefferson, to send a confirmation by express. This would strengthen their coming tenfold. This news sent the table into a whirlwind of conversation that brought life to us.

When Colonel Fitzwilliam and I were able to talk together in the stables as he tended to his horse, we were very verbose on the subject.

"I must say," Colonel Fitzwilliam commented, "that Pemberley has never been this alive with eagerness for a company to come visit."

"Really?"

"Yes. Before now, parties have always been the traditional people to come. They could never be described as...exciting. And yet, here we are, about to entertain a sailor, a widow, and two misfits, where one was so notorious, his actions found its way into the newspapers. We're living in strange times where flaws are counted for more than virtue."

"I have a theory for why that is," I noted as he showed me how to clean a saddle. "And I believe that it makes all the sense in the world."

"Go on," Colonel Fitzwilliam said, putting the yoke on the horse. "I am listening to this theory, you little imp."

"Thank you, you stodgy codger. Henry Crawford has a side of him that is, perhaps, villainous, by what is described. If Mary Crawford is a villain, well, that will surprise me. For we have seen nothing but the good in her when she visited Hertfordshire. Sometimes her opinions can be jaded and inconsiderate, but welcome to being young, I daresay! Well, have you ever noticed that it is the most flawed individuals who are the most fascinating? And when I mean flawed, I do not refer to criminals who commit atrocities. That is horror. I speak of people who make mistakes that indicate that they are not perfect, that they sometimes have moral slips of the tongue or technique to morality. I mean they commit gradual sin but are neither murderous, malicious, nor violent."

"I understand the meaning of your sentiments."

"Thank you. Forgive my wordiness, but it is so easy to be misunderstood, that one must be thorough in one's explanations."

"I am willing to know the recesses of your philosophy. You can only inform me by actually *talking*. Silence is praised but it brings nothing more than misunderstandings."

"THANK YOU! Well, think of images of perfection. And people who are perfect. How long will it be before you get bored being in their presence? For the only way that a person can be perfect is if they don't ever do anything. They do not move, they do not choose, they never have a belief. They are reactive in life because they have no choice."

"That is actually true, from an objective standpoint. Virtue and perfection are the aspiring goals, and they ought to be. But when you are always perfect, what stories of your own actions do you have to talk about?"

"Precisely. Mistakes breed stories. Errors from one's past breed personal growth. And when others falter, fail, and acknowledge their failure, we can walk down that path with them. You see, their faults are like a trial that we can learn from, and experience through *their* experiences. But if a person is perfect, what experiences can they share with us, that proves cathartic? We can marvel at them, but we can't grow with them. There is nothing to grow from."

"You present the idea that images of perfection can be a little cold to connect to, even though it's what we should try to emulate?"

"Yes."

"It makes sense. We humans are dual creatures. We aspire to greatness, to that one guiding light, but the guilty side of us will always be there, and we will give into it."

"And what can help you feel justified or purge your guilt, but the guilt of another person? Misery does love company. And as a result, the Crawfords will be fascinating when they come here. Mrs. Grant will be fascinating because she was the one who invited them to Mansfield Park. William Price will be fascinating, because he is engaged to a woman who his brother-in-law used to court. Within these four are four portraits of very interesting characters, because of the struggles that they have had to undergo, due to their own choices. We, therefore, have no choice but to anticipate their arrival. And for all we know, maybe we need a little spice of imperfection in our company. Without knowing it, it can bring us new life. Especially if we can help them in some way."

I turned to him.

"Do you still understand me?"

"Your logic is very sound. I can't argue, because the darker and more 'flawed' parts of myself understand that theory. And from what I have seen, the Crawfords coming has already proven to liven things in a way that suits me. After all, it made me feel some sort of connection to your sister."

"My sister? Which one."

"Jane. Here is the strange thing about her. She is a beauty, yes. A great beauty."

"She looks like my mother," I said, not jealous at all. I had grown so used to Jane's beauty being the most prized part of us Bennet sisters, that time taught me indifference to it all now. I knew my self-worth. Nothing would shake me anymore.

"Ah, that explains why your father married her. Either way, Jane is beautiful, and yet, I never cared."

"Really?" I asked, stopping cleaning as I looked up at him, fascinated. "Well, that is unique."

"Not as unique as you would think. She is lovely, she is wise, practical, and practically perfect in every way. And yet, whenever

I am around her, I can never be fully comfortable or think of anything to say, because I cannot connect with her on a level of conversation that interests either of us. The serenity of her countenance makes it difficult to dissemble if she is interested in anything I say. On the other hand, you have yourself, Elizabeth, and Mary. When I speak with you three, there is a light. I see your eyes light up in a desire to know me. When I first met you, I fell in love with you because of your vivacity, which some regard as a flaw. But without it, I could not connect to you. But when she spoke about the Crawfords, and her undying intention to try and reconcile their mistakes to helping them improve, something awoke in her."

I was merry, happy to see that our minds were alike again.

"You saw it too?"

"Yes."

"That spark of life?"

"Yes! Suddenly, Jane's whole character and countenance just woke up and she had that spark in her, that showed a woman who was not afraid of how she would look. She had a cause, and she would commit to it. It forced her to lift her voice and do something strange: risk looking ugly. And then... I finally felt a connection to her. It can never be the way I feel with you, but at least it was nice for a moment."

I smiled.

"You poor boy; you love women so much, and inheritance is not on your side."

"Oh, I am meant to have daughters alright." He laughed. "Your father will never understand his good fortune." His eyes grew misty. "You would have given me happy children, you know."

"I know," I replied, sorry for him. "They would have been happy. Yet, there is one benefit to this all."

"What?"

"When you do marry, your children would not have my cough."

We smiled sadly at each other because that was all that we could do.

After I finished cleaning the saddle, Colonel Fitzwilliam inspected it.

"Very good," he said, hanging it up so that no dirt got on it. Next, he turned to Leonidas, patted his nose, and began to speak sweet nothings in his ear. Watching him stand there, getting the horse to love him, I had a sudden thought.

"Richard?" I asked.

"Yes?"

"In the little time that you are here, can you spend every day teaching me about how to ride a horse better?"

His eyes sparkled at my request.

"Why do you wish to do that?"

"I don't know. A sudden thought suddenly has come to me."

"And what is that?"

"I just realized that I want to know all the practicalities of life. What I mean is, I am not talented at all. I am not accomplished in any respect. And there is the possibility that I may never marry."

"Don't talk like that."

"I am not afraid of the possibility that I could be the only Bennet sister who never takes a husband. I accept it. But it just occurred to me that maybe my sisters might not always want me at their home. Or, if I stay with Mary or Lydia at some point, I will have to earn my keep. If I can assist in many respects, when regarding the bare necessities of life, then there would be use for me. And if the worse happens, and I have to live alone, then I can do it, because I learned to provide for myself."

"Elizabeth or Jane would never abandon you."

"Yes, but one must prepare for every eventuality."

He sighed, feeling sorry for me. Sorry—because he knew that I was right.

"Very well. Besides, you're asking me to teach you something that I already enjoy. At least we have this together."

"I'd embrace you if I was allowed."

He looked back and forth.

"No one is here," he whispered.

Rolling my eyes, I ran to him, wrapped my hands around his

waist, he closed his arms over my shoulders and rested his head on my hair.

"We are always teetering on the edge of breaking decorum to its utter ruin, aren't we?" I asked.

"Yes. You are right. Folly loves company."

～

My sudden desire to improve myself did not just end there. This conversation was repeated:

"You want to learn how to fold, sort laundry and how to make the bed?" Betsy said to me when I asked her and Sarah to show me basic living customs.

"Yes," I answered. They both had accepted that they would live with Jane, so I didn't have much time.

"And why would you want to do that?" Sarah asked. "Are we not enough?"

"Yes! Aren't we doing our duties well? And you know us. Sarah and I hate agreeing with each other."

I looked at them archly.

"You do know that you both will be at Godfrey Park, and I won't get the chance to have this firsthand instruction again, right?"

They suddenly realized how foolish they were being and decided to help me.

～

"You want me to teach you how to wash laundry?" Samantha asked me when I would visit the regiment's headquarters.

"Yes," I answered, "and you can gain much by doing such. You can teach me by making me help you with the officers' laundry, without me asking you to pay me anything."

"Why, in the name of St. Mary, would you want to put yourself through such an ordeal?"

"Because I just realized that I might not always be so lucky in life. I need to find a place to fall. Being independent is as good as any reason."

"Oh, well, I won't look a gift horse in the mouth. I'll take you on as an apprentice."

❧

"You want me to teach you how to cook and clean?" Lucy asked me.

"Yes," I responded.

"Why on earth do you want to learn to do that?"

"It's simple," I said, now accustomed to this response, "Lucy, you know as well as I that I am not like Miss Darcy or my sisters. I need to think practically. Now it's time for you to teach me how to be practical." She looked dubious. "Unless you don't want me to be in your company."

She groaned.

"Of course, that's not what I mean. Very well. You need to take time out of your day, because it's not going to be easy to master cooking. Cleaning is pretty comprehensible after a first lesson. But cooking, well, that is an artform."

"I never was good at learning artforms." I groaned.

"You never had me for a teacher. That's a difference."

Of course, my desires for educating myself would not go unnoticed. Before I undertook lessons from Colonel Fitzwilliam, Betsy, Sarah, Lucy, and Samantha, I had to tell Darcy and Elizabeth. Initially, this unsettled Darcy. After all, what powerful Master of a great estate wants the world to be aware that he is having his sister-in-law learn to work and toil. But when I explained it all to him, he saw the reasoning and Elizabeth only had one thing to say:

"You and your sparks, Kitty. You're always bursting around somewhere."

This did not deplete my time with Georgiana. On the contrary, she often accompanied me to the regiment's headquarters where she watched me learn to clean and even kept

Samantha and I company. When she tired of that, the four knowing women would invite her inside for some tea.

While Colonel Fitzwilliam instructed me on horse-maintenance, she would groom and tend to her brown mare.

When Lucy took me to the kitchens to learn to cook—it got interesting. Georgiana actually would take lessons as well and began to learn to cook herself.

Somehow, it made our friendship stronger.

While I did laundry, Finlay occasionally would find reasons to take moments from his duties to spend time with me. By God, he was beautiful!

Elizabeth was becoming somewhat proud of me. Jane, despite my shortcomings, was always proud of me, therefore, I had neither gained nor lost anything.

Darcy, in his own way, approved of what I was becoming.

Enara and Arthur just viewed it as losing my company for hours at a time. They missed me. How flattering!

Chapter Twenty-Five
VICES & VOYAGES

I n all this time, between my lessons, and my time seeing Finlay and Colonel Fitzwilliam intermittently, it led to being a proper distraction for how long we were anticipating the Crawfords' arrival.

Despite all the horrible remarks said of them, their company was much remarked on day in and day out.

Sometimes I wondered what our mother and father would think with us entertaining such company. But then I recalled Lydia, and I realized that they couldn't have much to say on the matter. It didn't do well for them to ever fully be hypocrites.

Yet time moves eventually, even though it may appear slower to some and faster to others.

However, the day did arrive where we all were dressed in our second or third best clothing, we awaited the appointed hour, and it duly came when we heard a carriage coming down the lane.

In anticipation, I went to the window while everyone else was seated in the main parlor.

"Kitty," Elizabeth advised, "do come away from the window."

"I will in one second," I said, dismissively, "I will once I get one quick peek in, to make sure that it is them."

The carriage pulled up in the front of the house, some servants tended to it, the door opened, and Mr. Henry Crawford emerged, followed by William Price. Both men offered their arms to help Mary Crawford and Mrs. Grant down from it.

"It's them!" I cried, rushing back to the group, and taking my place by Enara and Arthur. "It really is them."

"Did you see Mrs. Grant with them?" Jane asked.

"Yes, I did. She is come."

Jane smiled, happy that she would get to see Mrs. Grant, as much as myself.

For some reason, when we heard their voices as they entered the house, we all breathed in a sigh of nervousness. All of us, except Mr. Darcy.

Looking around at all of us, he was unique in that he was surprised by our reaction.

"Honestly," he remarked, joking, "you act as if we are the ones visiting *their* home."

"I just...want this to begin and end well," Jane said, nervous.

When seeing Jane's apprehensions, Darcy's tone shifted to gentleness.

"It may, sister."

Soon the door opened, we all stood up and turned to see the new arrivals.

~

There they were.

Mary Crawford, with her arm wrapped in William Price's. He looked handsome in his naval uniform. Mary Crawford, also, was in the very best of looks. She had an immediate striking demeanor that put her on Elizabeth's level. While her beauty could never fully be on Jane's level, it did not lessen her impact. Seeing her again immediately made us all have a difficulty in thinking anything but the very best in her. Hopefully one day, I would see her objectively, but it was not easy.

Next, Henry Crawford entered with Mrs. Grant on his arm. Henry was dressed well, which found a way to diminish or lessen his ugly looks. His posture was erect, his hat sat atop his head perfectly, and Mrs. Grant looked as plump and quaint as ever.

When seeing Jane and me, her eyes lit up and she forgot the traditional habit of waiting for us all to bow and curtsy before she spoke.

"Jane and Kitty!" Mrs. Grant cried. "Oh, my dears!"

Oh, thank God for the Mrs. Grants of the world! If it weren't for her improper outburst, we would have begun quite awkwardly, with no one knowing how to proceed or what was the best way of beginning. But since she had struck up such a familiarity with us, it made it impossible for us to fully stand on ceremony.

"Mrs. Grant!" I cried, moving away from where I stood and approaching her. Sensing my willingness to embrace her, she hugged me, and I responded in kind.

"It has been too long, hasn't it?" Mrs. Grant said.

"Yes, it has."

"Well," Jane said, "if my sister gets to behave so…"

Jane joined us and Mrs. Grant opened her embrace to bring Jane inside of it.

"Oh, dear Jane! I have heard that you are to be a mother soon."

"If God sees fit, then yes, I will be."

"I cannot think of a woman who would be a better mother."

"Thank you, Mrs. Grant, but I can." Jane turned and gestured to Elizabeth. "My sister and I are with child at the same time, and I do believe that she will best me."

"My sister does me too much credit, as usual," Elizabeth retorted.

"Jane has a way of doing that to many of us," Mary Crawford replied, "she would make a sinner into the best saint."

"That is a statement that could not be truer," Mr. Bingley said, eyeing Henry Crawford kindly, but also a little wary.

Henry Crawford was not ignorant of this reaction, and rather than ignore it, he bowed his head gently to Bingley, to openly acknowledge what was being referenced.

"I am remiss in my manners and am doing everything backwards," Jane said, turning to us all. "Family, you recall Mr. Crawford, Miss Crawford, and Lieutenant William Price. But this is Mr. and Mrs. Crawford's half-sister, Mrs. Grant. Mrs. Grant, this is my family." Jane introduced everyone to whom Mrs. Grant was not familiar with.

"Mrs. Grant, Mr. and Miss Crawford, and Lieutenant Price," Elizabeth greeted, "welcome to Pemberley. Please do be seated."

All sat down, and Elizabeth ordered tea to be brought, along with refreshment.

"Unless you would prefer coffee," Elizabeth said, "Do not be shy. I'd like to know what sort of preferences you have here, if we are to suit your palate."

"Tea is delightful," William Price responded, "thank you for caring for our preferences."

"Of course. If I did not, what sort of mistress would I be?" She asked this with levity, and this brought the company more at ease.

"Mr. and Mrs. Darcy," Henry Crawford said, "as tedious as such flattery may sound, I can assure you that it is sincere when I say that I thank you so much for the honor of seeing my sisters, my soon to be brother, and myself. We did not expect such an honor from one of the most illustrious of persons in England."

"You are too kind," Mr. Darcy responded.

"I am not but thank you for saying such."

"Ah," Darcy said, penetrating, "you are aware of yourself. That is good. This gives me the right to begin where I can."

We all looked at him, and very well were aware of what he was referring to.

"My love," Elizabeth said to Darcy, "you jest."

"I do not. You know that I do not. And you are right to chide me." He turned to our guests, and to Henry Crawford in particular. "And something tells me that, the more I delay the matter, the least beneficial it will be for all." He looked at Elizabeth. "Do you support me in this?"

The question was so direct, so exacting, that it would have overwhelmed any other woman. But Elizabeth, always willing to rise to a challenge, considered this.

"Do I support you in this?" She echoed his words. "Now that is a question for the ages." She turned to the Crawfords. "We do welcome you here, but whatever happens next, my husband is correct to begin. And I sense that you are aware of what is about to happen. But I still am a mistress, and I request that we at least wait till the tea is brought in before we begin."

William looked confused.

"I confess that I am quite at a loss," William Price asked. "What is happening now?"

"They are about to question us on our past," Mary Crawford deduced, shrewd as ever. "That is what is about to happen, isn't it?"

"Yes," Mr. Darcy responded, "I confess, that I would never forgive myself if I did not. You shall learn this soon about me, as the Master of Pemberley. I seek the truth, of all things."

"This really must happen?" Jane asked, uneasy.

"Jane," Elizabeth said, "I confess, that I am of my husband's mind in this. It is correct for us to ask them to explain themselves."

"No," William Price said, "I will not have my fiancée be interrogated as if she has done anything wrong." He stood up, bitter. "I tire of her being judged."

My heart felt for them immediately.

"I promise," Jane said, "no one will judge Mary."

"Yes," I said, finally finding my voice. "Mr. Price, no matter what happens, Mary and Mrs. Grant have friends here. And my brother merely wishes to know the truth of it all." I turned to Mary Crawford and Mrs. Grant. "We will always think you worthy. My brother simply must speak to your brother."

"He will not be happy until he does," Elizabeth said about Darcy. "And my husband has that right."

I looked around at the rest in our company. They all looked a little out of their depth.

"We were brought here to be interrogated," Mrs. Grant said, heartbroken.

"No, not you," Jane assured her. "Oh, this has all overwhelmed me."

"My love," Bingley said, holding her, "please sit down and calm yourself. For our child."

She sat down and the tea was brought in. This gave us all the time to calm ourselves and gather our resolve.

When the servants were dismissed, Mr. Darcy was about to speak. Henry Crawford did so first.

"I know," he began, "what you are feeling, sir. I confess myself surprised only that you wished to confront the matter so quickly into our visit, and with so many present."

"I thought it right that I would speak to you myself," Darcy acknowledged, "but then I realized that it wasn't fair to the rest of my household. They have just as much a right to know you as I do. Mrs. Bingley has told me all your histories, but I feel that you have the right to tell me yourself, in your own words."

"Then I thank you for giving me the right to explain myself," Mr. Crawford said. "Very few have given me the opportunity, after my plight of villainy. Many have suffered for it, from my sisters to others associated with me. I have been judged, yes, but my wealth and station in life has cushioned me. But my actions have led to the ruin of the women in my life. It took me a while to see the weight of that, to consider how my actions hurt them, but now I do. Therefore," he said, standing. "You are right. It is time that I finally answer for all that I have done. And I tell all, in hopes that one day, I may find forgiveness."

"Mr. Crawford," Mr. Darcy said, still seated, "I confess that I have a temper, and resentment is part of that. I detest men who have done what you have done. I find your sort to be the negative aspects of our times. But I am prepared to listen, to judge you fairly," and he looked at Jane, Elizabeth, then Mary Crawford and Mrs. Grant. "For the love of our sisters, who want us to understand each other, I do it for them. Therefore, you may proceed."

All of us—Darcy, Bingley, Arthur, Enara, Georgiana, Jane, Colonel Fitzwilliam, and myself were leaning forward, internally. Every word that would now be spoken, every moment that this story would be unfolded, and every second that took place for now, was our largest interest.

It felt like we were watching the pendulum of judgment, the attempt for understanding a demonic habit, the willingness to listen...it felt as if our eyes were watching God as It spoke up and said 'It is time. Time for you to judge, as I have done so often. I bid you good luck, for there is nothing more dangerous than punishing a sinner who wishes for redemption *or* forgiving a villain who knows how to talk fair.'

Henry Crawford folded his hands in front of him to begin. And thus, here at Pemberley, the trial of Henry Crawford began.

End of Book Six

Afterword

Reader, we are on Book Six of this series, and for the love of Dumas, you few, you happy few who still sojourn onward, willing to read a series that keeps going like this, are the stuff of legend.

This series is meant to not only chronicle a young woman amidst the very middle of the Regency era, but she is also meant to display the constant emotional plateaus that faced the average woman and man at that age group, and how the mundane and everyday habits of our lives are quite the marvel in themselves. The everyday deeds and mental destruction that we all undergo, on a daily basis, is meant to walk the reader through those same situations that Kitty experiences. I know that it would be easier to skip to who Kitty marries, but another writer once wrote something that I paraphrase all the time: when love is found, adventures end. Kitty's adventures are the ones that we all face daily. Her story is not the stuff of an epic. Her story is the stuff of commonality and reality. Can there be happiness found in the traditional throes and findings that we all usually experience? After all, many of us didn't find love, true love, for quite a while. And some of us may be waiting for years. Kitty has to wait for those years with *us*. She has to be torn away from things like we have. And so, her trick is that she is reality itself.

I hope the reader is not too annoyed by me for giving her this journey. Because we've all been there and back again. By going there with Kitty, we recall when we were once her. Memories can be fun to walk down because they present a scene where you can see your whole life mapped out in front of you. Kitty's journey is a map of its kind.

Of course, I am aware that this entry was quite the complex set in the series, because of the references made to Miss Austen's other works.

Yes, 'Mansfield Park'!

First, those of you who wonder why I referenced things that were not mentioned much earlier in this series, such as Kitty knowing the Crawfords. I promise, this is not an oversight but was intentional.

In the next book, it will be split between Kitty's continued story, and Jane's tale from when Mr. Bingley left Netherfield Park after the ball, and Jane was heartbroken. Then it's going to continue to when Jane stayed with the Gardiners at Cheapside, and she met Mary Crawford. I knew, early on, that I wanted to include the Crawfords, Mrs. Grant, and William Price in Jane's tale. I did this, because I felt that Mary Crawford was like a foil, who I thought was waiting to have a friend like Jane Bennet; a woman who was very principled, but also was kind and forgiving. Jane and Mary Crawford become great friends, and eventually Jane meets Henry Crawford, much to her apprehension. Yet, they develop an understanding of each other.

So why didn't I mention this much before in Kitty's adventure?

There was only one reason: I wanted to surprise readers. When I published Kitty's story first, if I included the Crawfords in it, the reader would not be surprised if/when they read the next chapter. After all, they would see it coming. Never get in the way of letting a reader have fun and remove the element of surprise.

And when a reader requested a sequel to *this* series, it gave me the ability to intertwine Jane and Kitty's stories in a way that I always wanted to. Therefore, I stole an idea from Phyllipa Boyens, one of the screenwriters from the 'Lord of the Rings' films. In Tolkien's books, there is an important character named Tom Bombadil, who saves the hobbits' lives when they were lost in the Forest and were being attacked by the monster called the Barrow Weights. For anyone who has seen the LOTR films, Tom Bombadil makes no appearance, despite his role in the books. It's natural and it makes sense, because the character ultimately did not have a huge impact on the overall story, but Boyens said 'in the film, we don't know that the hobbits didn't go into the forest and met Tom Bombadil. (paraphrase) The hobbits could have, but we just left it untold'. What she meant was that something does happen in a story, but it was left out of the chief narrative. So, it existed without being mentioned.

Readers, I'm not going to lie, I totally took that idea and ran with it. When Jane was in London and befriended these characters, it actually happened in this series as well, but I left it unmentioned until recently.

But of course, the main reason was just simply to give readers a surprise between both Jane and Kitty's stories. Nothing is worth ruining that sort of thing for a reader.

However, if you did not prefer the tale told this way... then darn. Sorry about that. Oh well, I'm human, not a saint.

Mansfield Park Adaptations

Reader, I have only seen two Mansfield Park adaptations in my time.

The BBC miniseries adaptation from the 1980s.

And the 1999 theatrical version starring Frances O'Connor.

I know of another BBC version, with Billie Piper as Fanny Price, but I have never gotten around to seeing that. But I acknowledge that after the two I saw, I never had the impulse to see another version. Mind you, this is coming from a person who still has not seen the 2020 'Emma' adaptation, despite hearing great things about it. Before you cast aspersions on me, it's simply that I have five versions of Emma. The 1970s version, the Kate Beckinsale version. The Gwyneth Paltrow version. Clueless. And the Romola Garai version. After those five versions, I am sound as a pound. Seeing another 'Emma' will take a little time before it sparks my interest, just because I already enjoy those versions. It's also the same feeling I get when I watch the 1980 Pride and Prejudice, the 1990s Ehle and Firth P&P, and the 2006 Knightley version: I'm good, and I've seen all I want to see. Heck, I've only seen two versions of Persuasion: the 1970s one and the Hinds/Root one, and that was all I needed.

Long story short (forgive me, that was long), I just need a little time before seeing the new 'Emma', and the same goes for MP adaptations. I am also aware that there is a new version of MP that is underway. I was told that it might star Benedict Cumberbatch, but I could be mistaken.

When it comes to the two versions of MP that I have seen, I am a strange little critter. I like both versions for two different reasons. I like the 1980s BBC MP miniseries, because of how loyal it is to the book. Then I love the 1999 version because of how creative it is and how well P. Rozema did with directing it.

For those who have already read this in another afterword of mine, forgive me. I have a high tolerance for older BBC miniseries adaptations, because I am well aware of the production value. Therefore, I firmly believe that the miniseries did a fantastic job at adapting the book, with the little money it had. In fact, I thought it looked quite good, the casting was well done—truly, they literally got the right actress to play Fanny Price. The writers/director didn't even try and attempt to demonize Mary Crawford, but just had her be as she was. Everyone, I felt did a great job with it. The acting was also superb all around.

When it came to the 1999 version, Rozema wrote and directed it. It was beautiful to look at, but purists must have been screaming at the screen when they saw it.

For those who don't know my advice on viewing it, I would always recommend not looking at the lead as Fanny Price, but rather taking Jane Austen and putting her in Fanny's place. By turning Fanny into a writer with gusto, Rozema was clearly writing Jane Austen in Fanny Price's place.

Also, fun fact: Johnny Lee Miller played Edmund Bertram in the 1999 version. He also was in the 1980s BBC adaptation. He played one of the Price children in Portsmouth. It's always fun when things come full circle in that fashion.

Also, the 1999 adaptation went in depth with the Bertrams' owning of enslaved people. I am also aware that the slavery topic can be a little touchy to some viewers. It's very easy to ruin a fun experience, and it can look like virtue-signaling. Even when it's the right thing to bring up, it still is just so... polarizing. You don't want to alienate your audience, even when it's historical and it ought to be discussed. In life, we all don't mention these difficulties that we have when reading this subject matter, because if we do, it's easy to come across as 'petty or non-progressive'. If you feel guilt because you come to romance for the sake of that escapism and, as a result, it tries your nerves when you get a pandering social message, I'm here to tell you that it's okay. You are not a bad person. We're all human, and we don't want anything ruining our escapism.

But sometimes, reality does have to rush in. When that happens, confront that side of yourself, and weigh out that situation. Take into account how the author approaches the subject, can you find something about the story that is enjoyable, and see if the author is just trying to respect the history and care about proper representation. We all can tell when a writer is giving us true history to frame the story and augment the narrative, or when they just feel like preaching a sermon to you, without any sense of how to phrase it. It is very easy, as a writer, to fall into that trap. I admit, it took me time to see the difference and learn accordingly. In fact, I'm still learning how to achieve it myself.

Therefore, back to the topic of the Trade, I am aware that it can be a hard subject to dwell on when you came for romantic escapism. But how much romance is in 'Mansfield Park'? Like actual romance? It's more of a saga following a family's comings, goings, and habits, with a love story to be the frame.

And Jane Austen did have the Bertram family receive their income from the plantation that they had, because slavery was still legal in most of Britain. However, with the effect of abolitionists like William Wilberforce, a lot more Brits were pushing for slavery to be abolished in all of Britain. By the time 1840 rolled around, London had hosted the World's Antislavery Convention where abolitionists came from all over the world to discuss the evils of the Trade. American abolitionists, in hopes of slavery ending in North America, also came over to strengthen their foundations. But, during Regency Era, it was still a practice. It's not easy, when you are a modern writer, to ignore an issue like that.

So that's my long explanation for why I understand why Rozema did what she did when she adapted the 1999 MP. In Miss Austen's time, such topics were taboo for a lady to sometimes talk too much about in their books, and also, that's not Jane Austen's focus. And in many respects, that's a good thing, because her subjects are very general, it has led to her immortality and international appeal. Anyone, anywhere, can grow fond of her, and it's because she touched on qualities that we all have.

However, I will always understand Rozema's intention when she adapted MP. Especially since she delivered the subject in a way that helped people see the horrors of reality, while still being committed to the storyline. She walked a fine line, and I have to respect that she was able to pull it off. I don't think I would have been able to achieve it.

Now it comes down to my final thoughts about 'Mansfield Park', the novel. First, I acknowledge that it's very well-written. In fact, I would say that the last chapter of the book is one of the best well-written final chapters of a book, ever. Structurally, it is creative, shows how Jane Austen was a master for observation and storytelling.

Yet, I admit, that I will never love it as much as I love reading P&P, Persuasion, or Emma. I think the reason for such is because, in each of those stories, I am more invested in the love story. I think the principal reason is because I am not overtly fond of Edmund Bertram at all, and it shows. I don't hate him, but I confess that I do not like him, and I like the other heroes more. Maybe it's because the other heroes are more tolerant of the heroine's flaws/understanding that flaws happen in women. Knightley, Colonel Brandon, Henry Tilney, and Wentworth, all become tolerant of the heroine's mistakes. Even Darcy, who acknowledges his resentful nature, is lenient towards Elizabeth's misunderstandings of him. He even sees how he made mistakes himself. There's a greater sense of forgiveness involved.

With Edmund Bertram, I admire his virtues, but not many of his puritanical habits. As a homebody, I love peace and tranquility, but I understand the right for people to have fun, to find diversions in life and to chase down gaiety. It makes sense to me. Edmund's ways are too strict for me.

But I've talked your ears off long enough, and I will speak more on this in the next book, which will introduce the Bertram family into the narrative.

As for inclusion of 'The Watsons', never fear, those characters will be more realized in later books in the series, and I hope you will not be against me discussing that unfinished gem to our hearts' content.

I hope that these Afterwords are not tedious to you lot. I just remember, when I read books I liked, it would just end and I had all these things I wished to discuss, but the authors were no longer alive, or did not have discussions when the book ended. In case you all wished to have them, I figured that I'd always take a chance. I can't speak with you directly, so this is all I can do.

I hope it does something.

Friends, satisfied readers, or dissatisfied readers...till the next time!

Ney Mitch

Don't miss out on your next favorite book!

Join the Satin Romance mailing list
www.satinromance.com/mail.html

~

THANK YOU FOR READING

Did you enjoy this book?

We invite you to leave a review at your favorite book site, such as Goodreads, Amazon, Barnes & Noble, etc.

DID YOU KNOW THAT LEAVING A REVIEW...

- Helps other readers find books they may enjoy.
- Gives you a chance to let your voice be heard.
- Gives authors recognition for their hard work.
- Doesn't have to be long. A sentence or two about why you liked the book will do.

About the Author

Ney Mitch has been a long-standing Jane Austen enthusiast, having written forty novels that were inspired by her various works. Since stumbling on Miss Austen's books after graduating from college, she has always dabbled in Austen inspired literature, ranging from writing works for teens to adults. Originally, her desire was to adapt Jane Austen's writing in a way to help young adults connect with her, however over time, she has spread her aims to other genres and styles. Having received her BA Degree at Desales University, she is a writer, both literary and dramatic, as well as being a Historic Reenactor.

facebook.com/courtney.mitchell.589

x.com/CMMitchelPsyche

pinterest.com/shebaanna

Also by Ney Mitch

WITH SATIN ROMANCE

Austen Gaskell Series

Curiosities & Contemplation

Resolved & Resigned

Triumph & Tragedy

∽

Kitty Bennet Adventure Series

Vanities and Vexations

Forms & Fashions

Romance & Recklessness

Nuance & Novelty

Doubts & Difficulties

∽

Romance & Revolution Saga

The First Impression

∽

The Memory Series

Moments of Moments Past

Moments of Moments Present

Moments of Moments Future

Moments of Moments Infinite

∽

Pride & Prejudice Reimaginings

Rapture & Rebellion

Fortune & Misfortune

Desire & Destiny

Pride & Peace

Resolve & Revelations

Hope & Hopelessness

Follies & Forgiveness

❧

Chances Series

Chances Are

Chances Come

Chances Fade

Chances End

❧

Novels

The Tale of Mr. & Mrs. Bennet: A Pride & Prejudice Christmas Tale

Considerations Near Christmastime